THE GUY NOT TAKEN

Jennifer Weiner

THE GUY NOT TAKEN

POCKET
BOOKS

LONDON • SYDNEY • NEW YORK • TORONTO

First published in the USA by Atria Books, 2006
First published in Great Britain by Pocket Books, 2007
An imprint of Simon & Schuster UK Ltd
A CBS COMPANY

5 7 9 10 8 6 4

Simon & Schuster UK Ltd
Africa House
64-78 Kingsway
London WC2B 6AH

www.simonsays.co.uk

Simon & Schuster Australia
Sydney

A CIP catalogue record for this book is available from the British Library

ISBN-13: 978-1-4165-2770-1
ISBN-10: 1-4165-2770-2

Printed and bound in Great Britain by
Cox & Wyman Ltd, Reading, Berks

For Adam

Happiness

There's just no accounting for happiness,
or the way it turns up like a prodigal
who comes back to the dust at your feet
having squandered a fortune far away.

And how can you not forgive?
You make a feast in honor of what
was lost, and take from its place the finest
garment, which you saved for an occasion
you could not imagine, and you weep night and day
to know that you were not abandoned,
that happiness saved its most extreme form
for you alone.

No, happiness is the uncle you never
knew about, who flies a single-engine plane
onto the grassy landing strip, hitchhikes
into town, and inquires at every door
until he finds you asleep midafternoon
as you so often are during the unmerciful
hours of your despair.

It comes to the monk in his cell.
It comes to the woman sweeping the street
with a birch broom, to the child
whose mother has passed out from drink.
It comes to the lover, to the dog chewing
a sock, to the pusher, to the basket maker,
and to the clerk stacking cans of carrots
in the night.
     It even comes to the boulder
in the perpetual shade of pine barrens,
to rain falling on the open sea,
to the wineglass, weary of holding wine.

—Jane Kenyon
1947–1995

Contents

JUST DESSERTS

It was a late June afternoon. Jon, Nicole, and I were scattered around the pool in our backyard, watching our mother swim laps. Jon, who was almost fourteen, kicked rhythmically at the foot of his chair with his bright yellow Walkman earphones over his ears. "Cut that out," my sister snapped. She was almost seventeen, and had felt entitled to boss our little brother around since his arrival had displaced her from her crib, even though he was taller than she was and muscular from a spring on the lacrosse team.

Jon kicked harder. Nicki leaned forward, brown eyes glaring, skinny shoulders tensed. "Stop it, you guys," I murmured, as our mother touched the edge of the pool at the deep end and began another lap. The flowered skirt of her swimsuit flapped in her wake. Nicki sank back against the slightly mildewed cushion of her chaise lounge, which seemed to sag under the humid, gray sky. Even the leafy trees and lush lawns of our Connecticut suburb looked despondent in the heat. It had been over ninety degrees every day since June, and it hadn't rained once, although there was thunder every night.

Mom flipped over again and started another lap, switching from the crawl to the breaststroke, with her sleek head bobbing in and out of the water. Underneath the tinted plastic of her goggles, I couldn't tell whether her eyes were open or shut.

"Why doesn't she wear a decent bathing suit?" Nicki grumbled to no one in particular. Nicki herself was clothed in a scrap of a bikini, neon green with black polka dots, cut high on the thigh and low on the chest.

I unlaced my workboots with grimy fingers and wiped my forehead on my sleeve, smelling the gasoline that had seeped into my clothes. I'd taken a women's studies class that spring and had come home from college determined not to take any stereotypically female job. I'd passed up a chance to babysit or peddle perfume in the air-conditoned mall, and had gone to work for a commercial landscaping company, earning six dollars an hour pushing a big red mower up and down endless corporate office parks. It was miserable work, and I wouldn't even have a good tan to show for my troubles: Lavish Landscaping rules dictated jeans, not shorts, because the mowers would kick up stones or broken glass—whatever you'd run over—and spit chunks of it back at your shins.

I yanked my shirt down over my hips and started fanning myself with my Lavish baseball cap.

Nicki glared at me. "Get downwind," she commanded.

"I'm striking a blow for gender equality."

"You sure smell as bad as a man," said Nicki.

Jon settled his earphones around his neck. "Mom bounced a check to the car place," he said.

Nicki made a disgusted hissing sound. "Oh," I said. I twisted my shirt, feeling a mixture of sorrow and indignation. Sorrow that my family, my mother in particular, kept finding itself in situations like this; indignation that, somehow, I'd become the one who was supposed to do something about it. Down in the deep end, Mom's arms moved like pistons in a slow machine, up and down, entering the water without a splash. When they'd dug the hole for the pool and filled it with concrete, the five of us had used a stick to write our names in the yielding gray sludge. Under the water and the tiles, our names were still there.

Nicki raked her pink-tipped toenails through the gravel. "I need a job," she said.

"The babysitting thing didn't work out?" I'd passed along all of the job offers I hadn't taken to my sister, and as of that morning, she'd been working for a family down the street.

Nicki shook her head wordlessly, leaving me to fill in the blanks—the father had tried to grab her butt, the mother wanted her to empty the dishwasher while the kids were napping; the kids were brats; or some combination of A, B, and C. Or, more likely, one parent or the other had asked, with too much cloying sympathy, *How are things at home?*

"Lavish Landscaping's always hiring," I offered. Nicki grunted something unintelligible and arranged a towel under her head. Even when she was annoyed, she was adorable, with her brown hair permed into corkscrew curls, and a tiny heart-shaped face to go along with her slender frame. All of the cute genes floating around in our collective pool had gone to Nicki, whereas I'd cleaned up in the big, bosomy, awkward, and acne-prone department.

"No physical labor!" she pouted.

I reached for the newspaper our mother had tucked underneath her chair and flipped to the classified ads. "Avon Convalescent Home. That would be easy. Just feed the oldsters their mush, wheel them around a little bit."

Nicki's scowl deepened. "Josie," she breathed in the fake-patient tone that signaled a full-blown tantrum was on the way. "You know how I feel about old people." She reached for her baby oil and smoothed a dollop onto one hairless calf. "About all people, actually."

I turned back to the ads. "The state parks system is looking for seasonal workers."

"No people!" said Nicki, shuddering. "I don't want to spend my whole day telling a bunch of idiots where they can swim or how to find the hiking trails." She grabbed the tube of generic suntan lotion and squirted it vigorously onto her chest.

I pressed on. "It says here they're looking for maintainers."

"What's that?"

I took my best guess. "You wouldn't have to deal with the people, just their messes."

Nicki gave a noncommittal snort.

"You might not have to talk to anyone. You could just walk through the woods all day, and spear garbage on a stick."

She sat up, intrigued by the image of the cool woods and a job that would pay her to poke things. "Huh."

"Outhouses," said Jon.

"What?" asked Nicki.

I explained, "Well, there probably aren't bathrooms in the woods."

Nicki grimaced. *"No outhouses!"* she cried. She flung her suntan lotion onto the gravel and flopped furiously onto her stomach. "Why, oh why, do you all torture me so?" she murmured into the cushion. Milo, our bulldog, strolled over to investigate the commotion. He approached cautiously to sniff Nicki's foot, but his stentorian breathing gave him away. Nicki waved her arm. "Go away, dog!" she yelled. Milo shuffled sadly down the sloping hill that led to the deck at the back of our house, as our mother raised her head from the water.

"You could work at Friendly's," she said.

Nicki was momentarily silenced, as if the irony was too

great for her to decide immediately between one of several replies. Finally she arrived at "Who invited you into this conversation?"

Mom smiled and shook water out of her ears. "I was listening to you when I was swimming."

Nicki was spoiling for a fight. "You can't hear underwater."

"Sure I can." She did a showy backward somersault in the shallow end and popped her dripping head back up. "You could work at Friendly's," she repeated. "They need an ice-cream scooper."

It was left to me to point out the obvious. "The thing is, Nicki's not very friendly."

Nicki swung around eagerly. "I am friendly!" she insisted. She peered into the backyard until she located Milo on the deck, underneath the shade of the picnic table, splayed on his belly and snoring.

"Come here, sweet puppy!" she cooed. Milo continued to snore. "Milo!" she called. The dog lifted his massive head and stared at Nicki distrustfully. "Oh, sweet Milo!" she sang. Mom watched from the water as Milo lowered his head until his jowls rested on the deck, and went back to sleep. Jon laughed. Nicki shoved herself off her lounge chair and stomped across the gravel to the fence dividing the pool from the yard.

"*Dog!*" she hollered. Milo heaved himself to his feet and trotted briskly toward the back door. Nicki spared me a murderous look. The cordless telephone on top of Mom's towel started ringing. The sound cut through the sticky air, silencing Jon's laughter and Nicki's yells. My sister stiffened. Jon turned away, and Mom ducked back under the water, gliding down the length of the pool without a breath.

When the ringing finally stopped, my sister stomped back across the gravel and snatched up the telephone. She flopped onto her chair, punched in some numbers, and said, "Yes, in Avon, Connecticut, a listing for Friendly's, please?"

This was the summer of 1988. I was nineteen years old, thick of thigh and sunburned of face, home from my freshman year at college. My parents, who'd still been, at least nominally, together in the fall, had both dropped me off on campus in September, but when the school year ended, I took trains back home—the little train from campus to the Princeton station, a bigger train from the station to New York City, then an Amtrak train up past New Rochelle and New Haven to Hartford. My sister met me on the sidewalk and drove me home to Somersby, and our big yellow house with the black shutters on Wickett Way.

Nicki had gotten her license that spring, but she still looked like a little kid pretending to drive as she sat behind the wheel of our mother's green station wagon. "Brace yourself," she said, as she swung the car, tires squealing, down our street and into our driveway. The paint on the house was peeling, the lawn was ragged and overgrown, dotted with dandelions and Queen Anne's Lace. Someone—Nicki, I suspected—had backed into our mailbox. The wooden post supporting it was splintered and listing to the left, looking like at any minute it would just give up and collapse onto the street.

Things inside weren't much better. By my first night home, I'd realized that my brother had basically stopped speaking; my sister seemed to be a perpetual ten seconds away from punching someone; and my mother spent more of her time under water than on land. When she wasn't doing laps, she was teaching summer school algebra to kids who'd flunked it the first time around, and ignoring the telephone.

I mowed my way through June and July, reading the entire oeuvre of Judith Krantz in my spare time in the air-conditioned library, scrunched into a carrel along the back wall, trying to avoid my current neighbors and former classmates. When Jon got invited to a dance at the country club, I used a library book to figure out how to tie a tie. When the water heater broke, I cashed in the State of Israel bonds from my bat mitzvah and gave my mother the money to repair it. I'd been expecting an outsize emotional outpouring of gratitude, something like the scene in *Little Women* where Jo sells her hair to pay for her mother's trip to her sick husband's bedside. Instead, my mother had just slipped the money under her towel, nodded her thanks, and done a shallow dive back into the deep end.

She swam, and seemed not to notice that the azure-blue tiles were falling off the edge of the pool and the water was an odd shade of green now that we could no longer afford the maintenance service and couldn't get the chemicals quite right ourselves. She'd do laps until eight or sometimes nine o'clock at night, after the sun had set and the thick night air came alive with fireflies. Once a flock of bats had exploded up from the field behind the house and fluttered over the water, flapping their wings and squeaking. She'd churn out lap after lap, mile after mile, as the telephone shrilled and then subsided, and the three of us sat on our lounge chairs, bundled up in damp towels, watching her.

Nicki shocked all of us by making, and keeping, an appointment for an interview at Friendly's, where she was hired on the spot as a scoop girl. It was, she assured us, ideal for her. She'd be working in front of freezers, to keep her cool, and behind a long, stainless-steel counter, to keep the pesky people at bay. Waitresses passed her written slips or called out their requests; Nicki made the requisite dish, and then flicked a switch that lit up a number on a flashboard, and the waitress would come and whisk the sundaes and cones and Fribbles away.

I'd stop by for lunch between lawns and find Nicki, clad in a short blue-and-white gingham dress and a frilly white apron, bent over the caskets of fudge ripple and strawberry delight, the muscles in her skinny arms working valiantly to dislodge the ice cream. "Get out of there, you!" she'd mutter into the tubs. When she'd gotten the ice cream loose she'd stand up with the dish in her hand, pivoting swiftly on sticky sneakers between the hot fudge dispenser and the plastic containers of jimmies and Reese's Pieces and maraschino cherries.

On her chest, like medals for valor, she had pinned brightly colored Friendly's-supplied buttons, a new one each week, bearing slogans like "Buy one get one free! Ask me!" or "Try a cone-head!!" The one pin that should have been a constant was the plastic rectangle reading simply "Hi! I'm" with a space left for the employee to write in his or her name, but Nicki, perversely, would change names every night. She'd be Wendy on Monday, Juanita on Tuesday, and Shakina the day after that. She hated the implied familiarity when customers requested things from her by name, and she took a great deal of delight in watching people who would mistakenly approach the counter thinking she would serve them, or help them in some way, struggle with unfamiliar monikers to which she'd never respond on the first try.

Spying on Nicki at work became a regular summer event for me, Jon, and our mother, one of the few pleasures those hot months held for us. After dinner and *Jeopardy,* Mom would survey the family room. Jon would usually be sprawled on the brown leather couch in khaki shorts and a too-tight polo shirt, tossing a tennis ball toward the ceiling with his Walkman headphones over his ears. Milo would be dozing on the floor, and I'd be in a corner of the couch with a book or a magazine in my lap.

I'd take the quizzes in *Cosmo*. *It's in your kiss! Does your smile say "Sexy?" Are you the life of the party or a wet blanket?*

"OK, kids," Mom would say, "who wants a Fribble?" We'd pile into the station wagon, drive past the leaning tower of mailbox, and make the fifteen-minute trip to Route 44, past the brief strip of chain stores and fast-food restaurants, and turn into Friendly's parking lot.

Nicki's manager was an ex-teenage wasteland turned born-again Christian named Tim, with the ravages of bad acne still apparent on his newly baptized brow. He knew us well. Dispensing with the menus, he would lead us to a booth that offered the best view of Nicki scooping ice cream, refilling the napkin dispensers or salt shakers, or grimacing as she wiped off the counter or directed lost diners to the bathrooms.

One Thursday night, as Nicki squirted whipped cream on top of banana splits, a birdlike old lady waiting at the cash register tried to get her attention.

"Excuse me," she called across the counter in a high, reedy voice. Nicki ignored her and reached for the hot fudge. With shaking hands the woman fumbled her chained bifocals to her eyes. "Miss?" she called, squinting at the name tag. "Esmerelda?"

Mom set down her coffee spoon. "Esmerelda?"

The old woman waved her check at Nicki, who shook her head. "I don't do checks," Nicki said. "Just desserts." The old woman heaved a well-practiced sigh. "Young people today . . ." she began, as Tim, sensing trouble, hurried out of the kitchen. Nicki turned, ladle in hand, and glared at the old woman.

"Begone!" she thundered. A glob of hot fudge flew off the ladle and was headed straight for the woman's withered bosom when the manager interposed himself between topping and target. He snatched the bewildered customer's check. "It's on the house tonight, ma'am. I apologize for your wait."

Nicki bent contritely over the wet walnuts as Tim sponged fudge off his shirt. "Behave," he muttered. "Esmerelda."

"Hey, Nicki," Mom called, "not too friendly." Jon pointed his spoon at her. "Begone!" he said, and I laughed. "Nicki Krystal, defender of the young people today."

Nicki clicked on the Fribble machine, which roared into life with a wall-shaking racket.

"You know who has power?" she yelled over the din.

I did. "Whoever's got the money."

Nicki shook her head. "Nope. It's actually whoever's making the food."

Nicki lasted for almost the entire summer at Friendly's. In August, after his fourteenth birthday, Jon got a job, too. He'd wake before the sun was up and pedal past the pristine, sprinklered lawns and freshly painted houses, with his tennis racket strapped to the back of his bike. There were a few farms in town happy to hire fourteen-year-olds to pick strawberries and green beans and corn, and he worked at one of them. By noon, the sun would be high in the hazy sky. Jon would collect his pay in crumpled dollar bills and head off to meet his friends.

Work wasn't going well for me, not because of my foundering feminist ideals, but because of the weather. The dry spell stretched through July into August, and my hours at Lavish Landscaping dried up right along with all of that corporate grass. I'd pick up babysitting jobs when I could find them. When I couldn't, I'd stay home, angling fans on either side of the heavy fringed rug in the family room for some cross-ventilation, glued to the couch by inertia and my own sweat, waiting for Mom to come home. When her car turned into the driveway, I'd unstick my legs from the leather, pull on my own suit, and swim with her until my arms burned and my legs felt numb. Then I'd turn on the underwater lights and sit with my feet dangling in the water until she was done. I'd ask careful, leading questions. *Had she heard from my father? Had the lawyer called yet?* She gave vague answers without meeting my eyes, without seeming upset or sad or worried or anything that would have been appropriate.

Even when she was inside and upright, dumping chicken and Italian dressing into the chipped green bowl to marinate, or whispering to her lawyer behind the closed door of the stifling, curtained living room where no actual living ever went on, her movements and her speech had a dazed, distant quality, as if she were observing the world through goggles and three feet of artificially warmed, weirdly green water.

Her friends were constantly on the phone, but none of them seemed to stop by anymore. The neighbors would watch us as we backed the station wagon out of the driveway or crossed the street to get the mail from the ruined mailbox, then look away quickly, as if divorce was some kind of contagious skin condition that they could pick up just by looking. The telephone would start ringing at seven in the morning, a constant reminder of our father's absence, and it would ring all day long.

My father hadn't left the way other neighborhood dads had, with regret, a nice speech about how he'd always love us, and a new address at a condo across town. He had simply gotten up from the table after Thanksgiving dinner, tossed his napkin into the congealed gravy on his plate, and said two words: "That's it." My mother, at the other end of the table, had gone pale and shaken her head. Tears filled her eyes. I felt my stomach clench. I'd heard them fighting at night, his hissing whispers and her tears, and I knew that for the last month he'd come home late, and for the last week not at all, but I'd been telling myself I was worrying about nothing, that they were just going through a rough patch, that things were going to be fine.

"Ready for dessert?" Nicki had chirped, and Dad had glared at her so furiously that she cringed in her seat.

"That's it," he'd said again, and walked away from the table, set with the fancy white lace tablecloth and the good china, laden with roast turkey, sausage stuffing, asparagus and corn-bread and bottles of wine. He stomped through the kitchen and the laundry room and into the garage, slamming the door be-hind him. We'd sat there, stunned, as the garage door opened and his sports car roared into life. "That's it," he'd said . . . and that was the last we'd seen of him. But his mail—and, then, his creditors' calls—still came to the house on Wickett Way.

The calls always started the same way. The person from the collection agency would ask to speak to Gerald Krystal. I would say, "He's not here."

"Well, when do you expect him?" the caller would ask.

"I don't." Then I'd recite his office number, which would provoke angry sighs.

"We already have that number. We've left numerous mes-sages."

"Well, I'm sorry, but he's not here, and that's the only num-ber we have for him."

"It can't be," a man from Citibank whined in my ear one morning. He had a grating New York accent, and he'd called at 7:10 a.m. "He's your father, right? You must have some idea how to reach him."

"That's the only number we have," I'd repeated woodenly.

Citibank tried seduction. "There's no point in lying."

"I'm not. That's the only one we've got."

Citibank pressed on. "Doesn't your father ever stop by? Doesn't he call you?"

I squeezed my eyes shut. He hadn't called. Not once. Not here, not at college, not me, not Nicki, not Jon. I thought

I could understand a man not wanting to be a husband anymore—certainly I'd seen enough of my high school friends' fathers bail over the years, taking up with colleagues, with secretaries, with, in one memorably scandalous incident, the guidance counselor at our high school. What I couldn't understand was a man not wanting to be a father anymore. Especially not our father. I'd scoured my memories, turning each one over beneath the hard light of hindsight, but I couldn't convince myself that he'd never loved us, that the first sixteen years of my life had been an elaborate sham.

He'd taken us all on special trips, little adventures. He'd drive me to the library three towns over that had comfortable couches and the best collection of current fiction. He and Nicki made visits to the toy store, where she'd spent hours playing with the marionettes and the Madame Alexander dolls. He took Jon to hockey games and football games, and to help Mr. Kleinman down the street, who was engaged in a never-ending and, so far, quixotic attempt to steal cable. ("Gendarmes!" Mr. Kleinman would shout when he thought he'd spotted a police car, and Jon and my father, who'd sometimes made it as far as a third of the way up the telephone pole, would drop their pliers and wires and sprint back to the safety of our garage.) My dad would remember the names of our teachers and our friends, and our friends' teachers, too. He told Nicki she was smart. He told Jon he was an excellent athlete. He'd told me I was beautiful. And he was the one who'd taught all three of us to swim.

"You could save him a lot of trouble if you'd just tell us how to reach him, honey."

"That's the only number we have." I twisted the phone cord around my finger and swallowed hard against the lump in my throat.

Citibank heaved a sigh. "We'll find your father," he promised me.

"Well, when you do, could you tell him his kids say hello?" I said, but got nothing but a dial tone in response.

Mom used to tell us that the calls were nothing to worry about. "Be polite but firm," she said, looking each one of us in the eye over dinner one night. But then a smooth-talking operator from a collection agency in Delaware tried to convince Jon that our father had won a brand-new car, which would be given to the next person on her list if Jon failed to immediately provide her with our father's most recent contact information. "I gave you everything we've got," Jon said, just like our mother had instructed.

"Doesn't your father want a new car?" the woman asked. Jon, who'd been the only one home when our father's Audi sedan got repossessed, said, "Yeah," and the woman had said, "Didn't anyone ever tell you that it's wrong to lie?" Jon had hung up the phone, walked through the kitchen, past our mother ("Jon? Who was that? Is everything okay?") into the garage and onto his bike. Mom spent the next two hours either on hold or talking in low, furious tones to the woman's supervisor's supervisor. When it started to get dark, she threw me the car keys and pointed toward the driveway. Nicki, who had the night off work, rode shotgun. We drove for an hour and finally found Jon at the country club, slamming a tennis ball into the backboard with a borrowed racket. The night was dark and humid, but the courts were brilliantly lit, empty except for my brother, as we pulled up beside the courts. "Jon?" I called through the open window. "Are you okay?" There was no sound but the crickets' chirping and the thud of the ball against the wood.

"Get in the car!" Nicki yelled. "I'll give you beer!"

"Nicki!" I said. "You are not giving him beer!"

Jon yanked the car door open, threw himself into the backseat, and slammed the door without a word. He didn't say anything to any of us for the next week.

Nicki, on the other hand, seemed to relish the calls. "Hello-o-o?" she'd begin, lipsticked mouth smiling, eyelashes fluttering, as if the caller could be one of the half-dozen boys who'd flocked around her that summer. Her face would darken as the collection agent of the day began his or her pitch. "As one of us has undoubtedly informed you already, Jerry Krystal no longer lives here," she would say. "And furthermore, I find it abysmally rude of you to persist in what I see as simple harassment!" She took great pleasure in pronouncing *harassment* in the English manner, with the accent on the first syllable: *har*assment. Jon and I would gather around to marvel at Nicki's phone manner and she, obligingly, would ham it up. "To think that you people see fit to continue pestering innocent children in light of our father's unfortunate and precipitous departure . . . are you familiar with the recent ruling of Sachs versus Engledorf!"

Generally, the caller was not.

"Wherein a large collection agency was sued for the sum of seven jillion dollars for contributing to the delinquency of a minor, after they made the poor child feel so guilty about not knowing his father's telephone number that he turned to a sordid life of crime . . . yes, that's correct . . . and don't call back!" Nicki would slam the receiver down in its cradle.

"My pride wins again!" she proclaimed, breaking into an exuberant boogie, bony elbows akimbo, skinny legs bopping over the floor.

"Nicki," Mom would say sternly, "those people are just doing their job."

"And I," said Nicki airily as she strutted up the stairs in her ruffled miniskirt, with her Friendly's uniform hanging over her arm, "am just doing mine."

By the middle of August, the dry spell showed no signs of breaking. Heat lightning crackled through the sky every night, and we'd wake up to the sound of thunder, but the rain never came. One Monday night, Nicki and Mike, her boyfriend of two weeks, were in the family room with the videotape of *Jaws II*. I was huddled in my customary corner of the couch, curled up near the glow of the reading lamp with a scholarship application that had come in the mail that morning, trying to figure out how I could spin my father's six months in ROTC in a manner that would convince the Veterans of Foreign Wars to pay for my books sophomore year.

"Look, Miguel, the shark's coming!" Nicki pointed at the screen as violins screeched in the background. She shook her head and spooned up a mouthful of Swiss Miss pudding from a plastic cup. "I don't know why those people went waterski-ing on that beach in the first place. Didn't they see the first movie?"

Jaws surfaced and made quick work of the pyramid of scant-ily clad lady waterskiiers. Milo rested his snout against my bare leg, and Mike, whose summer job in construction started at six a.m., let his spiky blond head fall back on a stack of pillows. His lips parted and he began, almost imperceptibly, to snore. Nicki gazed at the carnage, face lit by the blue glow from the screen, her spoon in her hand, the pudding forgotten.

"Wow," she breathed as blood clouded the water. She grabbed the remote, rewound the tape, and replayed the mas-sacre in slow motion, scrutinizing each shriek and severed limb.

"Fake," she concluded in disgust. "Josie, look . . . you can see that the blood was just painted on that leg there. . . . Hey!"

she barked as she noticed that my eyes were on my application. "You're not watching!"

I acknowledged that the scene is, if anything, too realistic for my tastes, and pointed out that her boyfriend was asleep.

"No, he isn't," Nicki proclaimed. She leaned back until her head reclined on Mike's chest and began to prod his midsection vigorously with her elbow. His eyes flew open, and his hands went first to his carefully gelled hair, then to Nicki's shoulders.

"Ow, quit it!" he begged.

Nicki beamed at him angelically. "Wake up," she coaxed, "or I'll get the dog to lick your face. You," she said, pointing at me. "Wimpy. Make us popcorn."

Mom entered the room wearing a swimsuit, wrapped in a towel, frowning and smelling of chlorine. She had a stack of mail in her hands and a letter pinched between her fingers. "Nicki," she said, peering at the letter. "Did you tell someone from Chase that Dad was in the hospital, dying of testicular cancer?"

"Perhaps," Nicki allowed.

"You can't lie," Mom said.

"They lie," said Nicki.

"Well, don't you want to be better than a bunch of underpaid collection agents?" my mother asked.

Nicki scowled, then turned back to the screen, where a handsome man was lying on the beach beside a woman in a bikini, caressing her arm. Mike couldn't resist teasing my sister, who loathed skin-on-skin contact above almost everything else. "Look, Nicki. Unnecessary touch!"

"She gets eaten soon," Nicki snapped. She pointed at me again. "Popcorn!" I hurried to go make it as Mom drifted out the back door. I'd gathered the popcorn and the big red bowl when Jon's bike came crunching up the driveway. He walked through the garage door, loped into the kitchen, and stood in front of the refrigerator, considering his options.

"I heard Mom on the phone today," he said. He pulled a stick of butter out of the refrigerator and tossed it to me. I unwrapped it, put it in a bowl and then into the microwave to melt. Mom had left the lights in the pool on, and the greenish glow of the water filtered through the window over the sink. The Hendersons two doors down had one of those electronic bug zappers, and its sizzling sound punctuated the hot, still night.

"What'd she say?"

"That she's going to have to put the house on the market in the fall. She can't afford to keep it."

I pulled the steaming butter out of the microwave. I'd known that things were bad from the creditors' ceaseless calling, from the absence of the lawn service and the pool guys and the cleaning ladies. Late at night, I'd woken up from bad dreams listening to the sound of my mother walking downstairs, from room to room, past the painting my father had bought for their tenth anniversary, past the kitchen table where we'd all had hundreds of meals together, up to that fateful Thanksgiving feast, and past the photographs on the wall: Jon in his high chair and Nicki and me on the swing set, and Milo dressed in a baby bonnet for Halloween.

"It'll be okay," I said. It sounded like a lie even to my ears. Jon glared at me. He'd gotten taller that summer, and tanned from all the time on the farm, but at that moment he looked like he was five years old and we'd just dropped him off at summer camp and he was trying not to cry.

"It's okay for you, you know. You get to leave. Nicki's going to leave, too. You don't have to live here with . . ." He cut his eyes toward the staircase, lowered his face, and shook his head.

"I'm out of here," he muttered, and slammed the back door hard enough to make the cabinets rattle.

When I came back to the darkened family room with the bowl of popcorn, Mike was asleep again, sprawled on the couch. Nicki was standing in front of the television set in a short denim skirt and halter top, her finger on the fast-forward button and an angry look on her face. "I want some blood!" she said as scenes whipped by. "This is ridiculous. Where's the damn shark?"

As if in response to her words, the image of a shark filled the screen. "Yeah!" Nicki cheered. "Finally!" But the shark swam away to the strains of the familiar danger theme without doing any damage. Nicki hit the fast-forward button again. "Rip-off," she muttered. I handed her the popcorn. Mike betrayed his somnolence with a rasping snore. Nicki whipped her head around and glared.

"Well, I warned him," she said. She dipped into the bowl of steamy, buttery popcorn and began to delicately apply kernels to Mike's slack lips. "Milo!" she called softly. Milo trotted over, his truncated tail making vigorous circles and saliva dripping from his wrinkled jowls. He propped his stubby legs on the edge of the couch, then, with a grunt, heaved his entire body up, gave a few noisy snuffles, and began licking Mike's lips. Mike woke up, spluttering, to find Milo's muzzle poised as if for a kiss.

"Gross!" was all he managed before dashing to the bathroom. Milo gazed after him sadly. Mom walked into the family room dressed in a faded pink bathrobe with ripped lace on the collar, holding the telephone.

"What's going on in here?"

"Shh," Nicki hissed. "We're watching the shark."

Mom squinted into the darkened room, peering at Nicki. "Did you unplug the phone?" she demanded.

Nicki fluffed her perm, stretched her bare feet on the coffee table, and ignored her.

"Nicki?"

"Bug off," my sister grunted.

"Look," Mom said, "I don't like these calls any more than you do. But we can't unplug the phone." She looked at Nicki sternly. "What if there'd been an emergency? What if someone was trying to call?"

"He never calls," said Nicki, her eyes on the screen.

Our mother sighed as if she were being deflated. "Plug it back in," she said.

"Fine!" said Nicki. "Miguel!"

Mike scrambled out of the bathroom. "Sorry, Mrs. Krystal, but . . ."

"She told you to," Mom finished. "Nicki . . ." she began.

"Bug off," Nicki repeated. On screen, the giant white shark was in the process of devouring what looked like the entire populace of a New England beach. The camera angled in for a close-up and the shark's eye, obviously plastic, gleamed in the wavery underwater light. I slumped back onto the couch, with my pen and my application. The truth of our situation was so obvious it might as well have been engraved over the fireplace. Dad was never coming back. Mom was going to have to sell the house. I was never going to lose the twenty-five pounds I'd gained from too many late-night pizzas and bowls of cafeteria ice cream, and the cute guy in philosophy class was never going to see me as anything more than a girl who'd lent him a pen once, and I sure as hell wasn't going to get a VFW scholarship. My family was falling apart, and all the good intentions and State of Israel bonds in the world would not be enough to save it.

Nicki froze the frame and snatched the bowl of popcorn away from Milo's questing nose.

"Fake," she said, holding the bowl against the scant curve of her hip. "Fake, fake, fake."

It wasn't the fake names and bad attitude that eventually spelled the end of Nicki's tenure at Friendly's. It was the satanic coneheads.

Nicki never liked the coneheads to begin with. "They're very hard to make," she complained of the children's dessert made of a scoop of ice cream with whipped cream and an inverted cone on top. She'd describe to anyone who would listen how painstakingly she had to squirt the whipped cream so that it looked like hair, and dig through the bin until she found two matching M&M's to serve as eyes, and how gently the cone had to be placed on top of the whole affair to simulate a witch's hat. "My cones always slip," she fretted, "so they look like sloppy witches. Or else I put too much hot fudge at the bottom and it winds up looking like its face is melting."

But the kids of the Farmington Valley loved coneheads, so Nicki was compelled to make them by the dozen. Or at least, the kids loved coneheads until the last two weeks of August 1988.

It started innocently enough. Temporarily out of hot fudge, Nicki decided to improvise and place the head of the conehead in a pool of cherry sauce.

"And what shall I say this . . . item is?" asked the waitress, who was in her thirties with two kids and not much patience for the summertime help.

Nicki thought fast on her feet. "Conehead with severed neck," she proposed. "Maybe you could call it a be-head?"

The waitress shrugged, ambled off to the table, and plunked the conehead down in front of a five-year-old dining with his mother.

The mother stared at the dessert, then at the waitress. "Miss," she said, "this dessert doesn't look the way it did in the picture."

"It's *bleeding*!" her son said.

"Oh, it is not," said the mother sharply. As if to prove the conehead's innocence, she dug in with her long silver spoon and took a big bite of vanilla ice cream and cherry sauce. "Tastes fine!" she proclaimed with a cheerful smile. The boy began to cry . . . perhaps because, unbeknownst to both waitress and mother, Nicki had picked up the large, lethal-looking knife used to slice bananas and was capering behind the counter with a crazed grin. No one could see her but my mother and Jon and me, seated at our customary booth, and the little boy with the be-head, whose wails pierced the restaurant.

"Cut that out," I mouthed. Nicki shrugged and put the knife down.

"Honey, what's wrong?" demanded the exasperated mother.

"Really, it's only cherry sauce," the waitress insisted.

The little boy was unconvinced. "Blood!" he yelled.

"Fine!" said his mother. "No dessert, then."

This suited the little customer just fine. He bolted from the booth and dashed toward the door, leaving a melting conehead and an inspired Nicki behind him.

For the two weeks that they lasted, Nicki Krystal's creative coneheads became the talk of the town. Nicki styled herself the artiste of ice cream and, with coneheads as her canvas and a thirty-seven-flavor palette, she was wildly inventive. The specials, which she'd display on hand-lettered cardboard signs affixed to the "Flavors of the Day" list, were increasingly gruesome, which made them, of course, tremendously popular among the town's teenagers.

There was the Asphyxiated Conehead, made with blueberry

ice cream; and the Apoplectic Conehead, made with strawberry ice cream; and the Conehead with a Skin Condition, made with peppermint stick. A Conehead with Lice had white shots in its whipped-cream hair. The Bloody Conehead featured strawberry ripple ice cream and strawberry sauce; the Drooling Conehead had caramel oozing over its chin.

Nicki's friends loved it. They'd line up at the counter and cram six or seven to a four-person booth, demanding all manner of diseased, deformed, and dying coneheads: Conehead with a Cold (marshmallow topping dripping from where the nose should have been), Cyclops Conehead (one eye, a Hershey's Kiss), Nauseous Conehead (gaping chocolate syrup mouth spewing great frothy quantities of Reese's Pieces and whipped cream). Business was booming. Tips were stellar. The manager, Tim, didn't know what to do, but he was certain that my sister's inventions were far from standard Friendly's procedure.

He sat Nicki down over a late lunch one Friday before her shift began. Tim was having a Big Beef Patty Melt with a double order of fries. Nicki, a picky eater, was having a scoop of tuna fish, a pickle, six olives, a handful of crackers, and a conehead of her own creation for dessert.

She came to the table expecting praise, perhaps even a promotion. "So, Tim," she said, spearing an olive with her fork, "I hear we're about to be named Friendly's of the Month in the Farmington Valley region."

"Nicki," said Tim, "just what is going on with the coneheads?"

Nicki gave a nonchalant shrug.

"Are you making them the way the manual says?"

"I may have taken a few liberties," she said.

Tim shook his head. "Liberties." He picked up Nicki's dessert and turned it slowly in his hands: a Satanic Conehead, with beetling black licorice brows and "666" written out in chocolate shots underneath its cone hat. For a long, silent moment he perused the conehead, considering its every angle. "This is no dessert for a Christian."

"I," Nicki pointed out, snatching her conehead back across the table, "am not a Christian." She spooned up a big mouthful of ice cream and sauce. "Mmm-mmm good!"

Tim sighed. "Make the coneheads regular, okay? Like they show them in the manual."

Nicki shook her head. "That would thwart my creativity."

Tim clasped his hands in an attitude of prayer. "Nicki," he said, "maybe you should consider looking for a job at a place where your creativity will be more appreciated. For now," he added, "regular coneheads. I insist."

Nicki got to her feet, untied her apron, and flung it on the floor. "You know what? I don't need this crap. I don't need this job," she said. "I quit."

For the last week of summer Nicki spent her afternoons in front of the TV, reacquainting herself with the doings of the denizens of Santa Barbara and Springfield and General Hospital. When the sun set and the temperature dropped, she'd make her way to the kitchen to work on her magnum opus: Portrait of a Family in Coneheads.

When she'd gone to Friendly's to pick up her final paycheck, she'd taken a few items home with her: a round ice-cream scooper and a whipped-cream dispenser. To this arsenal she had added some new toys: a series of small tubes full of food colorings—red and brown, neon green and electric blue.

Four coneheads were already lined up in the freezer. Jon's conehead had brown M&M eyes and the hopeful caramel hint of a mustache above its upper lip. My conehead had green LifeSaver glasses and pointy banana chunks for bosoms. The Mom conehead had shredded coconut hair and floated on watery waves of blue icing, while Nicki's self-portrait, the Beauty Queen Conehead, had an updo of the glossiest Hershey's syrup topped with a tiara made of crushed toffee. There was only one conehead left to make, and Nicki took her time as she crafted the glasses and selected the perfect chocolate shavings for the beard.

Finally she called the family into the kitchen, and the four of us stood around the butcher-block island, staring at her final creation.

Mom, in her swimsuit, pronounced it a perfect likeness.

"It's really good," I said, picking up discarded chocolate shavings with a fingertip and slipping them into my mouth.

"Not bad," Jon acknowledged, leaning his tennis racket against the wall.

We considered the conehead until it started to melt.

"We should dump it in the garbage disposal," I said.

"Send it to the collection agencies," said Jon.

"Or maybe we could feed it to Milo," I said.

Nicki smiled as she handed out the spoons. "We can't let good ice cream go to waste." She filled her spoon with ice cream and sauce and raised it in a toast. "To us," she said. Four spoons clinked together over the figure of my father in ice cream. Mom and Nicki and Jon each took a single ceremonial bite before drifting away—my mother back to the pool, Nicki back to the television set, Jon back onto his bike and out into the night. I stayed in the kitchen with my spoon in my hand and the dog hovering hopefully at my feet, and I ate, scooping up ice cream faster and faster as an icepick of pain descended between my eyebrows, spooning through the hair and the eyes and the nose and the mouth, eating until I felt sick, until every bite of it was gone.

TRAVELS WITH NICKI

I stood in front of gate C-12 in the Newark airport, waiting for Nicki. I had taken the train from Princeton to Newark. My sister was soon to arrive from Boston, and, after an hour layover, which we'd planned to spend in the frequent-flier lounge, we'd be on our way off for a week in Fort Lauderdale with our grandmother and, eventually, our mother and our brother, Jon.

From my vantage point at the floor-to-ceiling glass windows, I watched my sister's plane lumber toward the gate. Passengers struggling with luggage or wrangling fussy babies piled out of the walkway. I shifted my backpack from one shoulder to the other and checked my watch. When I looked up, Nicki was stomping into the lounge, dragging her duffel bag, looking mightily displeased.

At nineteen, Nicki could probably still pass for a twelve-year-old, in her ratty canvas sneakers, white overalls, and faded Run-DMC T-shirt, and with an oversize lime-green windbreaker tied around her waist. Her purse, a little number in black silk and gold sequins, which I recognized as one of our mother's ancient cast-offs, was slung across her chest, and dangling from a leather cord around her neck was a tiny plastic vase with fake flowers and blue plastic water. Her dark brown curls were piled haphazardly on her head, and her little mouth was pursed in its customary frown.

I bent down to hug her. "Hi, Nicki."

She sidestepped my embrace, air-kissed my cheek, and pushed her duffel bag into my arms.

"I have a kidney infection," she announced by way of hello. She pulled her backpack off her shoulders and shoved it on top of the duffel bag. "Take this, oaf," she said, and headed off down the hall.

The frequent-flier lounge, a study in tasteful beige carpet and gray couches, was filled with businessmen murmuring into the telephones or talking to one another. It had an open bar that I hastily steered my sister away from, and a number of snacks laid out buffet-style on a table in the center of the room. Nicki plopped down on a couch across from two businessmen in blue suits, while I fixed myself a plate.

Nicki looked at it longingly. "Can I have your plum?" she wheedled.

"Get your own," I said, sitting down beside her and pointing to the fruit bowl. "Kidney infection!" Nicki said loudly enough to cause the businessmen to stop their conversation and stare at her. She gave them a cordial wave and stared meaningfully at my food. I handed it over. She accepted it with a brief inclination of her head, devoured the plum with noisy relish, then grabbed my hand and spit the pit into my open palm.

"Oh, for God's sake!" I said. The suits grabbed their briefcases and departed for a quieter couch. Nicki gave them another wave as I tossed the pit and scrubbed my hand with paper napkins. "Bring me some salted almonds, Josie," she instructed. "I'm sick."

My mother had never provided me with a plausible explanation as to why Nicki and I were born a scant eleven months apart. "I loved being pregnant," she told me when I was fourteen and we were jogging side by side in the swimming pool.

"Ma, nobody likes being pregnant that much."

"Well, I did." She pumped her arms up and down over her head. Her breasts, restrained by her thick-strapped, practical tank suit, heaved in the water, churning up miniature whirlpools. I tried not to look, knowing that mine were doing the exact same thing. "I loved being pregnant, I loved being a mother." She smiled dreamily. "After you were born I couldn't wait to have more kids."

I kept my mouth shut without observing that there were almost four years between Nicki and Jon. Whatever mother lust she'd had, however she'd enjoyed her pregnancies and her newborns, it seemed that Nicki's childhood had cured her but good.

My sister and I shared a bedroom until I left for college, which should have at least given us a shot at friendship. In fact, we were nothing alike. I was quiet, bookish, and so shy I once rode the school bus all the way to the terminal because I couldn't work up the courage to tell the driver he'd missed my stop. Most of my friends were imaginary. I'd been that way since I was a baby. "You slept through the night at two weeks," my mother told me. "Instead of giving you midnight feedings, we'd wake you up every two hours to make sure you were still alive. You weren't really into interaction," she concluded. "You just liked your mobile a lot."

Nicki, in contrast, clawed the mobile off the ceiling before her six-month birthday, and flung herself out of her crib before she turned one. She was into interaction: the more violent, energetic, and potentially painful, the better. Family myth had it that her first word was not "Mommy" or "Daddy" but "gimme." Our vinyl-covered photo albums show a delicately built girl with long lashes and dimples, usually in motion. The strained, weary expression of whichever parent or relative was in the picture with her told the story better.

Nicki and I found our seats in the back of the plane. I fastened my seat belt low and tight around my hips and pulled *Madame Bovary* out of my backpack. Nicki slapped it out of my hands. "Vacation!" she said, handing me a copy of *People*. "I can't wait to see Jon."

"And terrorize him," I muttered, bending to retrieve my book. The passengers in the row ahead of us took their seats: a mother with a flushed, cranky toddler in her arms. The child had a phenomenally wet, deep cough, and within minutes of takeoff Nicki dubbed him the Exorcist Baby. Every time he coughed, she shuddered, then giggled. The mother looked at us with a tired smile. "I bet you're waiting for something to come flying out of his mouth," she said.

"No," Nicki whispered to me, "I'm actually waiting for his head to spin around."

I shoved my book into her hands. "Here," I said. "Improve yourself."

Nicki tucked the book in the seatback pocket and adjusted her snug shirt, then the straps of her overalls. "I don't need improving," she said. I sighed and pulled *Heart of Darkness* out of my backpack. Five pages later, Nicki was slumped on my shoulder, her mouth open, her eyelids a dark fringe against her cheek. When the flight attendant zipped down the aisle, I asked her for a blanket, and when it came, I pulled it around my sister's shoulders and clicked off the light over her head.

Nicki woke up with a start as soon as we'd started our descent, rubbed her eyes briskly, and opened the window shade to peer down at the cars inching along the highway. "Check it out," she said. "You can see how bad they drive from all the way up here. Also, the stewardess did not offer me the beverage of my choice."

"I think we're supposed to call them flight attendants. And you were asleep," I pointed out. "I got you a Diet Coke."

"Well, that's the beverage of your choice. Not mine. I wanted Chardonnay." She rummaged around in the seat pocket and finally found an evaluation form. Under the section on "flight attendants," she checked off "poor." In the comment section, she scribbled, "Was not provided with drink." A picture of the founder of Northwest Airlines appeared on the form's front page. Nicki drew horns and a beard on it and a balloon coming out of his mouth with a statement urging the reader to perform an anatomically impossible act. "Nicki," I said, "I don't think they'll take that seriously." She scowled at me, lips pursed, plucked eyebrows drawn, and jabbed one pink-tipped finger at the call button so she could hand the flight attendant her form.

Nanna, our mother's mother, greeted us beside the baggage claim. At seventy-six, she was small and trim, with carefully styled frosted hair, wearing one of her array of pantsuits that spanned the spectrum from pale yellow to beige and back again. She tucked her purse carefully under her arm—a precaution against the thieves she believed roamed the world outside of her gated retirement community—and gave us a quick once-over. "How are you?" she asked, kissing us each once on the cheek. "How's Mother?"

"Fine," I answered. It wasn't exactly true. When I'd gone home for Thanksgiving there'd been a "For Sale" sign stuck in front of the house but, Nicki had told me, nobody had made an offer yet. In the eight months since their divorce had become official, my mom had dragged my father into court twice. Each time he'd promised to pay her the child support and alimony he owed. He'd send checks for a month or two, then he'd stop, and the whole process would start again, with court orders and subpoenas and staggering lawyers' bills. He hadn't sent the tuition check to Princeton that fall. My mother and I had gotten a loan as a stop-gap measure until my financial aid application went through. I remembered her detached expression as we sat in a back office of our Connecticut bank, the way her lips had twitched underneath an unfamiliar coat of lipstick as she stared blankly at the stack of documents until the loan officer handed her a pen and pointed out the space for her signature.

Nanna smoothed her short hair. "Mother told me you have a kidney infection," she said to my sister. Nicki rolled her eyes and grabbed at her back dramatically. "I'm dying," she groaned. Nanna glared at me. "How could you let her come here with a kidney infection? Take her luggage!" Meekly I complied, heaving both of our backpacks over my shoulder and struggling with the straps of Nicki's duffel. Nicki smirked at me, but was quickly distracted by an elderly woman driving a golf cart.

"Oh, can we get one of those?" she asked.

"The car's just across the street," Nanna said. Nicki weighed her options and elected to continue walking. "I called my doctor," Nanna continued. "We can see him first thing in the morning. How's school?" she asked, peering at Nicki through her bifocals.

Nicki scowled. "It's a dump," she cried, and began enthusiastically listing her university's shortcomings: bad food, ugly guys, clueless roommate, library too far from her dorm, unsympathetic RA, girl across the hall plays Janet Jackson incessantly, infirmary sucks. We walked through the glass doors into the inky Florida night, and the humidity hit us like a fist. I shifted Nicki's bags in my arms as sweat trickled down my back.

Nanna led us toward her enormous cream-colored Cadillac sedan. The car had belonged to my grandfather, who'd died in

1985, and it still smelled faintly of his cigars. It wasn't the most practical vehicle, getting, as it did, approximately eight miles to the gallon, but Nanna kept it and drove it at least once a week, all the way to the car wash a mile away from her condo, to have it waxed and vacuumed.

She unlocked the car doors and stared at Nicki, frowning. "Just what's wrong with the infirmary?" she asked.

"Well, for one thing, I had to wait for two hours before I saw anyone," Nicki said. "Then they said there was nothing wrong with my kidney. They didn't even give me a blood test! They didn't even ask me the right questions!"

Nanna pursed her lips. "So you don't have a kidney infection."

Nicki didn't back down. "I might have one," she said. I wiped my face and heaved Nicki's backpack into Nanna's immaculate trunk, right next to the first-aid kit and emergency gallon of bottled water. "They forgot to ask me if I was experiencing pain upon urination."

"Well, are you?" I asked.

"No, but that's not the point."

Nanna threw up her hands in despair. "Nicki, Nicki, Nicki," she said. "What are we going to do with you?"

But Nicki wasn't listening. Kidney pain forgotten, she opened the heavy car door and flung herself into the backseat, behind the cramped, skinny, bald, Sansabelt-slacks-clad figure of Nanna's eighty-three-year-old gentleman caller, Horace. "Let the games begin!" she cried. I stowed the rest of our luggage and slammed the trunk shut.

My sister's earliest childhood memories were of torture. She talked frequently, nostalgically, about the happy days of her youth when she'd give Jon his bath and pour alternating pitchers of hot and cold water over his back—never hot enough to burn him, just hot enough to make him extremely uncomfortable. "I liked the noises he made," she said. She hid my books, stole my diary, listened in on my telephone conversations, and finally found her niche and calmed down a little when she landed a spot as the coxswain for the varsity crew team, where she was actually encouraged to scream insults at people. She'd sit in the tiny seat at the stern of the boat, knobby knees drawn up to her chin, a headband holding a miniature microphone perched on top of her curls, red-faced and cursing inventively, utterly in her element (especially when I was the stroke and she could direct her insults, and her threats to tell our mother about the copy of *Delta of Venus* she'd discovered under my mattress, specifically at me).

But high school was over, the crew team was gone, and I sensed that my little sister's college experience wasn't turning out as well as her time in high school had. We'd run up a shocking phone bill her freshman year, working through her assignments long distance. Every few weeks she'd mail me a paper to proofread (translation: rewrite), but when we'd been home for Thanksgiving, she'd just shrugged when I asked how her classes were going. Since then, she hadn't sent anything to read, and when she called it was mostly to complain about her geeky roommate, who used up her hair mousse and slept with a retainer and a night-light. "Fine, fine," she'd say, every time I asked about her classes and her coursework and whether she'd gotten her grade on her Introduction to Sociology class yet. "Everything's fine."

"Horace!" Nicki crowed. She flung her arms around his neck and planted a loud kiss on his sun-spotted pate. "My man!"

"Hello, Nicki!" Horace boomed. He worked his way out of his seat and around the car so that he could hold the door for my grandmother. He gave me a hug on the way back, and I breathed in his smell of mothballs and Hall's eucalyptus cough drops. Horace had survived two wives, several strokelets, a heart attack, and quadruple bypass surgery and, along the way, experienced what his doctors and our grandmother politely referred to as a substantial hearing loss. In other words, Horace, despite the finest hearing aids Medicare can buy, was as deaf as a post. But he was a sweet man who loved my grandmother and could put up with my sister (perhaps because he couldn't really hear her).

"How are you?" he asked Nicki when he was back in the car.

"I'm having a sex change!" she shouted.

"Glad to hear it!" he replied.

Nanna shook her finger at Nicki, who stuck out her tongue in reply.

"Your mother worked hard so that you girls can have a nice vacation," Nanna said, undeterred. "I want you both on your best behavior." I rolled my eyes. I didn't need to be told to behave myself, even if Nicki was another story.

My sister adjusted her necklace, fluffed her curls, and pinched my thigh as she groped underneath me for her seat belt. "Cut it out!" I said.

"You know you liked it," she said.

"What's that?" asked Horace.

"Nothing," I yelled. I rolled down my window, yawning. I wasn't very well rested, thanks to my roommate, who slept with neither a retainer nor a night-light but, rather, a rotating cast of our classmates, whose ranks had most recently swelled to include my crush from philosophy class freshman year. After two and a half years of staring, I'd finally worked up the courage to talk to him. Sadly, our first and last conversation had occurred in the quad in front of my dorm room. Sally, my roommate, had sauntered by, and that was the end of that. The three of us went to dinner together where, over pork chops and green beans, the two of them had discovered a history class in common. They'd skipped dessert and gone to the library to study, leaving me alone in the room. At two in the morning, they came giggling through the door, clambered into the top bunk bed and noisily consummated their relationship, apparently unaware of, or untroubled by, my presence in the bottom bunk, three feet away. I'd given Sally a stern talking-to in the morning. She'd sniffily loaded up her purse with her toothbrush and a fistful of satin underwear and departed, presumably for the philosopher's single across campus. Every night since then I'd barely slept at all, waking up once or twice every hour at the sound of laughter or a door slamming, thinking it was the two of them showing up for an encore.

As we drove down the palm-tree-lined streets of Fort Lauderdale, Horace noted the passing attractions in a booming voice. "Heavenly Delights," he read as we motored past a billboard. "Nude Oil Wrestling Nightly. Now Hiring."

"I could get a job!" said Nicki.

Horace, who caught only the last word, nodded his approval. "Jobs are wonderful." Nanna's lips tightened.

"Why I let your mother talk me into this," she said. She glared at the two of us in the rearview mirror. "You'll have to share the pullout couch, and I don't want any complaints."

"Forget it," said Nicki. "She could accidentally kick me in the kidney."

Nanna zoomed onto the freeway. "Too bad."

Our grandmother's guest room hadn't changed in the fifteen years she'd lived in Florida. It was decorated in shades of sea green and coral, with family pictures in frames on the bookshelves and crocheted samplers hanging on the walls, and there was a pullout couch against one wall and a tiny television set on a dresser against the other. I pulled out the bed and piled the pillows neatly in the corner. Nicki unzipped her duffel, stacked her clothes on Nanna's card table on the screened-in porch, placed her cosmetics and a Walkman on the bedside table, and scooped up all three towels on her way to the bathroom. After some perfunctory bickering about whether this bed is really the most uncomfortable one we've ever slept on (I argued in the affirmative, my sister maintained that the ones at Camp Shalom were worse), I pulled the blinds shut and we fell asleep.

At three o'clock that morning, Nicki poked me in the side. "Josie?"

I grunted and rolled over. She poked me again. "Josie, wake up!"

I opened my eyes. "What?"

"Can you die from a kidney infection?"

I exhaled and flipped my pillow over. "No."

She shook me again. "If I needed a kidney transplant, would you donate one of yours?"

"Nicki, it's three in the—"

"Would you?"

"I'll give you a kidney first thing in the morning if you'll please just let me go back to sleep."

There was silence until 3:02. Then Nicki asked, "Do you think there are alligators in the pond?"

I flicked on the light and glared at my sister, a hundred and five pounds of distilled pain in the ass in a pair of boxer shorts and a tank top with "Where's the Beef?" emblazoned across the chest. "Nicki, we're on the second floor."

"Oh."

I turned off the light, flopped down hard on the bed, which

creaked in protest, and shut my eyes. I'd finally managed to drift off when Nicki whispered, "I'm failing everything."

I sat up in the darkness with my heart pounding, thinking that I might still be asleep, that this might be the continuation of a bad dream. "What?"

"It doesn't matter. Dad never sent the tuition for the next semester. I'm going to have to leave anyhow."

I flicked the light on again. "Turn it off!" Nicki snarled, and rolled over so that I was talking to her back. Her boxers and tank top were striped with light and shadow from Nanna's plastic blinds, and her head was tucked into her chest like a turtle's.

"Nicki, have you talked to anyone? Does Mom know?" I winced, imagining how our mother was going to react to this news, now that she'd finally started getting herself together. She'd planned a vacation, and even if it was only to her mother's house, and Nanna had probably paid for our plane tickets, that counted for something. "You can apply for a loan, you know, or maybe emergency financial aid."

"I'm dropping out," she said. "It doesn't matter. I don't even like it there."

"Nicki . . ."

"Forget it," she said, and reached across me to turn off the light.

"You can't just drop out of college."

"Yes, I can." Her bony shoulder blades pulled together. "Not everyone needs to go to college. Not everyone's like you." She yanked the covers up to her chin. "Can you bring me a snack, please?" All those years of training had conditioned me well. I got out of bed, padded to the kitchen, located crackers and juice, a glass and a napkin. By the time I got back to the guest room, Nicki was sleeping. I set her snack on the table, pulled the blankets up to her chin, and eased into bed beside her.

———

When we woke up at eight in the morning, Nicki was raring to go, as if our late-night conversation had never even happened. She yanked the covers off me and hooted at my drab cotton nightshirt until I grabbed my swimsuit and slunk off to the bathroom. "How's your kidney?" I inquired on the way.

"Much better, thanks," she replied. She'd turned her back to me and was wriggling into the scraps of screaming yellow spandex that constituted her bikini. "In fact, I think I am well enough to take some sun."

Nanna dropped us off at the beach at ten, along with an ancient red-and-white Thermos full of ice water, a beach blanket, and a bottle of sunblock. "Be good," she said, as we stood on the sidewalk in flea-market sunglasses and flip-flops, and sun hats that had once been my grandfather's. As soon as Nanna's Cadillac pulled away from the curb, Nicki shucked off her tight pink tank top and stalked along the sand in cutoff shorts and her bikini top, basking in the sun and the admiring glances as she looked for the perfect spot. Laden with the blanket and the Thermos, my bag and my sister's, I struggled to keep up. "How about here?" I asked, jerking my chin toward the scant shade of a palm tree.

Nicki nixed it. "We have to find interesting people."

I put down the bags and wiped my face. "Why?"

She stared at me as if I'd lost my mind. "So we can eavesdrop, of course." After ten minutes, she found three bathers who suited her: a very skinny blond girl in a white string bikini sharing a blanket with two short, swarthy, heavyset men whose chests and backs were thick with hair and whose necks and wrists were festooned with gold.

"Ew," I whispered. Nicki motioned me to be quiet, and helped me spread out our blanket.

"Drama!" she said, her brown eyes sparkling.

"Enjoy," I told her. I smeared sunblock on every body part that wasn't covered by my extra-large T-shirt and plodded past the palm trees down to the edge of the ocean. Maybe I could call the financial aid office on Nicki's behalf, I thought as the blue-green water churned and waves sent grit and seaweed splashing over my ankles. Or call the bank where I'd gotten my loan and see if they could arrange one for my sister. Or maybe I'd just drop out and give her my loan, and start again next year. My roommate would undoubtedly be delighted to have our double to herself.

When I got back to the blanket my calves and thighs were aching, and Nicki was full of news. She rolled over to face me, words tumbling over one another as she filled me in on the tenants of the blanket next to ours. "The girl—her name's Dee Dee," she whispered out of the corner of her mouth, as if spies from *People* magazine were lurking in the palm trees, waiting to catch every word. "Well, she went up to their hotel room to get some Cool Ranch Doritos, and as soon as she was gone, they both started talking about all the action they were getting. Not from her."

I looked over at the hairy guys with new interest. One of them was asleep on his back, his mouth lolling open and his hands loosely cradling his hairy belly. The other was lazily flicking through an issue of *Playboy*. Dee Dee sat between them, her bony chest dusted with Cool Ranch Dorito debris, smoothing suntan lotion over her arms. "You should hear how she pronounces Bain de Soleil!" Nicki whispered. She fished the ten dollars Nanna had given us out of her pocket. "Now go buy me a hot dog."

"Don't you want to come with me?" I asked. Nicki flapped her hands impatiently, waving me away. "I wish I had binoculars" was the last thing I heard her say as I headed off down the boardwalk.

When I returned with lunch, my sister had torn a page from the back of *Madame Bovary* and was busy composing a letter. "Dear Dee Dee," she'd written. "Your boyfriend is seeing other women. Ban de Soleil is not pronounced exactly the way it is written. You can do better than Richie."

"How do you know his name is Richie?" I asked. Nicki nibbled daintily at her hot dog.

"Because I am a champion spy."

"But of course," I said. I pulled off my T-shirt and put my head down for a nap.

When I woke up two hours later my face was drool-glued to my forearm and my back was on fire. I looked around for Nicki, whose own skin was an unhealthy maroon. "You need sunblock," I said, grabbing the bottle.

"Oh, no," she said, wriggling to the far edge of the blanket. "No unnecessary touch!"

"It's not unnecessary. You're getting burned and so am I, and we're sisters!" I tossed her the bottle. She flung it back.

"Forget it."

I knew when I was beaten. I slathered myself as best I could, stretching my hands as far as they'd reach down my back. Then I put my shirt back on, pulled the blanket over my legs, and read until pickup time.

When Nanna arrived at four p.m., she was deeply displeased. "I told you two not to get too much sun!" she scolded from underneath her own wide-brimmed sun hat. She pointed one manicured fingertip at me. "Make sure you get the sand off that blanket before you put it in my car!"

I shook the blanket vigorously toward the street. "Nicki wouldn't touch me."

Nanna was bewildered. "What? But she's your sister!"

"Doesn't matter," said Nicki, hissing as her legs hit the cream-colored leather of the backseat.

"*Meshuggenah!*" Nanna snorted.

"*Oy vey!*" Nicki replied

Dinner was late—five fifteen—at Nanna and Horace's favorite Italian restaurant, the Olive Garden. Nanna and Horace both ordered eggplant parmigiana. I got rosemary chicken, a desiccated breast the size and consistency of a hockey puck centered on an oversize plate. "Should have gotten the eggplant," Horace boomed. Nicki poked halfheartedly at her meatball.

"Eat!" said Horace.

"*Ess!*" said Nanna, pointing her own fork at my sister's plate.

"*Mangia!*" said the waiter, zipping by holding a platter laden with pasta.

Nicki shredded the meatball with the tines of her fork and asked for a doggie bag. "She barely ate a bite!" Horace whispered loudly enough for people in neighboring restaurants to hear.

"She doesn't like food," I explained.

"I don't like chewing," Nicki amplified.

"I don't understand," said Horace.

"Crazy," said Nanna. The meatball was stowed in Styrofoam and a plastic bag, and off we went to the movies, with Nicki toting her leftovers along, in case she got hungry during the feature.

We got seats on the aisle (to accommodate Horace's long legs), about three rows back from the screen (a nod to Nanna's eyesight), with plenty of space on either side (because Nicki didn't like people sitting next to her, or really, as she explained to Horace, people under any circumstances). As the lights went down, a couple attempted to ease past us to the seats next to Nicki. "Excuse me," the man said, stepping first over Horace, then over Nanna. The man stumbled over my feet and then, having failed to notice her, sat down squarely on my sister.

"Hey!" Nicki yelled.

The man bolted to his feet. "Excuse me!"

"Shh!" Horace said.

Nicki, outraged by this gravest of unnecessary touches, whacked the man's Bermuda-shorts-clad bottom with her meatball bag. "You pervert!"

Half of the theater turned to look. The man sank into the seat beside Nicki with an air of abject humiliation as the lights finally, blessedly, went down.

The first ten minutes of the movie were uneventful, but slowly Nicki and I began to notice something strange. As the actors on the screen said their lines, about half of the people in the theater repeated them in a loud whisper to their hard-of-hearing companions, resulting in a kind of three-part harmony.

"I'll be going now," said the handsome leading man.

"What did he say?" whispered half of the theater.

"He says he'll be going now," said their seatmates. Nanna was busily translating for Horace. Nicki's eyes gleamed in the light from the screen. Unceremoniously dropping her meatball bag on the floor, she leaned over in her seat and began feeding Horace misinformation.

"I have good news," breathed the leading lady.

"Huh?" asked Horace.

"She says she wants blue shoes," whispered Nicki.

Horace's brow furrowed in puzzlement as Nicki's whispers grew wilder.

"I love you," murmured the leading lady.

"What?" whispered Horace.

"She's having his love child," said Nicki. Nanna, who had finally figured out what was happening, pursed her lips and reached over to pinch Nicki's arm. She got mine instead. "Ow!"

I yelped. The two rows in front of us went "Shh!" at once. Nicki picked up her meatball bag and whacked me smartly on my sunburn. "Stop disrupting the entertainment," she said.

The next morning, we were going to the flea market. By eight a.m., the temperature was inching toward ninety, and we'd poured enough black coffee into Nicki that she consented to getting dressed and exiting the condo. Nanna opened the door of her Cadillac, staggered backward two steps, and screamed my sister's name.

Nicki flung her hands defensively in front of her face. "What'd I do?" she demanded. Then, wrinkling her nose, she said, "Jesus, what's that smell?"

"My car!" Nanna groaned. I looked over her shoulder and noticed that my grandmother's splendid Cadillac no longer smelled like her late husband's cigars. Instead, the air was filled with the overpowering scent of oregano and decaying meat, emanating from Nicki's abandoned meatball in the middle of the backseat.

"Are there maggots?" Nicki asked, peering eagerly into the car.

It was not the right question. Nanna turned toward her, lips pursed, hands balled into fists on her Capri-clad hips. "How could you be so careless? What is the matter with you, Nicki?" She stamped one Easy Spirit–shod foot on the pavement. "I'm never going to be able to get that smell out of the upholstery!" She flung open her door, shoved her keys in the ignition, and bent over as she rolled down all four windows. "Where was your head? Why don't you think?"

Nicki's lip quivered. She ducked her head and stared down at her devil-red toenails. I quickly grabbed the offending meatball and deposited it in a trash can labeled "Keep Our Community Clean!"

"Sorry," Nicki muttered as she climbed into the reeking backseat without even making a play for the front. Nanna blasted the air conditioner and didn't say another word to either of us until we'd pulled into the parking lot.

The trip to the flea market was uneventful, save for my sister being on her best behavior. She wore her sun hat without protest, offered suggestions on watches and T-shirts, promised that if Nanna dropped us at the beach again she'd put lotion on my back, and went on and on about the improving effects the Florida weather had had on her troublesome kidney. She even offered to drive to the airport that afternoon to fetch our mother and Jon.

"Not a chance," said Nanna, gathering her purchases in their skimpy plastic bags. "I'm taking you out to breakfast, I'm dropping you off at the beach, I'm going to get the car cleaned, and I'm turning you over to your mother as soon as she gets here. No wonder she's—"

She pressed her lips together.

"No wonder she's what?" asked Nicki. Nanna just shook her head.

"It's not Nicki's fault," I said, too softly for anyone else in the car to hear me over the roar of the Cadillac's air conditioner.

"What?" asked Nanna. "Josie, speak up."

I shook my head. In the backseat, Nicki closed her eyes and rubbed the heels of her hands against the puffy pink flesh of her cheeks. "You okay?" I asked quietly, and she rubbed her face again, then turned toward the window.

"I'm fine."

On the way to breakfast, Nicki rallied, chattering about her roommate, the parties she'd gone to, the guys she'd dated and dumped. Once we were there, she ordered the lumberjack special and proceeded to eat almost everything: eggs, bacon, homefries, pancakes. She dropped her fork queasily, silent for the first time since her plane had landed. "Ugh." The waitress was sympathetic. "You want me to wrap that for you, hon?" she asked, pointing to Nicki's bagel. Nanna snapped the clasp of her purse.

"Absolutely not," she said.

An hour later, we were back at the beach. The sun was shining. Families were sharing picnics or tossing Frisbees; girls in bikinis oiled themselves and stretched out on bamboo mats. I was lying on the blanket in my swimsuit, while Nicki, still in her shirt and shorts and sun hat, was huddled miserably beneath a palm tree, groaning that her stomach hurt. "I would say that that's the least of your problems," I told her.

"I wasn't that bad, was I?" she asked.

I propped myself on my elbow. "Hmm. Let's see. You faked a major illness, left clothes and wet towels all over the place, got us both the worst sunburn of our lives, convinced Horace that *Working Girl* is actually a movie about Elvis and prostitutes, and Grandpop's car smells like a rotting corpse that was sprinkled with oregano." *And you're flunking out of college, which our father won't pay for anyhow, and it's going to break our mother's heart.*

Nicki shrugged. "At least Nanna has something to remember me by." Cheered, she spread her towel on top of the blanket beside me and stepped gingerly into the sun.

Soon, things were back to normal. I was back with *Madame Bovary* and her endless discontent, while Nicki kept trying to pull the book out of my hands in order to regale me with recent doings on her soap opera, which she unfailingly identified as "the Emmy Award–winning *Santa Barbara*." "Okay, so Gina's house burned down, but Abigail owns it and won't give her any of the insurance money 'cause she knows that Gina once had an affair with Chris—Abigail's ex-husband, really her brother, but she didn't know. . . ."

Suddenly Nicki stopped talking. "Oh, dear," she said.

"What?" I asked . . . but then I saw. Through the white glare rising off the sand, marching toward us like soldiers in resort-wear, were Nanna, Jon, and our mother. Judging from my grandmother's indignant gestures and my mother's quickening stride, Nanna was in the process of spilling the beans. "Mom had to ride all the way back from the airport in the meatball car," I whispered. Nicki grabbed my book and clutched *Madame Bovary* against her chest, while scanning the waterfront for the lifeguards.

"I'm doomed."

The two women drew closer, glaring at Nicki with unforgiving eyes. "She hasn't looked this mad since the last time she took Dad to court," I observed.

"She probably heard about the Horace thing," said Nicki.

"She probably heard about my sunburn," I said, twisting so the pinkest section of flesh was front and center. Nanna parked herself on a bench beside the palm tree while our mother plowed on toward Nicki, who was seized by a new fear. "Oh, God," she whispered, "what if she got my grades?"

"Take your medicine," I told my sister. Nicki gave me a desperate look, then pulled my giant T-shirt on over her bikini and slouched, head down, across the sand to meet my mother halfway.

I pulled a towel around my shoulders and hurried toward the water's edge, listening to Nicki's voice rising indignantly. My feet slipped in the warm sand, and the sun was warm on my face, as the words *meatball* and *kidney* and *utter ingratitude* followed me out to the sea.

THE WEDDING BED

It was the night before my wedding, and I should have been feeling any one of a number of things: nerves, joy, happiness, hopefulness, fear of the unknown. The truth was, the only thing I could really feel was hunger. In a last-ditch attempt to be the bride of a thousand fairy tales and a hundred thousand advertisements in *Modern Bride, Traditional Bride,* and *Martha Stewart Weddings,* I'd spent the last six months on Weight Watchers and the last five days subsisting on cabbage soup and seltzer water. The good news was, I was thinner than I'd been since my bat mitzvah thirteen years before. The bad news: I was crabby to the point of psychosis. Also, I couldn't stop farting.

"What died in here?" my sister demanded as she breezed into the honeymoon suite with two giant suitcases and my mother in tow. Nicki parked the suitcases by the door, marched through the living room, and flung herself into the center of the canopied king-size bed.

"So this is it?" she asked, bouncing up and down on the green-and-gold-silk comforter. "The wedding bed? The place where you will grant David your final favor?" She rubbed the corner of a pillowcase between her fingers. "Nice thread count. Too bad you'll ruin the sheets with your virginal blood."

"Please get off the bed," I said. "What are you doing here, anyhow? Isn't your room ready?"

My mother set the Playmate cooler she'd packed for the trip from Connecticut to Philadelphia down on the coffee table and wandered over to the window. It was my favorite time of year. Red and gold leaves were swirling in the air, brilliant against the bright blue sky. The stores along Walnut Street had pumpkins in their windows, and the air was crisp, with a cidery tang.

"Yes," said Nicki. "Well. About that."

My heart sank along with my blood sugar. "Your room's not ready?"

"Not at the moment," said Nicki, piling the pillows underneath her head.

"But you do have a room?"

Mom sat on the cream-colored armchair. When she flipped the cooler open, the sulfurous reek of hard-boiled eggs filled the room. "Who wants a snack?"

"Nobody's hungry," I said. "Nicki, what's going on? I sent you the information months ago! You were supposed to call and give them David's last name . . ."

"I got busy," my sister snapped.

"You can't stay here!"

She stared at me, brown eyes wide underneath meticulous eyebrows and layers of mascara. "Well, duh. I'm not planning on crashing your wedding night." She bounded off the bed, bent over the larger of her two suitcases, and started unzipping. "It would just be for tonight."

"Uh-uh. No way. Not happening." I looked at my mother desperately. She fiddled with her cooler, then took off her loose green linen jacket and hung it over the chair at the desk. "Do something!"

"Seriously," said Nicki, opening her suitcase and extracting her bridesmaid's dress, which appeared to have gotten radically shorter and much more low-cut since we'd picked it out together a few months before. "Open a window. Light a match. Anything."

I followed my sister into the marble foyer of the suite. "You can't stay here. I'm the bride. I'm supposed to be alone the night before my wedding."

"No," said Nicki, smoothing an invisible wrinkle on her skirt before giving it a final shake and hanging it in the closet. "That's not true. I checked the etiquette book. You're not supposed to see your husband the night before the wedding. It didn't say anything at all about siblings."

"Siblings?" I said faintly. Just then Jon, broad-shouldered and crew-cut, in camouflage pants and a black T-shirt, came barreling through the door. He dropped his army-issue duffel bag beside Nicki's luggage and swept the room with a practiced gaze before pointing at the couch.

"That had best be a pullout."

"If it's not, we'll get a rollaway," said Nicki.

I held my hands over my ears. "No. No. No, no, no, no . . ."

"Rock, paper, scissors," said my sister.

"Forget it," said Jon. "You cheat."

"*Mom!*" I screamed.

My mother was at the window with her back to us and her hands in her pockets. "Yes, dear?" she asked mildly.

"Get them a room!"

"Well, Josie, I would if I could, but the hotel's sold out."

"Well . . . well, then they can sleep with you."

"Ew," said Nicki, at the exact same time as Jon said, "Negative."

My mother's serene smile widened. "They can't share our room. Leon's coming down tonight."

"Jesus Christ," I muttered, edging back to the foyer, where I could fart in peace. Or so I thought.

"I heard that!" Nicki cackled.

"I'm not staying with Mother and her boy toy," Jon said.

"He's an old soul," said Nicki.

"Says who?" asked Jon.

"Says Leon," said Nicki. "He told me all about it over seitan crumble tacos Friday night."

"Could you guys please . . ." I began.

"*All* about it," Nicki repeated, with a Cheshire-cat grin on her face. My mother began to look faintly perturbed.

The couch in the living room was a spindly-legged affair with a striped white satin cover and a pair of fussy tassled pillows. Jon stacked the pillows on the floor and poked around in the cooler. "Rations," he said approvingly, and inserted an entire hard-boiled egg into his mouth.

"I don't believe this," I muttered. I locked the bathroom door behind me, fumbled through my purse, pulled out my cell phone, and speed-dialed David. But even as I was pouring out my tale of woe and desperately searching for a match, I knew with unalterable certainty that I would be spending my last night as a single woman in the company of my brother and sister.

Three hours later, my mother-in-law-to-be, swathed in mocha silk, far skinnier and miles more elegant than a lifetime's worth of cabbage soup could make me, tapped her champagne glass and beamed a little tipsily at the hundred guests assembled in the plush candlelit back room of her favorite French restaurant, where murals of springtime by the Seine decorated the walls and the appetizers started at twenty dollars. "I want to thank everyone for coming to David and Josie's rehearsal dinner," she said. I sipped from my own glass. Lillian's waist was as tiny as a child's, and the skin on her cheeks was stretched taut and shiny. I wondered, once again, just how much work she'd had done. "And I want to say how delighted I am to welcome Josie and her family . . ." She paused and worked up a smile for my mother (holding hands with a bearded, beaming, ponytailed Leon on my left side) and my siblings (whispering in front of the open bar, right by the kitchen door, the better to intercept the passed hors d'oeuvres as they came out) ". . . into ours. We are so happy to see David so happy!"

David smiled at Lillian and bent his head to whisper in my ear. Instead of *I love you,* I heard, *We should keep your sister away from the champagne.* I nodded my heartfelt agreement, squeezed his hand, and farted—quietly, I hoped—into my cushioned seat. David's mother smiled graciously into the overheated, dimly lit room that smelled of a dozen competing perfumes and the lilies that made up the centerpieces. "Would anyone from Josie's family care to say a few words?"

My mother and Leon were still huddled together, eyes locked, oblivious. Leon, I noticed, had fastened his ponytail with a bright green terry-cloth scrunchie that matched my mother's jacket. Sweet. I lifted my eyebrows, but neither of them noticed. Jon, never much for public speaking, finally ducked his head and mumbled, "Congratulations, you guys."

"Where's her father?" I heard David's great-uncle Lew whisper loudly. He was quickly shushed by cousin Daphne, who hauled him out to the lobby where, I was certain, she'd deliver into his tufted ear the thirty-second rundown on my less-than-conventional family (father bailed nine years ago, mother recently hooked up with a much younger man, brother on an ROTC scholarship, sister some kind of scandal although she certainly is a looker). I swallowed hard, feeling acid etch a burning trail up my esophagus. No more cabbage soup, I decided. In fact, no more anything until the vows were exchanged.

David squeezed my hand as his mother shuffled her feet, then sat down. I gave him a small shrug and a grateful smile. We'd announced our wedding in the *Times*. The item was supposed to run the following morning. *David Henry Epstein and Josephine Anne Krystal are to be married this evening, at the Rittenhouse Hotel in Philadelphia.* David had sent in our information at his parents' request. "You know my dad. All publicity is good publicity. Are you okay with it?" I told him, "Sure." I'd worked hard for my degree. I might as well have the pleasure of seeing in print the words *summa cum laude* and the names of the Ivy League institutions I'd be paying for decades to come.

But there was more to it than that. Secretly, I thought of that announcement, with the black-and-white photograph of David and me, posing with our eyebrows exactly level, per the *Times*'s request, the few lines of biography ("the bride and groom met in Philadelphia, where the bridegroom was pursuing a business degree at the Wharton School and the bride works as a stringer for the Associated Press"), as a flag. Sometimes it was a red flag, the one a matador snaps in front of a bull; sometimes a white flag, run up from a sinking ship, signaling surrender; but mostly it was the kind of flag you'd wave if you got lost in the woods and were hoping for a passing plane to spot you. *Here I am. Here I am.*

My father read *The New York Times*. Or at least when he lived with us, he used to. He'd walk to the end of our driveway early on Sunday mornings, magisterially clad in his black terry-cloth bathrobe, with Milo the bulldog trotting ponderously in his wake, and carry the newspaper into the living room, closing the door behind him so that he could absorb the news of the day without distraction. I don't know if his scrutiny of the paper extended to the wedding announcements, but ever since my engagement I'd had a fantasy of him showing up on my wedding day to tell me what a lovely and obviously accomplished young woman I'd turned into; how sorry he was to have missed the last eight years of my life; how lucky David was to have me. Sometimes, in my daydream, he would get choked up as he told me that he knew he didn't deserve it, but could he have the honor of walking me down the aisle? In the daydream, I never cried. Sometimes, I even told him no.

As the tuxedo-clad waiters whisked away my untouched plate of sautéed skate with hazelnut beurre blanc, asparagus, and pommes Anna and replaced it with a glass flute filled with cassis sorbet, David gave me a kiss. Then he sniffed, frowning. "Was that you?"

I shifted in my seat as Nicki breezed over from the bar to stand at the head of the table with her glass in her hand. "I'd like to say a few words, if I might."

"Ah," said Lillian. "The sister of the bride!"

"Fuck," I whispered, at the same moment David whispered, "Oh, no." Too late. Nicki clambered on top of her undoubtedly expensive upholstered chair to beam down at the assembled guests, most of them David's out-of-town relatives and his father's important clients. She wore a tight suede skirt and a clingy chocolate-brown sweater. Her hair, shiny and brown, swung around her shoulders; her high-heeled tight-fitting leather boots stretched to her knees and added three inches to her height.

"Hi, I'm Nicki Krystal. Some of you may recognize me from QVC," was how she began. David's mother blinked. I swallowed a mouthful of icy sorbet and pasted a smile on my face. After spending years lurching from one college, one city, one job, and one boyfriend to another, my little sister, now twenty-five, had finally gotten her act at least semi-together and landed a job modeling Diamonique jewelry on cable TV. She was by far the most famous member of our family. At least from the wrists down.

"I shared a room with Josie for seventeen years. I know her better than anyone in the world. And there are some things about my sister that I'd like to share with her new family."

I sank down in my seat, smoothing my pleated black-and-white-pique skirt over my knees and thinking that the less my new family heard from Nicki, the better it would be for all of us.

"First," said Nicki, thrusting her index finger dramatically in the air, "she's not normally this thin."

David's father let loose with a big, hearty *ho-ho-ho*. Lillian craned her neck around to stare at me in surgically perfected profile. I gave her a nervous grin, feeling myself start to sweat through the armpits of my black silk top.

"Now, I don't know how she did it!" Nicki said. "But seriously, David, if there's a buffet anywhere on your honeymoon, my advice is don't let her near it, because I don't know how many calories the human body can handle in one sitting."

I pretended to wipe my lips and groaned quietly into my napkin.

"Number two!" said Nicki. "She generally likes books better than people. I mean, I take it she likes you all right . . ." She favored David with a smile, which he weakly returned. "But as for the rest of humanity, forget it. If you ever have a party—and you probably won't, because my sister, as you've probably figured out, is not big on socializing—but if you ever do, she'll probably disappear about fifteen minutes into it and you'll find her in the bedroom with a book."

More nervous chuckles from the crowd. I shot my mother a beseeching look, which she either didn't see or decided to ignore.

"But," said Nicki. She lifted her chin, raised herself onto her tiptoes, and held herself perfectly still, in a pose demanding silence. The audience complied. "My sister Josie . . ." She bent her head, and when she looked up again, her eyes were glistening. "My sister Josie is loyal. She would do anything in the world to help the people she loves, even if it's at her own expense. She . . ." Nicki took a quick breath and looked at the crowd, then at me. "She's the best person I know and she deserves to be happy." She leveled her gaze at my not-quite-husband. "Take care of her," she said, and eased herself off the chair and strutted back to the bar.

"So I can stay now?" Nicki asked sweetly, trailing me into the ladies' room with a bottle of champagne that she'd liberated from the bar in her hand. "C'mon, it'll be fun! We'll order room service and tell ghost stories!"

A little girl in pink exited one of the stalls with her mother behind her. "I wear big girl underpants now!" she proclaimed. She looked up at my sister. "Do you wear big girl underpants?"

Nicki stared down at her. "No, I generally go commando."

The mother's eyes widened. "Jesus, Nicki," I said, and dragged her into the handicapped stall. ("What's commando?" I heard the girl asking as the door swung shut.)

"What?" Nicki asked. "What? Underwear gives me panty lines! Do you want me to lie to little children?" She turned her back, tapping her foot and exhaling impatiently while I took care of business.

Jon was standing at parade rest in front of the elevators, his feet planted hip-width apart and his arms behind his back.

When the doors slid open, the three of us piled in, along with a tiny white-haired lady in a pale blue pleated dress—a great-aunt or second cousin from the groom's side, I thought.

"So anyhow," said Nicki, as if the entire rehearsal dinner had merely been a five-minute interruption to her conversation, "the QVC thing's great. Did I tell you they're thinking of letting me do shoes, too?"

I nodded.

"But I think I need to be in Los Angeles."

"Oh, Los Angeles is wonderful," offered the aged party. "And if you really want to be an actress, it is where you need to be."

Jon grimaced. I held my breath. Nicki's eyebrows drew down as she turned slowly to stare down the little old lady. "Excuse me, but I was speaking to my brother and my sister," she said. "I don't believe you were invited into this conversation."

"Nicki," I said, and put my hand on her shoulder. She twitched it off.

The woman's chin and pearls and pleats trembled softly. "Well, I didn't mean . . ."

The elevator lurched to a stop at the third floor. The bridal suite was on twenty-one, and the woman had punched twenty-three. Evidence, as if I needed any more, that there was no God.

Meanwhile, Nicki had launched into a full-blown soliloquy. "Why is it," she asked the mirrored ceiling, "that people think that just because they overhear something they're invited to comment?"

The poor woman in blue was cringing in a corner of the elevator.

"Maybe it's Oprah," said Jon, trying hard to change the subject.

"No, it's me," Nicki spat. "Everyone thinks they've got

something to say. Everyone thinks they can just throw their two cents in. Tell me how to live my life, tell me what I'm screwing up, tell me what I should be doing better. You, Mom, everyone!"

"I'm very sorry if I offended you somehow," the woman said.

Nicki opened her mouth to snarl something in response as the doors slid open on the fifth floor and an aged couple—the man in a tuxedo, the woman in a beaded silver gown—shuffled in. I grabbed my sister's left elbow, Jon took her right, and I smiled at the little old lady as we pulled her into the hall. "We'll take the stairs," I said.

Up in the suite, the maids had piled blankets and pillows on the pullout bed. "Secure the perimeter!" Jon barked, and made a tour of the two rooms, peering out the windows at the buildings across the park as if there might be snipers targeting the room. I stood on my tiptoes to rub my palm against his buzz cut. "Ladies love the hair," he announced, and snapped a blanket over his bed. "Is there an open bar at this thing?"

"But of course," I said. David's family had spared no expense.

Jon gave a triumphant grin. "I shall have my choice of bridesmaids."

"I'm the only bridesmaid," Nicki called from the wedding bed.

Jon looked at her and stopped smiling. "Unfortunate," he said, and closed the curtained French doors between the living room and the bedroom.

In the bedroom, Nicki wriggled out of her skirt, shucked her sweater, pulled on a tank top and pink flannel pajama bottoms, and flopped happily onto the bed with her champagne and the telephone. "Hello, room service?" she said. I picked her clothes up off the floor and hung them neatly in the closet.

"Two cheeseburgers, an order of french fries, a hot fudge sundae, only please don't put the hot fudge on the sundae, um, one Heineken . . ." She put her hand over the mouthpiece. "Josie, what do you want?"

"Ice water."

"One chocolate malted and two Heinekens," said Nicki, hanging up. She grabbed the television remote off the bedside table. I pulled off my own clothes and slipped on a hotel robe, feeling anxious and antsy and strangely sad. There was nothing left for me to do. My dress had been steamed and hung on the back of the closet door, my hose and shoes and various constricting undergarments laid out carefully on a bench beside it. My pores had been squeezed, my bikini line waxed. My apartment was cleaned and locked up, and my cat boarded for the next ten days. I wouldn't have much to do but show up on time, strap myself into the big white dress, say "I do" at the appropriate moment, and remember the steps to the dance David and I had rehearsed.

"We need to talk," said Nicki. She grabbed my hands and tugged me to the bed. "Now, Josie," she said. "I don't want to frighten you, but there's something you should know before tomorrow."

I wriggled away to pull my suitcase out of the closet, heaving it onto the bed and starting an inventory. Swimsuit, SPF 45 for my body, SPF 30 for my face, sun hat, sandals . . . "Oh yeah? What's that?"

"David has a snake."

"Huh?"

"A snake," she repeated. "And the snake wants to hide in your cave."

"Oh, Lord," I muttered, carrying my cosmetic case into the bathroom. Toothpaste, toothbrush, mouthwash, dental floss . . .

"Don't be afraid!" Nicki yelled. "The snake means you no harm!" She lifted the champagne bottle and took a healthy swallow. "You must welcome the snake in order to be a good wife."

"I'll do that," I told her. I grabbed my razor out of the shower. When I turned around again Nicki was standing right behind me, smiling at me in the mirror.

"The snake will go in and out of the cave, and in and out and in and out and in and out . . ." She waved the bottle back and forth to suit the words.

"Okay," I said, and held out my hands for the champagne. Nicki ignored me.

"And then!" she said, starting to giggle. "It's going to spit up!"

I picked up the telephone. Room service greeted me with "Hello, Mrs. Epstein!" It took me a minute to realize that Mrs. Epstein was meant to be me. "Hi, can we add a pot of coffee to our order?"

Room service said no problem. Nicki giggled some more and hoisted herself onto the bed.

"I'm only telling you things you need to know," she said.

"Believe me, I'm grateful." I zipped up the suitcase and laid down beside my sister, who'd flopped on her belly to channel surf.

"Are you nervous?" she asked.

"Nah," I lied. "Piece of cake."

The food arrived. Nicki draped a towel over the bed, then set out each of the plates, lifting the silver lids with a flourish. "A prenuptial picnic!"

I told her I wasn't hungry. She waved her cheeseburger under my nose, fingers sinking into the soft seeded bun. "Just one bite," she wheedled, the way my mother used to coax her to eat when she was little. I shrugged, tried to take the tiniest bite I could manage, and groaned out loud as my teeth cracked the charred crust of the burger and the rich juices spilled into my mouth.

"Oh, dear Lord," I breathed, and gobbled a fistful of crisp french fries dipped in herbed mayonnaise. "If I don't fit into that dress tomorrow . . ."

"You'll fit," my sister promised. I drank a third of a beer in one gulp, then burped, wiped my lips, and licked salt and melted cheese off my fingertips. Five minutes later, I'd demolished the burger and was slowly spooning fudge over the dish of vanilla ice cream, promising myself that I'd skip breakfast and lunch the next day.

"How's work?" Nicki asked.

"Okay," I said through a mouthful of ice cream. I was the lowest person on the totem pole at the Associated Press offices, which meant I worked nights and weekends, running off to fires or car crashes or pier collapses, usually in bad neighborhoods where the witnesses were happy to give colorful, profanity-laced quotes about whatever they'd just seen, but clammed up when you asked for their names. "Call me Little Ray," a guy who'd been the single survivor of a six-car crash on Roosevelt Boulevard said the week before.

I'd patiently explained that the AP required both a first and a last name—preferably the ones he'd been born with. ("But everybody calls me Little Ray!" he'd insisted.)

I liked the work, though, and I liked writing, but two weeks into my tenure I'd done the math and realized that if I'd been making five hundred dollars less a year, I would have qualified for food stamps. It was a problem, given the student-loan situation. I dreamed of making more money, but so far the only thing I'd been able to think of doing was dropping out of journalism and going into advertising, where you could do quite well, if you didn't mind using your talent and creativity to sell tampons (for some reason, I was convinced that, no matter what city I worked in or which agency hired me, I would end up with the word *absorbent* figuring prominently in my future).

Of course I'd soon be a married woman, and David was set to start working as a venture capital consultant, which would be considerably more lucrative than my career as a cub reporter. Maybe I'd get promoted. Maybe David would make a killing. Maybe I could get my loans paid off on time. Early, even. Say, when I turned fifty.

Nicki watched girls in hot pants gyrating to rap songs where every third word was bleeped out while I polished off the ice cream. Then she reached over me for the phone. "Hello, room service? We're going to need another burger," she said in the same tone that the ship's captain in *Jaws,* upon glimpsing the great white shark, had said, "We're going to need a bigger boat."

"No more," I protested, sucking the last traces of chocolate off the spoon. "Seriously. I might explode."

"Fine," said Nicki. "I'll eat it myself."

In the bathroom, I took a twenty-minute shower in a stall that had half a dozen jets protruding from the tiled walls. I scrubbed myself with lemon-scented soap and washed my hair with rosemary mint shampoo. At the sink, swathed in a hotel bathrobe, I brushed and flossed, rinsed and spat, patted astringent and moisturizer onto my face, and considered my reflection. Things were as good as they were going to get. My eyebrows weren't lopsided, my complexion was clear, my teeth and hair were shiny. If I were a horse, I'd do just fine on the auction block.

I pulled on my ugliest, oldest, most comfortable flannel

nightshirt, tiptoed through the darkened bedroom, made sure the comforter was free of food and dishes, and slipped into bed next to my sister.

She rolled over instantly and tried to spoon me.

"Get off!" I whispered, wriggling away.

"Oh, Josie," she giggled, her skinny arms around my neck, "your nightshirt is driving me wild!"

"Stay on your side of the bed or you'll be sleeping in the closet," I said.

Nicki was quiet for all of thirty seconds. "Do you think Leon was a virgin before he met Mom?" she asked.

"Nicki," I said, "that is really not what I need to be thinking about right now."

My sister was undeterred. "I mean, he was her student."

"Student teacher," I said. It was a distinction I'd made many times in the two years since our fifty-six-year-old mother had taken up with a twenty-four-year-old.

"So young," said Nicki. "Too young."

"Not another word," I told her.

"Fine," she grumbled, rolling on her side and falling almost instantly asleep.

I shifted around in the big, high bed. It was 11:03 at night. T minus sixteen hours until my date with the white, tight, fitted satin, ridiculously expensive dress that hung over the back of the closet door like a ghost.

By 11:36 I had heartburn. By 11:38 I had doubts. By midnight I'd convinced myself that marriage in general, and David in particular, were bad ideas, and that the true love of my life was really Craig Patterson. I'd gone to high school with Craig, but we'd never actually spoken until our fifth reunion, when he'd followed me into the coatroom and slurred that I had the prettiest tits of all the girls in our class. Then he'd shoved his phone number in my pocket and lurched off toward the ballroom where, I heard later, he'd gotten sick in a potted plant.

At 12:15 I crept out of bed and stared at the empty streets around Rittenhouse Square, watching the lone traffic light tint the pavement green and yellow and red and green again. The treetops bent in the wind, and rain spattered against the windows. Was rain on a wedding day good luck? Bad luck? Nothing special? I couldn't remember.

At 12:30 I picked up the telephone. Craig's number was still in my wallet, on the napkin where he'd written it. I held my breath as I dialed his number. The telephone rang twice, then a woman picked it up. "Hello?"

My tongue turned to lead. "Hello-ooo?" the woman called. "Anybody there?"

"Sorry, wrong number," I blurted. I hung up the phone and took a few minutes to get my heart rate under control. Then I got back into bed and lay there, staring at the elaborate swags of the canopy, thinking about happy endings. Did I know anyone who'd had one? Not my parents, although these days my mother did seem pretty blissed out with young Leon. Not David's, either, I suspected. His father's eyes lingered on any woman older than fourteen and younger than forty, and his mother started sipping Sancerre at around four o'clock every afternoon and continued drinking right up until dinner, when she'd switch to vodka, toy with her food, and surreptitiously tug the flesh under her chin or pinch the skin of her upper arms, as if she was already planning her next plastic surgery.

But even so. I'd been at David's parents' thirty-fifth anniversary party, where they'd danced to "Fly Me to the Moon." His father had dipped his mother backward on her high heels, whispering into her ear, and she'd thrown her head back, laughing, and I'd thought, maybe a little sentimentally, that that was what love looked like. Even my parents, before my father had left and my mother had spent years in a chlorine-scented fog before emerging on Leon's arm, once had their moments. I remembered my father coming home from work, immaculately dressed in a suit and tie, setting his combination-lock briefcase down by the door and holding his arms open. "Wife!" he would call, and my mother would drop whatever she'd been doing and find him. They would stand there in the hallway next to the washer and the dryer, sometimes for just an instant, sometimes for much longer, holding on to each other at the end of the day.

They'd loved each other. They'd loved us, too, I thought, smoothing the pillows, remembering all of us sitting at the picnic table in the backyard, eating potato salad and barbecued chicken off the red plastic dishes my mom used in the summertime. My sister would be tanned in her white T-shirt, and Jon would be handsome in his baseball cap, and my mother and father would hold hands and laugh at my jokes. Now our father was gone. None of us had heard from him in years. Mom didn't appear to care about much besides her daily swim and Leon. I rolled over again, pulling the covers up to my chin. What if there was no such thing as happily ever after? What if Walt Disney and every romantic comedy I'd ever seen and all the novels I'd loved had gotten it wrong? What if . . .

"You know why I'm so angry?" Nicki asked in a hollow voice. I shrieked and almost fell off the bed. My sister didn't notice. "Because we got cheated," she said.

"Because Dad left?"

She didn't answer, but I imagined I could hear her *Well, duh* hanging in the air, just beneath the fringes of the canopy.

"Well, okay, it was hard, but we all pulled through. We all went to school. We're all doing okay."

"Mom is dating a teenager. Jon doesn't talk."

"Well, Jon's always been, you know . . . he's a guy. They're different. And Mom's . . ." I let my voice trail off. I still wasn't sure what to say about our mother. "And then there's me," I said. "I'm okay, right?"

Nicki said nothing.

"And you're doing fine."

"None of us are fine, Josie."

In the darkness, her words had the ring of prophecy. Outside, the wind rocked the big panes of the windows, and I could hear rain pattering down on the empty streets.

"What do you mean?" I asked.

No reply.

"What do you mean that none of us are fine?" She rolled over, sighing. I held my breath and then reached for her, gathering her scrawny shoulders in my arms . . . and, for a brief moment, she let her head fall back against my chest and let me hold her.

"Go to sleep," she said gruffly, wriggling away.

"Big day tomorrow," I replied, rolling back to my side of the bed. I closed my eyes and listened to the rain, imagining I could also hear the clicks of the digital clock ticking off the minutes until my wedding day.

I remember everything before the vows in snatches: the flower girl sobbing after a hot roller burned her cheek; my mother and Leon holding hands on a bench while the caterers bustled around them; David smiling at me as I made my way down the aisle with my mother on my left side and nobody on my right. In that moment, with two hundred and twenty guests looking at me from their ribbon-bedecked chairs, with tears on my mother's cheek and our announcement in that morning's *Times,* I wasn't thinking about love or happiness or how this was the ending the fairy tales had promised, the reward for the princess who survived the enchantment or the wicked step-mother or the hundred years' sleep. I was thinking, *I guess if this doesn't work out, we can always get divorced.*

Our first dance—per David's request, to Eric Clapton's "Wonderful Tonight"—went off without a hitch. David's father's toast was heartfelt, if a little generic. The salad plates appeared and then were replaced with the main course. David and I visited the tables, smiling, accepting congratulations and good wishes, thanking our parents, cutting the cake. Then it was midnight. The last guests collected their coats and umbrel-las, the caterers cleared the tables, the band packed its instru-ments away. I sank down on a beige velvet couch in the lobby, kicked off my shoes, and stared across the street at the empty benches and fountains of the park. It had rained on and off all day long and now it was pouring, a cold, driving rain that had cleared the sidewalks, except for a dogged trio of joggers in reflective raingear and a few homeless guys bundled up in trash bags. Wind lashed the trees and made the clipped hedges quiver.

"You ready?" asked David, smiling down at me, handsome in his tuxedo. He'd shaved so carefully that his cheeks were still pink with razor burn, and his bow tie was slightly askew.

"Sure," I said and got to my feet. We were heading toward the elevators when I caught sight of something through the double glass doors that made my heart stop. My feet, too. David, following behind me, bumped into my back.

"Josie, what . . ."

"Wait," I said, and spun around and dashed through the lobby doors into the cold, freezing darkness, running across Nineteenth Street barefoot in my wedding gown. Rain beat down, ruining my elaborately pinned and sprayed updo, sending my makeup sliding down my face, basting the satin bodice of the dress against me. In the center of the park, the man I'd seen was standing in front of the leaf-clotted fountain, with the headlights from the passing cars glinting off his glasses and his hands in the pockets of his overcoat.

"Dad?" I called, and wiped rain off my face.

It wasn't him, of course. Up close, the homeless man in the torn coat didn't even really look like my father. The dreadlocks should have been a clue.

The man's face broke into a smile as he looked at me, soaked and barefoot, shivering.

"Oh, now, look at you!"

"Yeah," I said, and I started to cry. "Yeah. Look at me."

He cocked his head and told me I was a beautiful bride, which only made me cry harder.

"You got any money, honey?"

I didn't. But I had a slice of wedding cake in my hands, a piece of cake in a wax paper bag upon which my name and David's were embossed in gold. We'd given cake to our guests on their way out the door. Single girls, I'd read, could put the cake under their pillows and dream of the man they'd marry.

I handed the homeless guy my slice. He thanked me and told me good luck. Then I lifted up my sodden skirt and, with as much dignity as I could muster, walked back across the street.

"What was that about?" my husband of four hours asked, with more than a little concern in his voice.

"I thought I dropped something," I said. "When we were taking the pictures." I stepped close to him, tilting my head up for a kiss, and as David's warm lips brushed my cold ones, I thought that every story I would tell for the rest of my life would somehow be about this: about the man who left and never came back. Except, possibly, the stories about guys calling themselves Little Ray . . . and, for all I knew, maybe those, too.

"I love you, Josie," my husband whispered. He lifted a lock of wet hair off my cheek and brushed at my skin with his sleeve, and I managed to smile.

"I'm all right now," I said.

SWIM

The girl's name was Caitlyn. That fall, it seemed like they were all Caitlyn, or some oddly spelled variation of the name. Judging from the way she kept crossing and recrossing her long, denim-clad legs and flipping her silver cell phone open to check the time, she wanted to be anywhere but in the Coffee Bean and Tea Leaf on Beverly and Robertson, sharing a table for two with my laptop and me.

"So in terms of a major? I'm thinking international relations? I want to be a diplomat?"

I nodded and typed it in. Every sentence out of her sparkly pink seventeen-year-old lips came out sounding like a question. I could just imagine her sitting across the table from some third-world potentate and toying with the silver ring through the cartilage of her left ear. *We'd like you to give up your weapons? Because biological warfare? Is bad?*

Patience, Ruth, I told myself. "Extracurriculars?" I asked, fingers hovering over the keyboard as the woman at the table next to mine, with bristly eyebrows and a bitter twist to her mouth, gave me a nasty look. I ignored her. Each Saturday I got to the coffee shop at seven o'clock, early enough to claim a prime corner table next to the big window, across the room from the blenders and the bathrooms, right near the store's single power outlet. The people who'd show up later—screenwriters or screenwriter-wannabes, most of them—were forced to play musical tables, inching closer and closer to my corner, stomping across the wide-planked hardwood floors or lingering ostentatiously beside the cream and sugar, their glares growing fiercer as their batteries slowly died. For six hours every Saturday, I would meet with my teenage clients, the ones who went to pricey private schools and whose parents had given them one more leg up on life by hiring an application consultant to help them get into college.

Caitlyn let go of her earring and tugged at a lock of glossy brown hair. She smelled intensely of coconuts—her shampoo, I figured—and the cloying, fruity scent emanating from the wad of Pepto-pink gum I glimpsed whenever she opened her mouth. I made a note to tell her not to chew gum at her interviews.

"Um, tennis?"

"You're on the tennis team?" I asked. *Please,* I thought. Something. Anything. So far her extracurricular page was completely blank.

"Um, no? I just like to play? Or I used to?"

I typed *tennis.* "How about clubs? Musical instruments?" I stared at her hopefully. She gave me a blank look back. "Piano lessons?"

Caitlyn made a face, pink lips wincing above her sweetly rounded chin. "When I was, like, six?"

"Volunteer work?" *Yeah, right,* I told myself. Caitlyn stopped smacking her gum, flipped her phone shut, and straightened in her chair.

"I have this friend? She's having surgery?" She lowered her voice. "A breast reduction? And I'm going to be taking care of her dog while she, you know, recuperates."

Jesus wept. I typed it in anyhow.

"Well, not, you know, technically. They've got a dog walker? But I'll be coming over to, you know, play with him?" She tugged the piece of hair down to her lips and started chewing it. "Or her?"

I made a note to remind her not to chew her hair during the interview, right beneath my note about gum. Then I saved her file, closed my laptop, took a gulp of the drink I'd ordered before this ordeal began, and gave her what I hoped was a friendly smile. She was all gangly limbs in tight jeans and a tiny pink T-shirt, with parents who'd happily agreed to my five-thousand-dollar fee. This guaranteed young Caitlyn three months' worth of my services, an hour-long videotaped interview coaching session, and a full review of up to five essays. We'd be in this for the long haul. I might as well try to find something to like about her.

"Well!" I said, trying to sound enthusiastic. "This is plenty for me to start with!"

She fiddled with her paper coffee cup, wiping sparkly pink lipstick off the rim with her pinkie. "Where'd you go to college?" she asked.

"In Connecticut. A small liberal arts college called Grant. You've probably never heard of it." Caitlyn's parents had told me that she wasn't considering any schools outside of California, and she had her heart set on Berkeley. It was a long shot, given her B average and solidly middle-of-the-pack test scores. Then again, Mom and Dad were both alums and, judging from the sleek gold Lexus their daughter drove, they could have been making major gifts to the endowment fund since Caitlyn was but a twinkle in their eyes.

"Did you like it?" She tilted her head, looking me straight in the eye, then letting her gaze drift sideways as she rested her cheek on her palm. My own hand inadvertently rose to my own face. With the Dermablend, my grandmother swore, you couldn't see the scar. With her vision, I told her, it was a wonder she could see anything.

"Yeah, I did. I liked it a lot." *Lie.* My first week of college I'd gone to a party in a fraternity house basement. It was hot and crowded and noisy, and I'd gotten separated from my roommate as we made our way through the forest of bodies toward the keg. I'd gone upstairs to hide in the frat house's library, which I'd figured, correctly, would be deserted. I was curled up in an armchair in a dark corner, planning on going back downstairs when the crowd had thinned out, when a girl and a guy had stumbled into the darkened room and flopped onto the couch.

"Jesus," said the guy. "Did you see that girl with, like, a crater on her face?"

My hands flew to my cheek. It did look like a crater. A shiny pink crater, the size of the bottom of a soda can, slightly indented, like someone had scooped out the flesh. The scar tugged the corner of my right eye down and extended across my cheek to the corner of my mouth. I'd fooled myself into thinking that I looked all right that night. I'd worn a cute halter top, pink sandals, jeans my roommate had lent me, and perfume and lipstick and eyeliner on my good left eye and my droopy right one.

"I wonder what happened?" the girl mused.

What do you think happened, dumb-ass? I got hurt! I wanted to say. I waited until they were too engrossed in each other to notice me. Then I crept out of the room, out of the frat house, down the sidewalk and over the hill and into the fitness center, which was open twenty-four hours a day and was one of the reasons I'd gone to Grant in the first place.

The pool was empty and glowing turquoise in the murky light. The familiar smell of chlorine, the feel of the water holding me up, eased my homesickness and my shame. I'd shucked off my borrowed finery, washed the makeup from my face in the shower, scrubbing extra hard against the disk of pink that no cosmetic could ever erase and no surgery could restore, and swum laps for two hours. Later, after I'd gotten dressed again, I stared at myself in the mirror. My wet hair clung to my scalp, and the scar was livid against my water-bleached skin. *Smile!* my grandmother always told me, her own face lighting up in demonstration. *If you'd smile, they'd see the smile, not the scar!* In the mirror, I attempted a friendly smile. A flirtatious smile. A charming little nice-to-meet-you smile. I saw the same pale, lightly freckled skin that my mother had, in pictures, the same clear blue eyes; a straight nose, full lips, eyebrows that refused to arch no matter how I tried to coax them. Good teeth, thanks to the braces; no zits, thanks to the Accutane. A cute face, or it could have been, without, like, the crater. I sighed, and turned away from the mirror and trudged back up the hill to my dorm.

"College was terrific," I told Caitlyn, and then, unable to help myself, I cupped my cheek with my palm.

She flicked her phone open and shut, open and shut, "I don't know," she said. "Berkeley's so big? Every time I go there with my parents, I just feel . . ." Her voice trailed off. She put the phone into her tiny pink purse and slid her cup across the table, shifting if from her left hand to her right, then back again. "Lost?"

"You'll make friends," I said.

She shrugged.

"Well, have you thought about other options? Maybe a smaller campus?"

"My parents," she said. The sour little smirk on her pink lips made her look much older than seventeen. "They're, like, obsessed. They both went there, you know."

"They mentioned it," I acknowledged.

Caitlyn bent her head and nibbled at a ragged fingertip. "I don't know," she said again.

"Well, maybe you should make an appointment with your school's guidance counselor. We're still early in the process, you know. It's not too late to change your mind."

She nodded, looking unconvinced. "Next Saturday I'll give you back the application. We'll go over it together, and I'll take a look at your personal statement."

"Can I ask you something?" I felt my shoulders stiffen. After all this time, I'd developed a pretty good sense as to when strangers were going to pop the question.

"Sure."

She swung one long leg over the other. "When you asked about volunteer work? I take care of my little brother sometimes? But it's not, like, an official thing."

"Well, that's nice of you, but I don't think babysitting's going to impress the admissions committee too much," I said, as gently as I could.

A pink flush crept up from her neck to her jawline. "Oh. Okay."

"But we could put it in there anyhow. It couldn't hurt."

She nodded, once, a princess dismissing a serf. Then she tucked her little purse under her arm and loped through the coffee shop, out to her fancy car with the Berkeley logo wrapped around the license plate. I wondered whether her parents paid her for the inordinate hardship of tending to her sibling. I bet myself that they did.

"So?" called my grandmother from her bedroom that night. "How was your day?"

"Fine," I said, setting down my laptop and piling my folders next to the bowl of wax fruit on our kitchen table, a heavy claw-footed mahogany thing that had looked much more at home in our four-bedroom colonial in Massachusetts than it did in our two-bedroom apartment in Hancock Park. I'd made it through five applicants that day, including an hour-long session with a boy who believed fervently—and, in my opinion, mistakenly—that he was going to get into Tufts, even though he had a B-minus average and had been suspended his sophomore year for selling oregano to his gullible classmates at a school dance. I rolled my shoulders, trying to work out some of the tension, as my grandmother shuffled into view, wearing her customary after-six attire: a lace-trimmed peach satin negligee, leopard-print mules, and Queen Helene's Mint Julep Mud Masque, which, she swore, kept her looking not a day over sixty. She looked like Miss Havisham in blackface. Greenface.

She teetered across the linoleum over to the stove. "Flanken?"

"I'll grab something on my way back from the pool," I said. We'd been in Los Angeles for years now, but my grandmother still persisted in cooking like it was Christmas in New England and we were expecting a hockey team or two to show up for dinner. She'd regularly prepare flanken with kasha and bow ties, or clam chowder and peppery cheddar-cheese biscuits. At least once a month, she'd stuff an entire leg of lamb with garlic and rosemary and wrestle it on the little hibachi on our tiny tiled porch.

I went to my bedroom for my gym bag. Grandma followed me in, a plate in her hands, concern on her face.

"Ruthie, when do you think you'll start writing again?"

"I'm writing," I protested, folding a pair of jeans and a black sleeveless turtleneck into my bag.

"Fixing college applications for spoiled rich kids is not writing, Ruth Anne." First and middle name. She wasn't messing around. When she set the plate down beside my bed, the minty scent of her mud mask mixed with the smell of buckwheat, onion gravy, and roasted meat.

"It pays the bills," I said.

"It's not what you want," she said.

"And where is it written that I get what I want?"

She grabbed my shoulders with her skinny hands and kissed my cheek, smearing me with green minty slime. "I wrote that," she said, and kissed me again, and shooed me out the door.

I belong to one of Los Angeles's super-trendy fitness hot spots, a club on Wilshire Boulevard with floor-to-ceiling glass windows on the cardio floor overlooking the bumper-to-bumper backup of luxury automobiles. It's expensive, especially because I don't take any of the fancy classes, or use the tanning booths or the sauna or the steamroom, or drop off my dry cleaning at their in-house facility, or hang out and surf the Internet in the juice bar. I was there only for the pool, and the pool was almost always empty, and probably would continue to be until an enterprising Angeleno invented some underwater regimen guaranteed to lengthen, strengthen, and eradicate cellulite.

I pulled off my clothes, pulled on my black tank suit, and tugged on my cap and my goggles while I stood under the running water. In Massachusetts, we'd belonged to the JCC. Over their Olympic-size pool was a quote from the Talmud, rendered in blue and green tile: *Some say a parent should teach a child to swim.* Here, all the tiles were blinding white, the better for beautiful gym-goers to glimpse their reflections glimmering back at them. No Talmud. I held my breath and did a shallow dive into the deep end. I started off slowly, getting used to the water, pointed toes fluttering, arms pushing against the resistance. Breaststroke first, to warm up, ten easy laps with racing turns at each end of the pool. Once my muscles were loose, I'd move into the crawl, and maybe throw in some butterfly if the spirit moved me. It was Saturday night. My fellow fitness buffs had already finished their workouts while I was in the coffee shop grappling with big dreams and bad prose.

After eighty laps, I pushed my goggles up onto my forehead and rolled onto my back, doing a lazy backstroke down the length of the pool and staring at the ceiling. More white tiles; no windows, and no sky.

My grandmother and I had moved out west when I was twenty-three and she was seventy. She wanted warm weather, and a chance to live near the movie stars, in what she routinely referred to, without any irony whatsoever, as the Glamour Capital of the World. I wanted to be a writer—movies, sitcoms, jokes, maybe even greeting cards if things got desperate. Los Angeles felt like the place to be.

We'd sold the house in Framingham—the one where I'd lived with my parents, before the accident, and where I'd lived with my grandmother for twenty years after that. At her insistence, we'd shipped almost every piece of furniture cross-country. I'd packed up the kitchen, the plates and pots and pans. She packed the photo albums, the precious handfuls of pictures of her daughter and son-in-law and me. "The Little Family," my mother had written across the back of one of the shots. Her name was Cynthia, and she'd been so beautiful, with pale blue eyes and hair that fell from a widow's peak high on her forehead. My father wore aviator sunglasses and had a goatee. I was usually snuggled somewhere between them, one thumb corkscrewed firmly in my mouth, my eyes wide and startled, one plump little starfish hand always touching one of them—my father's shoulder, my mother's hair.

My grandmother and I found a cozy apartment in a Spanish-style building in Hancock Park, with a tiled fountain tinkling in the lobby, terra-cotta floors, and high plaster arches dividing the rooms. Grandma signed up with a few of the agencies that hired extras for TV shows and movies, and worked three days a week. Just about every medical drama needed a few senior citizens to stick in the hospital beds for the background shots, and it made her enough money to kick in for the rent and, as she put it, keep herself in heels.

After a year of temping during the daytime and writing spec scripts at night, I found an agent. Three months after that, I landed a job writing for an hour-long drama (but a drama with jokes, our bosses anxiously insisted) called *The Girls' Room,* which was about four best friends at a boarding school in some unnamed town in New England. The show achieved the near-impossible by (a) actually getting picked up by a network, and (b) not getting canceled after it failed to crack the Nielsen top twenty in its first three weeks. The suits told us they wanted to give us time to find our way, to build an audience. They were giving us a chance.

Then one of the other writers, Robert Curtis—Robert with the crinkles at the corner of his eyes and the black hair laced with gray, Robert who smiled so rarely that you'd find yourself trying everything in your power to get to see him do it—parked himself in the chair next to mine during read-through one morning and asked if I'd help him with the scene he was working on. He leaned close to me and kept his voice low as he confided, "I'm having trouble thinking like a teenage girl." His incisors were crooked, one was longer than the other, which only served to make him more adorable.

Rob was a few years older than I was, and he'd worked on three other shows before landing in *The Girls' Room,* which, oddly enough, was written by a staff of three women and eighteen men. "You've never had a writing partner?" he asked me that first day, leaning back in the fantastically ugly orange-and-gold-plaid Barcalounger that someone had placed (ironically, of course) in the corner of the gray-carpeted writers' room, where it always smelled like garlic salami and dirty feet. "You want to give it a try?"

I nodded. I liked the way he looked at me, the questions he'd ask about where I'd come from, the way he'd slide a Diet Coke across the table when we worked late into the night, anticipating down to the second when I'd need a fresh can. I liked the big black plastic glasses he wore, and his rusty Karmann Ghia, and the way he honestly didn't seem to care at all what anyone thought of him (which, of course, made everyone like him, and want him to like them, too).

The first thing we wrote together was a prom scene, where Cara, one of the four girls of *The Girls' Room,* accepts two different invitations to two different proms, while Elise, her roommate, doesn't get invited at all and agrees to stand in for Cara at one of the dances. "This is nonsense, isn't it?" Rob asked, tossing his empty coffee cup into the trash can after six hours and four drafts.

"Don't ask me," I said, stretching and yawning (after six hours and four drafts, my self-consciousness had faded, right along with my Dermablend). "I never went to the prom."

"My school didn't even have one," he told me.

"Where'd you go? Some military academy?"

"Swiss boarding school," he said.

I stared at him. I thought he was kidding, but with Rob, you could never be sure. I didn't know a single thing about his history: not where he'd grown up, not where he lived now, not whether he was married or involved with anyone.

"All this stuff about dresses," he grumbled, glaring at the notes we'd been given. "Girls really care that much?"

I sat back down in my own chair, trying for grace. "Girls do."

"You know what we need?" he asked. "Pie. Come on. I'm buying."

"But this is due in . . ."

"We're not getting anywhere. We're spinning our wheels. We need a break." He jingled his car keys in the pocket of his khaki cutoffs that trailed threads down his hairy legs.

"You look like a lemon meringue kind of girl."

I got up and followed him as he did an exaggerated cartoon-ish tiptoe past the model-slash-receptionist. "I got your back," he muttered out of the corner of his mouth as he pushed the heavy glass door open and we race-walked into the sun-shine of the parking lot. "Head down, head down!" he whis-pered, opening his car's door and hustling me inside. "If anyone sees us . . ."

"It's curtains?" I said, getting into the spirit.

"Nah," he said as the car rumbled to life. "They'd just want pie, too."

We moved into a shared office a week later and worked to-gether for the next six months, bouncing ideas off each other, reading dialogue across the table, even acting out the parts. Rob kept balled-up athletic socks in his desk, and he'd shove them down the front of his T-shirt to impersonate Cara, the most im-probably endowed of the quartet, who was played by a twenty-four-year-old named Taryn Montaine. Rob swore he recognized her from a softcore porno that still aired late at night on Show-time. "I know it's her," he'd said after forty fruitless minutes scouring the Internet for a picture that would prove it. "She just got a new fake name to go with her new fake tits." When he got bored with searching for pictures of a pre-implant Taryn, he'd look at me with a lazy smile. "You know what you need?" he'd ask. He always did know, whether it was a burrito for lunch or a bag of chips or a butter rum LifeSaver, or a drive to Santa Monica. (Once he rented Rollerblades, and I sat on a bench and laughed at him stumbling around for half an hour.)

We were together for ten hours a day on normal days, something closer to twenty on the Thursday nights when we'd tape. I still didn't know much about his personal life, but I knew every T-shirt he had in his wardrobe. I knew that his cleaning ladies came on Tuesdays and that he had a poker game every other Friday, that his father had died of emphysema and his mother lived in Arizona. I knew how he looked first thing in the morning (rumpled, tired), and how he looked late at night (more rumpled, more tired, with more stubble). He called me Lemon Meringue, and once or twice he'd actually introduced me as his work wife, making my heart beat like a little girl who's gotten just what she wanted for her birthday.

I tugged my goggles back down, flipped over again, and kicked toward the end of the pool, forcing my aching arms high over my head, then knifing them into the water. Five months after we'd written it, the first episode Rob and I had collaborated on was scheduled to air on a Thursday night. My grandmother, who'd been as charmed by Rob as I was, decided a party was in order. She'd invited a bunch of her extra friends over to our apartment, and spent two days making brisket and borscht and potato-and-onion pierogies, covering the dark wood of our dining room table and sideboard with lace doilies, then loading them with platters of food. "A feast fit for a czar," I'd told her, straightening the plates, filling the ice bucket, too nervous to sit or eat a bite as her senior-citizen friends, with their canes and walkers and snap-brim hats, filed into the living room.

I'd perched on the edge of one of the dining room chairs, in a pretty pale-green sundress I'd bought for the occasion, counting down the minutes on the VCR's clock. Rob never showed. I left him three messages—two casual-cool, one desperate. I forced myself to watch the episode; then I'd hidden in my bedroom until the last of the extras, bearing Tupperware containers full of beet soup and sour cream, had gone home. I was under the covers in my sundress and my sandals when my grandmother crept into the room.

"You came home pretty late last night, Ruthie."

I groaned and opened my eyes. She was standing beside me, still dressed for the party in a vintage cocktail caftan, with diamanté hair clips and rhinestone-buckled shoes that clattered on the terra-cotta floors. "Did you sleep with him?" she asked.

I could hear Boston in her voice, and it made me ache for home as I nodded, too ashamed to say yes. *You know what you need?* I'd asked Rob the night before, at one in the morning, after we'd finished our script. He'd lifted his shaggy eyebrows. *Me,* I said, marveling at my own boldness, holding my breath until he grinned and said, *Well, Ruthie, I wouldn't say no.* I'd looked straight into his eyes, imagining—oh, it made my insides cringe to think about it—that I was Taryn Montaine as I unbuttoned my blouse, as I crossed the room, knelt, and unzipped his pants. His quick inhalation when my lips had touched him, the way, at the end, he'd groaned my name, all of it had made me think that he was feeling something more than mere gratification, or gratitude; that he was falling in love.

Afterward, snuggled against him in the Barcalounger, I'd been foolish enough to hope for the impossible: the workplace romance that actually worked. We were good together. Our months as writing partners proved it. And maybe, after one night of bliss on scratchy synthetic tweed, Rob would realize that I was the love of his life, that we belonged together.

My grandmother sat down next to me and stroked my hair. "Are you okay?" she asked, and I'd nodded again, without knowing whether it was true.

On Friday I'd gone to the office and Rob hadn't been there. I accepted congratulations numbly, nodding my thanks, asking everyone if they'd seen him. Nobody had. I spent the weekend in agony, looking at my cell phone every thirty seconds or so, imagining horrible scenarios: Rob dead in a car accident, Rob in a hospital with amnesia, or cancer, or both.

The show-runner, a twenty-seven-year-old named Steve, called me into his office first thing Monday morning. "So where's that partner of mine?" I asked with a smile.

"Sit down," he suggested. I sat down on an impressive, wildly uncomfortable Lucite and metal chair underneath his Emmys. "Rob and Taryn eloped over the weekend."

"He . . . Taryn . . . what?" This was a joke, I thought. Had to be. Rob barely spoke to Taryn during the read-throughs and rehearsals, and when he talked about her, it was usually to make fun of her implants or her pornographic past.

Steve kept a Magic 8 Ball on his desk (ironically, of course). He picked it up and shook it gently. "I guess she's pregnant."

I nodded numbly. I couldn't speak, couldn't move. I breathed deeply, hoping he wouldn't see that the blood had drained out of my face. I pictured Rob and Taryn together, his arm around her shoulder, one hand resting lightly on her belly. *The little family.*

"Hello? Excuse me?"

I looked up, startled, and sucked water into my nose. The janitor was standing by the side of the pool, pointing at the clock on the white-tiled wall as I coughed and spluttered. "Ten o'clock. We're closing now."

I shook the water out of my ears, took a quick shower, and

toweled off, avoiding the ubiquitous mirrors as I pulled on my clothes. On the way home I bought three fish tacos at Poquito Mas, and a chicken burrito for Grandma to eat in the morning. She was asleep when I arrived, snoring on the gold brocade sofa. My plate of flanken, covered in plastic wrap, sat on top of the stove. I put the food in the refrigerator, then eased my grandmother's legs onto the couch, slipped off her mules, covered her with a blanket, and flicked the television set into silence. My muscles were singing and my head still felt waterlogged. As I tumbled down into sleep, I remembered Caitlyn, the crack I'd made about babysitting. *I should get her a book,* I thought. *Let her look at all the colleges in the country. Let her make a real choice . . .* Then I was out.

"Excuse me?"

I looked up, ready to defend my right to the table I'd once again commandeered at 9:30 on the following Saturday morning. Mostly the screenwriters would just glare and mutter, but occasionally one of them would work up the nerve to walk over and demand to know when I'd be finished. *Sorry,* I'd say with a sweet and insincere smile. *I'm on deadline.*

"Yes?" I said, bracing myself.

The guy standing in front of me was tall and thin, with curly black hair cut so short I could see flashes of his scalp. He wore jeans and a faded gray long-sleeved T-shirt, and he had hazel eyes, pale skin, and little nick on his chin, probably from shaving, just above his pointy Adam's apple. "You were in here last week, right?"

I nodded. *Here we go.* He was probably going to tell me that hoarding the power outlet for two weeks in a row was such egregiously bad behavior I'd either have to move or he'd get management involved.

"You're a writer?"

I nodded a second time, a little quizzically. Yes, I was a writer. It was pretty safe to assume that anyone in Los Angeles who spent more than an hour sitting in front of a laptop in a coffee shop was a writer.

"Can I ask what kind of writing you do?"

"All kinds."

I'd left *The Girls' Room* with a nice severance check and my tail between my legs nine months before. Since then I'd been between shows, collecting enough unemployment to support myself, and Grandma, in reasonable style. The applications started out as a hobby, something to keep me busy and get me out of the house, but, just lately, I was making real money, with a lot less grief than writing scripts had wound up giving me. No Rob, no writing partners, no late nights or interfering corporate overlords. No complications. I gave the guy a polite smile and flipped open the screen of my computer, bracing myself not for a turf war over my table but for the other inevitable L.A. conversation, the one that started with a question about whether I was working on anything right now and ended with a naked plea for my agent's name and e-mail address.

The guy rocked back and forth on his sneakered feet. "You were in here with a girl last week. Dark hair? Pink shirt?"

Oh, Lord. This was even worse than getting hit up for my agent's number. "Dark hair? Pink shirt?" I parroted. "I was helping her with her college applications. She's seventeen." *You perv,* I thought, but restrained myself from saying, as I gave him my please-be-gone smile.

Instead of looking insulted, he smiled back. "That's what I thought," he said. "Did you help with her essays?"

"That's right," I said. "Essays and interviews. I videotape my clients, give them tips on how to present themselves, stuff like that. And I really should get back to work now." I looked intently at my screen, but he didn't leave.

"I've got kind of a business proposition for you. May I?" He looked at the other chair. I studied him more carefully.

"You're too young to have a kid applying to college."

"No kids that I know of," he said, taking a seat.

"So . . . you're applying to grad school?"

"Nope." He set his coffee cup on the table. "I'm setting up a profile for an online dating site, but I'm not a great writer. I could use some help."

I stared at him, making sure I understood. "You want me to script-doctor your online dating profile."

"Yes," he said, nodding and raising his coffee cup in a toast, looking pleased with himself, pleased with me, that I'd gotten the point so quickly. "I just think that, right now, it sounds a little generic. I just sound like anybody. Any guy."

"And you're not."

He shrugged. "I don't think I am, but who knows? Maybe I'm wrong."

I pulled a notebook out of my purse and flipped to a fresh page. Part of me thought this was the weirdest thing I'd ever heard. Another part—the part of me that had been eyeing a little Craftsman bungalow on Sierra Bonita—saw this guy as a potential gateway into a large and lucrative new market. There were only so many college seniors who needed my help and whose parents could afford me, and college apps would keep me busy only through the January 15 deadline. But personal ads were a year-round concern, and there was probably a limitless pool of the lovelorn and vocabulary-challenged who'd be willing to pay . . . let's see . . .

"How much work are we talking about?" I asked.

He'd come prepared. Reaching into a hard-sided backpack,

he pulled out a manila folder, and pulled from that three pages. The first one had a screen name (Lonelyguy 78) and a picture of the fellow in front of me, wearing a suit and a tie and a forced, dorky grin.

I stared down at the picture, then up at him. "Was that, by any chance, the shot they took for your employee ID tag?"

He squirmed, pulling the cuffs of his shirt down over his wrists. "You can tell? I know it's not the best picture, but they needed a head shot, and that was the one I had on my computer."

I shook my head, then studied his face. He was decent-looking. The photograph didn't do him credit. "That's the first thing. Get a new picture. One that doesn't make you look like a narc."

He pulled a pen out of his pocket and wrote the words *No narc* on the front of the folder. Then he pulled a plastic bag of red pistachios out of his backpack and offered them to me.

"No thanks," I said automatically, even though I adored anything salty, pistachios most of all—and of pistachios, my favorite were the ones with dyed shells that stained your fingertips red.

"You sure?" he asked, holding the open bag toward me.

"Well, maybe just a few," I said.

"Go nuts," he told me, and smiled. "Joke."

"Got it," I murmured. I picked up my pen and studied the pages he'd given me, zeroing in on his screen name. " 'Lonelyguy'? Good Lord. Was 'Desperateguy' taken? Or 'I might kill you and cut up your body in my basement guy'?"

"They only give you twelve letters for your screen name. What's wrong with 'Lonelyguy'?" he asked, offering me more pistachios.

"It's a little needy," I said, and tried not to sigh as my mind flashed to Rob. His confidence, the way he could walk into a room of overcaffeinated writers or anxious executives and lure them toward him with a self-deprecating joke, was what I'd loved most about him. I winced, and mentally swapped "liked" for "loved," and then downgraded "liked" to "appreciated," then reminded myself firmly that the most important adjective as far as Rob had been concerned was now, of course, "taken." I scanned the rest of Lonelyguy's profile. Turn-ons, turnoffs, preferred body type, hair colors and eye colors he'd consider, as if a woman could be ordered up like a meal at a restaurant, where a diner could swap french fries for mashed potatoes and insist on his dressing on the side.

Under "my date," he'd checked off ages from twenty-five to thirty-five. For body types, he was willing to consider "fit" and "slender." I'd urge him to throw in an "average," given that plenty of fit and/or slender women—didn't necessarily see themselves that way.

"It used to be swim."

I looked up, startled. "Huh?"

"Swim. My screen name. SWM. For Single White Male." He shook his head, embarrassed. "Talk about generic, right?"

"Do you like to swim?"

"Sure. I guess. But nobody here really does it. Have you ever noticed that? People go to Malibu and the only ones in the water are the surfers and the dogs."

I nodded. I'd noticed. I'd even bought myself a wet suit and spent a few Sundays bobbing around in the rough waves of the frothy blue-green water, figuring—hoping—I'd look like a surfer who'd lost her board, or, alternately, a dog owner who'd lost her dog.

"What's your name?"

"Ruth Saunders."

"Ruth the truth," he said, sweeping the litter of pistachio shells into his empty paper cup.

"Just Ruth will be fine," I said, and flipped briskly through the rest of the pages. "Okay, now . . ."

The sound of Caitlyn's high-heeled boots on the hardwood floor made us both look up. "Am I late?" she asked.

I looked at my watch. Ten a.m.

"She's all yours," said Lonelyguy.

"Are you trying to get into college?" Caitlyn asked him.

"No, he's trying to get into women's . . ." I stopped myself before I could say *pants*.

"Hearts," he said with a charming smile. "I'm Gary, by the way."

"Caitlyn," she said, smiling back. I sat there ("Like a lox!" I could hear my grandmother moan) while they eyed each other appreciatively. It made me wonder why Gary the Lonelyguy was lonely in the first place. Clearly, he wasn't having any trouble with Caitlyn.

Eventually Gary picked up his backpack. "Do you have anything free later today, Ruth?"

My last applicant was at one. "Would two o'clock work?"

"I'll be back," he said. "Do you have a card or something?" I did, a very nice one, with my e-mail address, and the words *application counselor* beneath my name. My grandmother had had them printed up at Kinko's the month before.

Gary slipped the card in his pocket, raised his coffee cup in another toast, and then was gone.

"Huh," said Caitlyn. "Cute." She reached into the tiny purse she'd carried last time and extracted a wad of paper that, once unfolded sixteen times, turned out to be her essay.

I sipped my coffee and read it through while Caitlyn wandered off to provision herself with a smoothie. "For a California girl, spending two weeks in Paris was a truly transformative experience," it began. Stifling a yawn, I arranged my face into a pleasant expression and broke things to Caitlyn as gently as I could when she came back with her cup.

"It's very competent," I began. "Very smoothly written."

She took a slurp of her smoothie. "So that's good?" She slipped off her cropped denim jacket, revealing an off-the-shoulder sweatshirt. Had the Flashdance look come back again? Had I missed it? I made a mental note to see if she was wearing leg warmers.

"Competent's okay, but okay's not going to get you into Berkeley." I tapped the first page with my pen. "Now, I can tell you had a great time in Paris."

Her brown eyes sparkled, and her hands danced in the air. "The flea markets were awesome! I found this cameo? On a silk ribbon?" Her fingers traced a line along her neck.

"That sounds beautiful. Really. But there's none of that passion on the page," I said. Her essay hadn't even mentioned the flea market. Instead, she'd written about the Louvre, and the Seine, and various and sundry cathedrals. The whole thing could have been lifted from a *Let's Go* guide.

Caitlyn gave me a blank look, pulled one knee up against her chest, and poked her straw deeper into her smoothie. "Passion?"

"If you loved the flea markets, you should write about the flea markets."

"But that's, like, shopping! No college is going to admit me because I like to shop!"

"They might if you can write persuasively and with passion. If you use this essay to tell them who you really are, what you really care about. If you . . ." I rubbed my cheek. Suddenly I had a headache. What if I was wrong? What if she wrote her essay about the flea markets and the admissions people decided she was an overprivileged brat?

I took a deep breath. "Okay. Maybe not shopping. But passion. Something else you're passionate about."

She shrugged, rolling her straw wrapper between two fingers. Her nails looked worse than they had the week before. "The thing about this . . ." I tapped my pen on top of her essay, remembering the word Lonelyguy had used: *generic.* "A hundred kids could have written this."

She shrugged. "There were only twenty kids on the trip."

"Well, twenty kids, then."

"Fine." She gathered her pages and began to refold them.

"Well, wait. We can talk about it, if you want. Try out some different . . ."

"That's okay. I know what I'm going to write about." The zipper on the purse was so loud I could hear it over the blenders, and over the two twentysomething screenwriters at the next table who were talking intently into the single cell phone that lay open on the table between them.

"Well, should we talk about the interviews? You've got one coming up in . . ." I clicked open her file. She shook her head.

"I'm okay. I'll just work on this for a while. See you next week."

"Caitlyn . . ." Too late. She was up, and she was gone.

I sat there for four more hours, for three more clients. I drank iced espresso and endured the glares of my seatmates until 2:45, when I packed up my laptop and eased out the door. Lonelyguy never came back.

"Nu?" asked Grandma. "Well?" It was October, seventy-two degrees under a cloudless blue sky. The breeze blowing through the opened windows carried the scent of lemons and jacaranda, and dinner: roasted turkey, with gravy, and stuffing, creamed onions, and cranberry sauce. Most Americans reserved

these items for Thanksgiving. My grandmother cooked them at least once a month, and served them in her gold-rimmed good china.

I dropped my keys into the blue-and-white-painted bowl by the door and followed her onto the terrace, where she'd draped our tiny metal-legged table for two in a festive orange tablecloth. She'd lit candles, too, and set the food out on platters on the little rolling drinks cart the previous tenants had left behind. I helped myself to a plate. "I think I've found a new line of work."

I expected my grandmother's eyes to light up when I told her about Lonelyguy, thinking of the money all that desperation could bring. Instead, she set down her fork and fixed me with a stern gaze that would have been more effective if she'd been wearing something other than a hot-pink kimono.

"Ruthie, you're spinning your wheels."

I patted my lips and looked at her calmly. "What do you mean?"

"This classified stuff, it's nice, you know. A mitzvah."

"Well, I wouldn't be doing it for free. I bet I could get people to pay five hundred bucks for a rewrite. Or maybe I could come up with some kind of contingency scale. Like, if ten people e-mail you when the new profile goes up, you pay . . ."

"What about your screenplay?" Grandma asked innocently, her pale eyes guileless under their false eyelashes as she spooned creamed onions onto her plate. She'd only blended her rouge on one side of her face. The other side was a clownish circle of pink. "The movie you were writing?"

I sighed. "I think I lost my inspiration."

"I think you lost your boyfriend," she said.

I set my knife down on a pile of green beans. "He wasn't really my boyfriend."

"If you fall off the horse . . ."

". . . you get back on the horse," I recited. "But guys aren't horses. I don't want to meet anyone right now. I'm very happy. Just because I'm single right now doesn't mean I'm not happy. I don't need a man to be happy!"

She pushed herself off her chair and drew herself up to her full height, giving the dragon embroidered across her chest a fond pat before she started talking. "When your mother, my daughter, was on her deathbed, I made her a promise," she began, her Boston accent turning "daughter" into "dodder" and "promise" into "prahmise."

Oh, God, I thought. Not the deathbed promise. That was Grandma's big gun, brought out once every few years, maximum. "You've taken wonderful care of me."

"I promised that I could always make sure that you were well taken care of and happy . . ." she continued as if I hadn't said a word, jabbing the air with her fork.

"I am happy."

"But you're not!" she said, dropping her fork onto her plate and glaring at me. "You're afraid! You think everyone's staring at you, judging you . . ."

"I am not afraid!"

". . . and spending your whole life underwater isn't natural, Ruth Anne!"

I raised my eyebrows and made a face, as if this was the most ridiculous thing I'd ever heard. "It's not natural to swim?"

"It's not natural to hide," she said. Her cheeks were flushed underneath the rouge, and a vein in her neck was fluttering. "Or to pretend you don't want love."

"I'm not hiding," I said, and shoved my hair behind my ear, off my scarred cheek, to emphasize the point. "And I do want love. Just not right now."

"So when, then?" she asked. "Next year? The year after that? Five years? I'm not going to live forever, Ruthie, and"—she reached across the table to grab my chin in her pincer grip— "nobody else is, either. You should know that. You, of all people."

I nodded, pulling my head away. "Okay," I muttered, sounding like a chastened teenager. "Fine."

She pretended she didn't hear me. "Decaf," she said, lifting her empty cup. "Please."

Later that night, I turned on my computer. There was one e-mail in my in-box, one lonely e-mail from Lonelyguy. "Sorry I stood you up," Gary said. "Something suddenly came up. I could meet you after work any night this week, or if you're free we could hook up tomorrow."

I stared at the message for a while. Maybe Lonelyguy was all there was for girls like me. Girls like Taryn, the gorgeous, confident ones, got the pick of the litter; girls like me got to choose among the also-rans and wannabes, the humor-impaired pistachio-eaters who'd think they were doing us a big favor by dating us and expect a lifetime of gratitude, not to mention oral sex, as recompense.

I thought of Gary in the coffee shop, all shaving cuts and eagerness, without any of Robert's edge, his black, cutting humor, and I wrote, "What occurs to me after a careful reading of your profile is that you were right. Sorry to be blunt, but there's very little here to distinguish you from any other guy your age. Do you have any hobbies? Pets? Passions? Talents? Anything?"

I sent it before I could reconsider. It was mean, I knew, but I was feeling like my heart had been shredded after my grandmother had accused me of hiding, of burying myself underwater and failing to make her happy before she died. If inflicting some of my misery onto Lonelyguy meant I'd be able to sleep, I wouldn't hesitate.

His reply arrived in my in-box five minutes later. "Can juggle a little. Can bake cookies. Have read every book Raymond Carver and Russell Banks have ever written. No pets, though. Should I get one?"

Christ. I typed, "I think getting a pet so you can pick up girls online is tantamount to animal abuse. PS: Please add reading stuff to profile. Chicks dig books."

"Will do," he wrote back almost instantly. "Re: pickup pet. I'd give it a good home and feed it that organic stuff they sell at Whole Foods. What do chicks dig? Cats? Dogs? Ferrets?"

"No idea," I typed back. I was wondering how much I could pour from Grandma's dusty bottle of Baileys without her noticing and thinking that, at my age, it was probably time for me to start buying my own nightcaps.

"Meet me at the valet parking stand at the Beverly Center at three o'clock tomorrow afternoon to discuss," he wrote. "It can be a consult. I will pay."

"Fair enough," I murmured, clicking on the X in the corner of his message and sending it to electronic oblivion.

"No. I won't do it," I said, and shook my head, refusing to move another inch closer to the pet-shop windows that overlooked the fourth floor of the Beverly Center shopping mall. "No, no, no. I'm not going in there, and you are not buying a pickup pet from a puppy mill."

"Lot of *p*'s in that sentence," said Gary, pulling a bag of nuts from a plastic bag looped over his wrist. "Pistachio?"

I looked in the bag. "Those are cashews."

"Yes, but pistachios sounded funnier." He bent down and

peered through the glass. A skinny Chihuahua looked out at us with wet brown eyes and wagged its thin tail hopefully.

I'd showed up at the Beverly Center parking stand at the appointed hour and found Lonelyguy waiting. I'd allowed him to steer me toward the escalators, then up to the fourth floor, where, on the way to the pet shop, he'd asked whether I'd ever done any online dating myself.

"No," I said. "Maybe some day. But I just got out of this long-term thing . . ."

He nodded sympathetically. "Prison?"

"A long-term relationship," I clarified. Okay, not technically true, but how was he going to know that? "Long-term relationship" definitely sounded better than "one misguided drunken blow job, given to a guy who eloped to Puerto Vallarta with Taryn Montaine two days later." The Chihuahua yawned and curled up on its side in a nest of shredded newspaper with its back to me. Fabulous. My pathetic excuse for a love life wasn't even interesting to lesser species.

"I've got a date tonight," he said.

"Well, that was fast," I replied, feeling an unpleasant twinge of emotion I couldn't name.

"Yep. I put a new picture up and added the stuff about the writers, and the cookies, and I got five responses by noon, and tonight I am seeing"—he stared at the shopping-mall ceiling, clicking his tongue against the roof of his mouth—"a d-girl named Dana."

"Well, good," I said, trying to sound enthusiastic. "That's great!"

"I could use some wardrobe advice. What do you think?"

I studied his outfit. From its glass enclosure, the dog appeared to be checking him out, too. Blue ring-neck long-sleeved T-shirt, khakis, orange Pumas. Official uniform of the

Los Angeles man-boy. The khakis were supposed to signal *I have a job,* while the funky shirt and sneakers said *but I haven't sold out.* Robert had worn the plaid shirts and concert T-shirts he'd had since high school. Nobody would ever mistake him for the Man. Once, he'd told me, he'd been sitting outside World of Pies and someone tried to put a dollar bill in his coffee cup. Which, he'd said, looking pained, was full at the time.

"Are you pro or anti cologne?" Gary asked.

"I'm indifferent."

His Adam's apple jerked and bobbed when he swallowed. "Help a brother out," he said. "It can't be any worse than listening to the hopes and dreams of seventeen-year-olds." He led me toward Macy's and got me to sniff half a dozen eye-watering potions that he sprayed into the air. "What do you think?" he asked after each one. "Is it doing anything for you?"

I rolled my eyes, and finally started laughing when he waggled his eyebrows and asked, in an atrocious Austin Powers accent, whether something that smelled aggressively of limes was making me horny. "Are you newlyweds?" the bespectacled, gray-haired saleswoman asked as she wrapped up Gary's Chanel por Homme.

He gave her a sweet smile and took my hand. "Brother and sister."

Back at the valet stand, I wished him good luck with his date.

"It's not too late," he said. He pumped my hand up and down once, and then he just held it.

"Too late for what?"

"We could go back in there. Buy that puppy. I'll ditch the d-girl. You'll forget about your unfortunate time behind bars. We could go to the beach and let the little guy run around."

I shook my head. "You need practice, and I've got plans." I

retrieved my hand and put it in my pocket. "You might want to take a shower first, though. You smell kind of confusing."

"Can't have that," he said cheerfully, and handed the valet his parking stub. "See ya."

"Good luck," I said, leaving him to his date as I headed for the pool.

"Phone for you, Ruthie," my grandmother announced, clutching the cordless as if it were a wild animal she'd managed to subdue with her bare hands. "It's a man," she emphasized in a loud whisper, as if I'd missed the manic glee in her eyes. It was Saturday, six days after I'd left Lonelyguy at the mall. We'd been e-mailing. His date, he told me, had been a disaster. Dana the d-girl had ordered a salad and spent the entire dinner shifting the leaves around her plate and complaining about, in order, her producer bosses, her most recent ex-boyfriend, her father, and her allergies. "By coffee, I was feeling like I was responsible not only for my entire gender, but the atmosphere, too," he'd said. But it hadn't stopped him from lining up somebody else. Actually, two somebody elses—a pediatric resident on Friday, for drinks, and a public relations executive for Saturday-afternoon coffee. I'd advised him on clothing, scents, and topics of conversation. *Make eye contact,* I said. *Look at them like they matter, like they're the only one in the room.* He'd thanked me and mailed me a check. No matter what my grandmother wanted to believe, it was a business relationship, nothing more.

I took the telephone, assuming that it was Gary, wanting to debrief in real time. "Ruthie?"

His voice, as always, went straight to my heart and my knees, making the first one pound and the second two quiver. I sank onto Grandma's fringed apricot velvet fainting couch, displacing two doilies on my way down. "Rob," I said faintly. "How are you?"

"Good," he said. Then, "Busy."

"I bet." I wasn't sure whether I wanted to sound snide or sympathetic. My voice cracked on the last word. *Pull yourself together,* I told myself sternly, picking doilies up off the floor.

"With a new show, actually," he said.

"Oh?" My tone was polite. I'd quit reading *Variety* in the wake of our whatever-it-was, and I'd assumed that Rob was still working on *The Girls' Room,* which should just be gearing up for its next season.

I leaned my cheek against the soft nap of the couch as he went into his pitch: a family dramedy he was preparing for pilot season. Hot mom, recovering alcoholic dad, dysfunctional sisters who managed a Miami lingerie boutique.

"Are you interested?"

"Do you mean, would I watch it?"

He chuckled. "No. I know you're not that much of masochist. Would you write it? We could use you, Ruth. We could use your voice."

"You can't have it," I blurted.

Rob's laughter was warm and indulgent, the sound of a father's amusement at a cute but willful child. "Well, not for keeps. But you're not working . . ." He let his voice trail off, turning it into a question. When I didn't reply, he pressed on. "Look, you can't just sit around all day. There's only so many laps you can swim." His voice softened. I pictured him in one of his ratty see-through T-shirts, five days' worth of stubble, his glasses, and his rare, delicious grin. "And I miss working with you. We were good together."

"We were nothing," I said. My grandmother was staring at me from the kitchen with a cordial glass of crème de menthe in her hand, eyebrows raised.

"Ruth . . . look. I'm sorry for what happened. I'm sorry if it gave you the wrong idea."

"Sure thing. Well, okay then! Thanks for calling!" I kept my voice upbeat. Maybe Grandma would think my gentleman caller was a telemarketer.

"I'll take that as a no, then," he said.

"No," I said, and then, because I was nothing if not polite, I said, "No thank you."

"Big surprise, Ruth," he said. Then he was gone.

I swam for hours that night, tracing the tiled lap lane back and forth until my arms were numb. When I got home, Lonely-guy had e-mailed. "Is it just me," he'd asked, "or is every woman out there a freak?"

"I'm not," I whispered at the screen. But I didn't write it. I typed in "See you tomorrow," shut off the laptop, and crawled into bed.

The next morning I drove back to the Beverly Center for a new swimsuit, thinking that maybe I'd stop by the pet shop and see if the skinny puppy was still there. I was walking down the bright, bustling corridor toward the escalators when I saw a familiar figure—long, denim-clad legs; skinny shoulders; a swing of shiny dark-brown hair. "Caitlyn?"

She turned around. "Oh, hi, Ruth." She was wearing a big gray hoodie that enveloped her torso and had "Berkeley" written across the chest, and she was pushing a small, candy-apple-red wheelchair that carried the twisted frame of a little boy. The boy wore a Berkeley sweatshirt, too, and stiff blue jeans that looked like they'd never been washed, or worn, or walked in. His head rested against the wheelchair's padded cradle; the mall's lights glinted off his glasses. He made a hooting noise. Caitlyn looked down at him, then up at me.

"This is my brother, Charlie. Charlie, this is Ruth? She's helping me with my essays?"

"Hi." I bent down so I was at eye level with Charlie. I looked up at Caitlyn, who nodded, then extended my hand and touched it to his. His fingers were folded tightly against his palms, and his skin was so pale I could see the veins underneath it. "Nice to meet you."

He gave another hoot, his lips working, eyes focused on my face. Caitlyn reached into her pocket for a handkerchief and wiped his lips. "Do you want lunch now?" she asked. I wondered whether Charlie was the reason she always talked in questions, the way she left her sentences open-ended, blanks that would never get filled in. "We're going to go to the food court?"

"Oh. Well, have fun."

Charlie moaned again, more loudly, struggling hard to make himself understood. Caitlyn bent her shining head to his, murmuring something I couldn't make out. Her brother's eyes stayed locked on mine, and I thought I could see where he was pointing, where he was going.

When Caitlyn lifted her head her fair skin was flushed. "I'm sorry," she said.

"It's okay," I told her.

Charlie's fist bounced on his chest.

"He has cerebral palsy," she said.

I nodded, looked at Charlie, and touched my cheek. "It's a scar from an accident. A long time ago."

Caitlyn sighed, then straightened up. "Do you want to get some lunch with us?" The three of us walked to the food court and sat at a metal-legged plastic-topped table, surrounded by chattering teenagers, mothers and daughters, women in suits and hose and sneakers lingering on their lunch breaks. Caitlyn bought herself a Diet Coke, and, for Charlie, a paper cone of french fries. She dipped each one into ketchup and lifted it to his lips with the same absentminded love as the mothers feeding their toddlers at the neighboring tables.

"When I was three my parents were driving on the Mass Pike to Boston for Thanksgiving. They were both teachers, they'd gone to school in Boston, and they were going to have Thanksgiving with some friends. Their car hit a patch of ice and rolled over into a ditch. They died, and I went through the windshield, in my car seat. That's what happened to my face."

Charlie twisted his head toward his sister, his mouth working. "Do you remember it?" Caitlyn translated.

I shook my head. "I really don't remember it much."

Caitlyn wiped Charlie's face with a napkin. "So who took care of you?"

"My grandmother. She was living down in Coral Gables, but she didn't think that was a good place to raise a little girl, so she moved up to my parents' house in Framingham, and we lived there."

They seemed to think this over while Charlie chewed another french fry. He had the same brown eyes and rounded chin as his sister. There was a smear of pink glitter on his cheek, where, I thought, she'd kissed him.

I got up.

"Well, Caitlyn, I'll see you on Saturday. Nice to meet you, Charlie. Have a good day." It sounded so stupid, so trite. I wondered what Charlie's life was like, trapped in a body he couldn't control, able to understand what he was seeing and hearing, unable to communicate. I was halfway out of the food court when I turned around and went back to their table and tapped Caitlyn on the shoulder. "You should write about this," I blurted. She looked up at me with her shiny brown eyes. Her tiny pink purse was hooked over one of the arms of Charlie's wheelchair, which had NASCAR stickers on the sides. "I was wrong about you," I said.

She nodded, unsurprised. "That's okay," she said.

———

I skipped my swim that night. After it got dark, I pulled on a sweater that had been my mother's. It was frayed at the elbows and unraveling at the hem. In a few of the pictures I had, she was wearing this sweater, and I imagined that even after all this time it still held some trace of her—a strand of her walnut-colored hair, the lavender smell of her skin, invisible handprints where my father had touched her, pulling her close. I curled up in a corner of the couch and told my grandmother about Caitlyn and Charlie. Halfway through the story I started to cry. Grandma pulled a wad of tissue paper from her sleeve and handed it to me.

"What's wrong, honey?" She was dressed in a white night-gown with mounds of lace at the neck and the wrists, and she looked like a baby bird peeking out of its nest.

"I don't know." I wiped my eyes. "People surprise me some-times."

She considered this. "Well, that's good," she said. "As long as people can still surprise you, it means you're not dead."

At midnight I was still awake, nerves jangling, muscles twitching, missing the water. I flipped open my laptop, clicked on "Documents," double-clicked on the file called "The Little Family." It was a screenplay I'd started years ago. I read through the first ten pages slowly. It wasn't as good as I'd hoped, but it wasn't as bad as I feared, either. It had potential. I hit "save" and then scrolled through my in-box, opening a missive from Lonelyguy that had arrived the day before. "Maybe we should have dinner."

I hit "reply," then scrolled up to find an e-mail from Caitlyn that had come that afternoon. "New Essay," the subject line read.

"My eleven-year-old brother Charlie will never visit Paris," she'd written. "He won't play Little League baseball or run on the beach. He was diagnosed with cerebral palsy when he was three months old. *Cerebral: of or pertaining to the brain. Palsy: a disorder of movement or posture.* My brother sees the world from his wheelchair. When I grow up, I will see things for him. I will go to all the places he can't go, places where they don't have curb cuts or wheelchair ramps, to flea markets and mountaintops, all the places in the world."

I buried my face in my hands. How did Caitlyn get so brave? Why was I so afraid? I opened my eyes and closed the window containing Caitlyn's essay, leaving up my unwritten reply to Lonelyguy's letter and remembering what I'd told her the first time we'd met. *We're still early in the process. It's not too late to change your mind.*

GOOD MEN

At just past three o'clock in the morning, Bruce Guberman and the rest of the liquored-up bachelors piled into a booth at World of Bagels and hatched the plan to kidnap Bruce's girlfriend's rat terrier, Nifkin.

There had been twelve of them when the bachelor party had started, in the rented back room of a bar in Brooklyn. First they shot pool, then they'd played poker with laundry quarters and subway tokens. Poker had seemed like a good idea when Tom, the best man, broke out the cards, only he'd insisted that the winner of each hand do a shot, which meant that by the fifth hand there was a lot of inadvertent bluffing going on.

Things deteriorated after midnight when four of the groom's fellow lab mates split a cab back to Manhattan and the room began to empty out. Clouds of smoke and the sour reek of beer hung over the bar's scarred wooden tables and overflowing ashtrays. Tom presented Neil, the groom, with his wedding gift, which turned out to be a three-quarter ounce of marijuana wrapped, as Neil described it, in a festive matrimonial Baggie. Tom, with his face flushed and long strands of brown hair sticking to his sweaty cheeks, liked the sound of that so much he

117

repeated it over and over as the first bowl was packed and the pipe went around: *Festive Matrimonial Baggie!*

Half an hour later the stripper arrived—dressed, for some reason, like Snow White, in a tight red top and a full blue skirt, with her lips painted into a crimson Cupid's bow. Bruce blinked, trying to make sense of the costume. Did she have a day job at Six Flags or something like that? Her black hair was glossy under the bar's smoke-ringed lights. It might have been a wig. Bruce was never sure of those things. Cannie, his girl-friend, would twirl around for him, grinning, asking, "What do you think?" He'd stare at her desperately. What had changed? Had she lost weight, or gotten her hair highlighted? Was she wearing a new coat or new shoes? Sometimes she'd take pity on him and tell him—"He cut three inches! That's this much!" she'd say, holding her fingers apart for emphasis. He'd nod and smile and tell her it looked great, when the truth was that the only time he could really tell for sure was when she'd had her hair permed, and then only because of the smell.

The stripper set up a boom box that blared rap tunes with X-rated lyrics—*put your back into it, put your ass into it.* Within minutes she'd wriggled free of her costume and was gyrating against all five feet, four inches of the groom as if she were riding a mechanical merry-go-round—up, down, up, down, staring at him with a fixed, rigid smile, as Tom dumped a forty-ounce bot-tle of malt liquor over the soon-to-be-bridegroom's head.

"I'm the eighth dwarf!" Tom hollered, waving his hands in the air. "Horny!"

"There is no dwarf named Horny," said Chris, sitting at the bar in perfectly pressed chinos and a crisp white shirt, looking as if he hadn't drunk more than the rest of them put together. "There's, let's see . . . Sleepy, Happy, Grumpy . . . Doc . . . Sleepy . . ."

"Dopey!" Tom yelled, flicking his hair out of his eyes and

rolling his meaty shoulders as if readying for a fight. "There's a dwarf named Dopey! How sweet is that?"

The stripper bent down, clamped Neil's chin between her fingers, and gave him a long kiss, mashing her lips against his and turning her head this way and that, as if she were trying to shake water out of her ears. The pipe went around again, and Bruce inhaled deeply. "Bashful," Chris said. Bruce handed him the pipe. Chris sucked in the smoke, held his breath, turned pink, and exhaled, coughing. Chris worked less and got high more often than anyone Bruce had ever met, but because he was blessed with the square jaw and fine features of a comic-book hero, and the dark-brown hair and bright-blue eyes of Superman himself, Chris got away with murder. "Happy . . . Doc . . ." Chris continued. The stripper disappeared into the bathroom, then returned in street clothes and demanded payment in a thick Long Island accent. Bruce, who'd somehow wound up the most sober of the bunch, hustled up twenty bucks apiece from the six remaining members of the bachelor party and handed it over. The stripper tucked the bills into her purse. "Good luck to your friend there," she said, smiling at him, then turning to wink at Chris.

She had her keys in her hand, and Bruce noticed that her key chain held a scuffed plastic square with a baby's picture inside. The little girl wore a frilly white dress and a sequined headband wrapped around her mostly hairless head. The stripper caught him staring and smiled with more animation than she'd shown to Neil during three songs and a simulated blow job.

"That's Madison," she said. "Isn't she a cutie?"

Bruce had smiled and nodded his assent, not particularly wanting to contemplate a world where women dressed up as Snow White, shucked off their clothes, and then headed home to little girls named Madison.

"You got any kids?" she asked.

Bruce shook his head. She reached up and patted his cheek.

"You'll have 'em someday," she predicted. "You'll meet someone nice."

He wanted to tell her that he already had met someone nice. He wanted to tell someone about him and Cannie, and the talk they'd had that Saturday night, which had begun with her bringing him a glass of wine and sitting beside him on the couch, close to him but not touching, and asking, "Do you ever think about where we're going with this?"

But the stripper was already shouldering her bag and turning to go. Neil was in the corner with Tom and Chris, smoking a cigar and swaying slowly back and forth, like a man trying to dance underwater. He had a beatific smile on his face, a garter belt hanging from around his neck, and malt liquor soaking his hair. "I love you guys!" he yelled. With his glasses askew, slanted sideways on his narrow face, Bruce thought he looked exactly the way he had when they'd met, in sixth-grade science class, pale and frail and destined to get the crap beaten out of him on any playground in the world. *Time to go,* Bruce thought, and went outside to call a cab.

Then there was another bar, and another one after that, and lots of tequila on the way. On one of the rides, Tom crammed his six-foot-tall, former-football-player physique into the front seat and tried to convince the cabdriver that Walt Disney was a stoner—"because how else do you explain a dwarf named Dopey?"

"You know who was definitely a stoner? Old King Cole!" Chris called from the backseat. "He called for his *pipe* . . . and he called for his *bowl*. . . ."

"What about the fiddlers three?" asked Neil, and Chris had shrugged, and said they were friends, he guessed.

At the final bar they'd encountered a table full of women who all had penis-shaped swizzle sticks in their drinks.

"We're at a bachelorette party," one of them explained, waving a dildo at them as the woman in the center with a veil perched jauntily on her head squealed over the edible underpants she'd just unwrapped. They bought the bachelorettes a round of drinks, and Tom asked if they'd had a stripper. When they said no, he stood on their table and actually worked his pants down over his hips, revealing a vast expanse of hairy white belly as he proclaimed himself, once more, to be the eighth dwarf, Horny. That was when the bouncer grabbed him around the waist, hoisted him off the table, and hustled all of them out the door.

And then there were five of them, crammed into a booth in the all-night diner at three a.m.: Neil, who was getting married in two days, sitting between Tom, who'd been Neil's college roommate and who now sold Hondas for a living, and Chris, who, along with Bruce, had known Neil since elementary school. At the far end of the booth was some guy from Neil's lab, a fellow postdoc named Steve, who was either passed out or sleeping at the table with his head pillowed on his forearms.

Bruce nudged him. "Hey, man," he said. "Are you all right?"

The guy looked up, bleary-eyed. "Order me a western omelette," he instructed. His head fell back to the table with an audible *thunk*.

They ordered. Neil pulled a handful of napkins from the dispenser and started to clean his glasses. Tom shivered in his undershirt, as if realizing for the first time that his shirt was still back at the bar with the bachelorettes. "Cold," he said, and gulped coffee. Chris grabbed for his mug.

"Not yet," he said. "We didn't toast!"

Tom lifted his coffee, brown eyes shining with warmth and alcohol. "To Neil," he began. "Neil . . . I love you like a brother, and . . . and . . ."

"Hold up," said Chris. He extricated his flask from his front pocket and unsteadily dumped whiskey into everyone's cup. "To the last best night of your life," he said to Neil.

Tom looked puzzled. "Last night?" he repeated. "He's not gonna die. He's just getting married."

"Last best night," said Chris. "I meant, that this is the last really good time he'll have." He thought that over. "The last best night he'll have when he's single." He looked at Neil. "Right?"

"I guess," Neil said. He burped. "It's been pretty wild."

"Tell me how you knew," said Tom suddenly. He planted his elbows on the table and stared at Neil with his bloodshot eyes.

"How I knew what?"

"That you wanted to get married," Tom said, and looked at him expectantly.

Neil hooked his glasses carefully behind his ears. "Because I love her," he said.

"Yeah, okay," said Tom. "But how do you know you'll still love her in three years or five years?"

Neil shrugged. "I don't, I guess," he said. "I just know what I feel now, and I hope . . . I mean, we get along."

Bruce nodded, although he privately subscribed to his girlfriend's belief that Saturday's festivities had little to do with love and everything to do with Neil's finally locating a woman who was both willing to sleep with him and two crucial inches shorter than he was.

"They get along," Tom repeated.

"That's important," Chris argued. "That's, like . . . a basis."

"Okay, for now. That's fine. But what about the future? You find someone, she turns you on, you get along, you spend some time, and before long . . ." Tom set two thick fingers on the table and made a humming noise as he slid them toward the ketchup bottle. "It's like this!"

Chris was puzzled. "Love is like your fingers?"

Tom sighed. "Love is like an escalator. Or one of those moving walkways at the airport. You start going out with someone, and it's like this unstoppable thing. You go out, you move in, you decide, why not, because you're getting it every night, and then you're married, and then it's five years later, and now you've got kids and you have to do kid things with them, and maybe she nags you or maybe she's fat, or maybe you just want your freedom back." He paused, swallowing coffee. "Maybe you want to be able to look at a girl on the sidewalk and think, *Yeah, it could happen, you could get her number and it could happen, it could work . . .*"

"Tom," Neil said, placing one of his hands on his friend's shoulder, "that isn't happening now."

"You're missing my point! My point is that it could! My point is that any single woman in here, in this, this . . . where are we?"

Bruce consulted his place mat. "World of Bagels."

"Any woman in World of Bagels could be the perfect match for Neil. Any woman in here could be his soul mate. And he'll never know, because that road is gone." Tom pulled something from his pocket and began waving it in the air in time with his words. " 'Two roads diverged in a wood,' and you took this one, and you'll never know about the other road."

Bruce squinted and realized that Tom was pointing with a penis-shaped swizzle stick.

"You'll never get a chance with . . ." Tom cast his gaze around the bar. A pair of heavyset men sat at the counter, buttocks overflowing their stools, and a waitress old enough to be any of their mothers was squirting the countertop with Windex.

"Tom," Chris said, "that is grim."

"It's the truth," Tom said. "I should know."

"Why?" asked Neil.

Tom shook his head and gulped from his mug. "I saw my parents," he said. "I saw how it was for them. They got married when they were both twenty-five, had me, had my sister, Melissa, and it was like they ran out of things to talk about by the time I was six. They were just two people who'd wound up in the same house, sitting across from each other at the same table every night."

"Did they get divorced?" Bruce asked.

"Whose parents didn't?" Tom answered. Bruce's parents didn't, but he knew better than to interrupt Tom. "My father cheated on her for years. Told her the most stupid lies. Told her he'd be working late, and she believed him. Fucking working late."

"Did they have fights?" Bruce asked.

Tom shook his head. "Not really. That wasn't the bad part." He reached across the table for the sugar and dumped some into his cup. "My dad started smoking again. This was right before he left, when I was, like, thirteen and Missy was ten. He'd take his cigarettes onto the deck and light up right under Missy's bedroom window. Do you remember how crazy they make you about cigarettes in school . . . how they tell you, like, one puff and it's instant death, and they show you those pictures of lungs?"

All of the guys at the table, except for the one who'd passed out, nodded. They remembered the pictures of the lungs.

"So he'd be out there and he'd light up, and the smell of the smoke would wake Missy up. She'd lean out her window and ask him to stop. 'Daddy, don't. Daddy, stop.' And he wouldn't. He'd just smoke and smoke, and she'd be up there crying, and he'd pretend he didn't hear, until finally he'd just get in his car and leave. Missy thought it was her fault. When he'd go away. She told me that a long time afterward. That she was the one who made him leave. Because she told him not to smoke."

The table sat silent, except for the faint snore of the passed-out guy.

"Where's your sister now?" Bruce asked.

"She lives in the city," Tom said. "She dropped out of college. She's mixed up, I guess." He paused, swallowed spiked coffee. "I think she never got over him leaving. Not really. She never stopped believing that it was her fault."

Neil took his glasses off and started polishing them again. Bruce thought that they all knew girls like that, girls in trouble. He'd sat across from girls like that in high school and watched them fill their notebooks with stars and hearts and scrolled initials, entwining their first name with the last name of the class president or the quarterback, without writing down a single word of what the teacher said; or they'd seen them in bars, laughing too loudly and drinking too much and leaving with the first guy who'd whisper the word *beautiful*.

Chris looked sympathetic as he whispered in Neil's ear. Neil lifted his orange-juice glass. "To Tom," he said, "the best man."

Tom waved the toast off grumpily. But Neil persisted.

"And to Chris, and Bruce, and Steve." Steve was the passed-out guy, Bruce figured. "Good men."

Chris liked that. "Mediocre men," he said, slinging his arm around the groom's shoulders. "Marginal men." When the food came, everyone was laughing.

Neil pushed back his plate and looked around the table. "So who's next?" he asked.

"Next? Not me, man," said Chris. "I can't even get a girl to stay around for, like, a week." This was sort of a lie, because, as good-looking as he was, girls fell in love with him after two drinks in a bar, but Chris got panicky if they started calling too often, and was usually the one to do the dumping.

"Tom? Nah, don't even answer," Neil said hastily.

"The thing is, I'd like to," said Tom. "I still believe in it. Like, maybe when I'm forty-five, and I don't want to do it all the time. Then it won't matter, if she doesn't want to either."

"Why don't you just find a girl who wants to do it all the time now?" asked Neil.

Tom shook his head. "No girl wants to do it all the time. That girl does not exist."

"So you'll just wait?" Neil asked.

"That's what my dad did. I mean, the second time," Tom said. "After he finally left, he was on his own for a while, then he married this preschool teacher. And she's pregnant now."

"You're gonna be a big brother!" said Chris.

"Yeah," said Tom sourly, shoving his hair behind his ears. "Lucky me."

"Bruce?"

Bruce looked at his plate, suddenly guilty at the relative tranquility of his own life. His parents had just celebrated their thirtieth anniversary. There were no affairs—at least none that he knew of—and no big fights. His parents still held hands when they walked on the beach; his father still kissed his mother first thing when he came home from work. And they were in agreement on most major issues he could think of: religion (Jewish, semiobservant), politics (Democrat, although his mother seemed to care more than his dad), and their regard for his continuing status as a graduate student (dim—Bruce had gotten adept at changing the subject when the question of his as-yet-unwritten dissertation came up, and after three years his parents had simply quit asking).

And things with Cannie were getting serious. When you

were twenty-eight and had been seeing someone for three years, things either got serious or they ended. At least that's what she said. "Eventually we're going to have to move forward, or . . ." She pushed her hands together, then let them slide apart.

Bruce had met Cannie at a party in Philadelphia, the kind of thing where he knew a friend of the hostess, and had nothing to smoke and nothing else to do with his Saturday night. By the time he got there, the party had been in full swing for hours. Cannie's eyes sparkled as she talked, gesturing with one hand and holding a glass of red wine in the other. People were gathered around her, and Bruce found himself joining the crowd, trying to get close enough to hear what she was saying.

They were in a typically tiny apartment, the room hot and crowded in spite of all the furniture having been pushed back against the walls. They'd spoken for a few minutes by the makeshift bar in the cramped kitchen, and Cannie leaned against him, shouting over the music. He remembered how her lips had grazed his cheek as she told him the most mundane facts—where she'd gone to school, what she did for a living. And he remembered how she'd laughed at his attempts at jokes, touching his forearm with her hand, leaning her head back so he could see the smooth, tanned skin of her throat.

He had tried to make her laugh, but she was really the funny one. "Oh!" she'd said the first time she saw him coming out of the shower. "It's your reclusive-billionaire bathrobe!" Once, she'd been babbling about some problem at the newspaper where she worked, and he'd put his hand playfully over her mouth, telling her there was only one thing he expected her to open that weekend. She'd looked at him, her eyes sparkling. "What's that?" she'd asked, her voice muffled and her mouth warm against his palm. "My wallet?"

She was funny and smart, ambitious and pretty, and desperately insecure—but in his limited experience, that was true of most women. He loved her. At least he was pretty sure that he did. But things weren't perfect. For one thing, they lived two hours apart, and saw each other only on weekends. Bruce liked sleeping in and smoking pot, and tended to leave things in his apartment about where they'd landed when he kicked them off or put them down. Clothes stayed on the floor until he ran out, and finally gathered everything into a laundry basket, which he drove home for his mother to wash. Dishes stayed in the sink until they drew flies. Food stayed in the refrigerator until it rotted or liquefied. At Cannie's apartment, everything was neat, and everything had a place, which meant that he was forever misplacing something, or knocking something over, breaking a glass candleholder or her favorite serving plate.

She'd accused him, more than once, of drifting through life, content to be a graduate student until he died, secure in the knowledge that his parents would continue to fund his education. He worried that she didn't know how to relax, that she saw life as one endless marathon and herself as a failure if she didn't finish first.

He worried about how sad she was sometimes. Depression ran in her family. She'd warned him of that the first time they slept together. "You should be careful," she whispered. "My whole family's insane. Clinically insane." He told her that he wasn't afraid. "My sister's on Prozac," she said, pressing her lips against his neck. "My grandmother died in an institution." He kissed her again, and she made a noise like a little bird, and he thought as he held her that this could be serious, that this was a girl he could love for the rest of his life.

And why not? They were both the right age, the right religion. She had a good job; he had (on paper, at least) a bright future. But when she'd looked up at him, curled on the couch with her eyes wide, tracing the tip of one finger around the edge of her wineglass, asking, "Bruce, where are we going with this?" he'd opened his mouth and found that he had no idea what to say.

"Fine," she'd said. "You're not sure. It's no big deal. I can wait." When she lifted her gaze to meet his, he'd been worried that she'd be crying, but she wasn't. She didn't seem sad. Just determined. "I can wait," she'd said, "but I can't wait forever."

"So?" asked Neil, his pale, sharp-featured face inquisitive. "Are you and Cannie next in line?"

"Maybe," Bruce said.

"Maybe?" asked Tom, raising his eyebrows and clenching his big fists on the table.

"Yeah, what's with maybe?" asked Neil.

Bruce said the first thing he could think of. "I can't stand her dog," he blurted. This, at least, was unambiguously true. Cannie had a tiny little yappy dog, a terrier mix she'd gotten secondhand. The dog had brown-and-white spots, and a sneer from when his mother had bitten him (showing more sense, Bruce privately thought, than little Nifkin had demonstrated in the three years he'd known the cur). He'd come with his name, a disappointment to his mistress, who'd told Bruce she'd always planned on calling a dog Armageddon, after the Morrissey song. "The chorus goes, 'Armageddon, come Armageddon, come Armageddon, come,' " she'd said. "I always knew that if I had a dog I'd want to call him that, so I could stand in the park and yell, 'Come, Armageddon!' " Bruce hated Morrissey, hated cutesy pet names, and thought that any dog under twenty pounds was more of a decorative cushion than anything else, but he'd been careful not to share any of that with Cannie.

"Nifkin?" asked Chris. "What's wrong with Nifkin?"

"Ah, you know," said Bruce. "He's got that yappy little bark, and he sheds, and he hates me."

"How come?" asked Neil.

"'Cause he gets to sleep with Cannie when I'm not around, but he has to sleep on his dog bed when I am. And when I'm at her place and she's not there, he just glares at me. It's scary." There was more. Cannie was always petting the dog, holding him on her lap and talking to him in a tender lisping baby talk that Bruce could barely decipher. She knew he hated Nifkin, which didn't improve the situation. Once, in a teasing mood, she said that if a genie came out of a bottle, Bruce would wish for her dog to be turned into a sack of weed. And Bruce, in a teasing mood, said, "You bet I would." Cannie still held his remark against him. She would bring it up in fights. "You look at my dog and I see murder in your heart!" she'd say, cradling the trembling terrier against her body, her tone sort of teasing, but sort of serious . . . the same voice she used when she was musing out loud about what they'd name their children.

Tom set his mug down on the table with a slam, flexed his bare arms, and stared at Bruce with bloodshot brown eyes. "The dog," he said, "must be eliminated."

"Huh?"

"Bruce," he said, "I'm doing this for your future. I'm doing it for the future of the *species*. No dog, no problem. The dog has got to go."

So there they were, the remaining good men, crammed into Neil's tidy silver Camry, which had been freshly detailed for the wedding, blasting Bruce Springsteen's "She's the One," doing seventy miles an hour on the New Jersey Turnpike on their way to Philadelphia for the liberation of Nifkin. Bruce sat shotgun and sipped from the bottle of tequila—not enough to incapacitate him completely, but enough to convince him that this was a good idea. Tom and Chris were in the backseat, and Steve was draped over both of their laps, head tilted sideways—"So if he pukes," Chris explained, "he won't choke on vomit."

"Hey," Neil said anxiously, "try to get his head out the window if he starts. I've got to take this car to the airport after the wedding."

"Lotta rock stars choke on vomit," said Chris, and then he fell asleep with his head against the window, mouth slightly open, chin resting on his pressed white shirt.

With the spring air rushing through the open windows and the miles slipping by, Bruce felt alive, almost electric, with purpose. They couldn't change the world that night, they couldn't rescue Tom's little sister, Missy, they couldn't solve the riddle of how to know when you were ready for marriage, but the problem of a ten-pound terrier with a bad attitude and a stupid name, this they could solve.

Their plan was for Bruce to sneak into Cannie's apartment and lure Nifkin into the living room with the remains of Steve's omelette. Once he'd gotten the dog out the front door, Tom and Chris would scoop him up in Neil's jacket and smuggle him into the car. Then they could drive him to Valley Forge, where Washington's troops had wintered, and set him free.

"He'll be out in the wild," Tom said. "Where he belongs."

Bruce thought there had probably never been a dog that belonged in the wild less than Nifkin, who dined on hamburgers and scrambled eggs and slept on an embroidered monogrammed pillow, but he kept quiet, and took another burning gulp of tequila. He'd almost gotten himself to the point where he believed the plan could work. He could picture the scene: the dog eliminated, Cannie distraught and desperate for comfort, as opposed to answers about how Nifkin had managed to unlock the apartment door and make his way outside.

"It'll be great," said Chris, who'd woken up at the exit 4 tollbooth just before the Ben Franklin Bridge.

"It'll be beautiful," said Tom, pulling the hood of Neil's too-small sweatshirt over his head and giving the ties a yank so that all Bruce could see was the tip of his nose and the Rasputin-ish glint in his eyes.

"But what if he comes back?" Neil asked, without taking his eyes off the road. "Like Lassie. Don't you hear about that sometimes? Those dogs who go across the whole country to find the house they used to live in?"

There was silence. Bruce thought about Nifkin. He wore a heart-shaped identification pendant on his rhinestone-trimmed collar, and on snowy days Cannie had been known to dress him in miniature Gore-Tex boots. He didn't think Nifkin was the sort of dog to cross the country in search of his mistress. He thought Nifkin was the sort of dog who wouldn't cross a snowy street without his boots on.

"Don't worry," Tom said finally. "He won't want to come back. He'll probably be happier out there . . . with the squirrels and all." He stared out the window dreamily. "Dogs love squirrels."

Neil killed the headlights as they pulled onto Cannie's street, and killed the engine as they approached her apartment building, so that the car glided over the pavement like a shark in black water.

"Go, men," Neil whispered, reaching across the gear shaft to grasp Bruce's shoulders in a half-hug. "And remember, you're doing this for love."

Bruce slipped his key into the door, padded softly up three flights of stairs, unlocked another door, and crept through the living room and down the hall of Cannie's apartment. He eased open her bedroom door. There was a pale pink dress hanging from the closet door, her dress for Neil's wedding. She was sleeping on her side, hair spilling over the pillow, her body a vague lump underneath her down comforter. Curled on the pillow beside her was Nifkin.

"Nifkin?" he whispered. He pursed his lips and whistled softly. The dog's ears twitched, but he didn't move. Bruce slipped his hands under the dog's warm, pliant body and lifted him into the air. Nifkin opened his eyes, yawned, and stared at Bruce. "Good boy," said Bruce. Nifkin yawned again, looking bored.

Cannie muttered something in her sleep and rolled over into the empty space the dog had left behind. Bruce stood beside her bed with Nifkin dangling from his hand, staring at him, unblinking. He thought about his parents, holding hands on the beach. He thought about Tom's father, standing on the deck with a cigarette while his daughter cried. He could do better than that.

"Marry me," he whispered. The words hung in the air. The dog stared at him. Cannie rolled over again, sighing into the pillow while she dreamed.

He set the dog down gently on top of his monogrammed pillow, pulled the covers over Cannie's shoulders, and bent down and kissed her cheek. "I love you," he whispered. His breath ruffled her hair. He closed his eyes and leaned against the wall, feeling the weight of the miles he'd traveled, everything he'd drunk and smoked that night, everything he'd heard, and he was more tired than he'd ever been in his entire life. But he didn't lie down. He didn't move. He stood there in the dark, with his eyes closed, waiting for his answer.

Buyer's Market

"I don't want to start off by saying that it's the dumbest thing I've ever heard," Namita said, adjusting herself on her bar stool and smoothing her tight wool pants. A guy at the pool table gave her an appreciative grin. Namita nodded back coolly, then returned her attention to Jess. "But it is. Seriously, it's the dumbest thing I've ever heard."

"I'm not sure I'm going to actually sell it," Jess shouted, in the vain hope of being heard over the thundering din of the jukebox and the chatter of the hundred or so people crowded around the bar. Every woman she saw appeared to be six feet tall and blond, which normally would have made Jess—at five-foot-two with brown curls—feel even shorter and mousier than usual, but that night she felt as giddy as if she'd drunk champagne, as if her heart was full of helium, as if she could float. "Probably I won't." She took a gulp of the Pabst Blue Ribbon Namita had ordered. "Ugh. This is warm."

"Sadly, refrigeration doesn't improve it much. And don't change the subject! You," she shouted, pointing an accusatory finger at Jess, "have the best apartment in the entire world."

"I know."

"Hardwood floors, views of the park, two full

bathrooms . . ." Namita's voice was rising as she ticked off the apartment's amenities. Light glinted off the gold rings on her thumbs as she gesticulated.

"I know," Jess said. Her friend was undeterred.

"An actual eat-in kitchen, a working—working!—wood-burning fireplace . . ."

"I know!" Jess had seen those exact words—albeit with fewer exclamation points—on the one-page sell sheet that Billy Gurwich had prepared that very afternoon on Hallahan Group stationery. "A triple-mint, spacious, light-filled, two-bedroom, two-bath prewar gem of an apartment in the fabled Emerson on Riverside Avenue," it began. She and Billy had worked on it to-gether over pizza the night before. She'd provided all the adjec-tives. He'd paid for the pizza and, on the way home, he'd hugged her against his side, telling her they made a perfect team.

"It's so beautiful there," Namita said dreamily. "You're never going to find anything better in that neighborhood. Or in the rest of the city. Or anywhere, for that matter." She took an emphatic swig of beer and turned on her stool, stretching and arching her back so that her figure was displayed to its best advantage.

"Which is why I'm not selling," Jess said. "We're just test-ing the waters."

"We," Namita said, rolling her eyes. "You're going to test the waters right into homelessness. You know what's going to happen?" The tip of her tongue flashed as she delicately licked beer foam off her lip. "They'll hold one open house, people are going to show up and fling piles of money at you, and you're go-ing to get swept away in the madness of it all."

"Namita. Please." Jess shook her head, then glanced at her watch (she was meeting Billy at ten to watch *Law & Order*).

"Have you ever seen me get swept away in the madness of anything?"

Her best friend leaned forward, took Jess's chin in her hand, and studied her carefully. "Yes. Now. There's something different about you." Jess tried to meet her gaze head-on as Namita studied her face.

"Did you have your eyebrows threaded?" she asked.

"Waxed, actually," Jess admitted. "And I had a facial."

Namita sniffed, as if this was the least she'd expect, and poured them both more Pabst. Jess smiled and hugged herself. In addition to the waxing and the facial, she'd sprung for a paraffin pedicure and an extremely painful bikini wax that she was pretty sure had left her bald as a baby bird down there. Not that she'd mustered up the courage to look.

"You're in love with your real estate man," said Namita. It sounded like an accusation.

"We're not in love," Jess said, but she couldn't keep herself from bouncing a bit as she slid off her stool and looked at her watch again, calculating exactly how long it would take her to get back home, to Billy. "We're just testing the waters."

"Lord, lord," said Namita, tilting her cheek for a kiss. "Same time next week?"

"Wouldn't miss it," Jess said. She pulled her hat over her brown curls and headed for the C train and the Emerson, her two-bedroom, two-bathroom triple-mint gem of an apartment with high ceilings and original oak floors and an actual working wood-burning fireplace.

The first time Jess passed through the art-deco doors of the Emerson, she was eight years old, a shy girl with unruly hair and glasses. Her parents had sent her to New York City to spend Halloween with Aunt Catherine. Jess had always been a little afraid of her great-aunt, who'd made no secret of the fact that she had no use for small children. "Sticky hands," Jess had once heard her say. "Even the cutest among them seems to have sticky hands." Aunt Cat had snow-white hair and cool blue eyes and, in the high heels she favored, she was as tall as Jess's father. Unlike the grandmothers Jess knew, cheerful dumpling-shaped ladies in pastel pantsuits, Aunt Cat was always elegant in her tweed pants, with a silk scarf elaborately knotted at her throat. But that first night she'd greeted Jess inside the Emerson's imposing marble foyer wearing a turquoise-and-gold silk sari.

"Where'd you get that?" Jess had asked.

"India," said her aunt, as if it were obvious. She had pearls twisted in her hair and a bright plastic pumpkin dangling from her wrist. "Here," she said, handing Jess the pumpkin. "For your candy." Jess had suddenly felt very ordinary in her tutu and ballet slippers. Unable to decide between being a witch, a princess, or a punk rocker, she'd wound up with no costume at all and had been forced to wear last year's ballet clothes. She surreptitiously wiped her hands on her tights to make sure they weren't sticky.

Upstairs, in the grand, high-ceilinged apartment, with its shiny, wide-planked dark wood floors and no television set anywhere Jess could see, Aunt Cat had given Jess a pair of wings made of wire and pale-pink mesh. She'd clipped a pair of gold chandelier-style earrings to Jess's earlobes, and she'd used a tube of tinted mousse she'd pulled out from underneath the bathroom sink to give Jess's mousy hair a pinkish-gold sheen. "Did you buy that special for me?" Jess had asked shyly, and Aunt Cat had given her a mysterious smile and said that it was always useful for a woman to have a few disguises lying around. "When you get older, you'll understand."

She led her great-niece down the long, green-carpeted corridors of the Emerson, and every door they knocked on was opened by someone smiling—the young couple two floors down; the two handsome young men in 8-C ("This is Steven, and this is his husband, Carl," Aunt Cat had said so matter-of-factly that it never occurred to Jess to ask how men could be married to each other); tiny, wizened Mrs. Bastian, who lived in the efficiency on Aunt Cat's floor between the elevator and the trash chute. Everyone knew Jess's name, and everyone had treats. Mostly they offered the normal, miniature Halloween-size bars, but at least once per floor Jess would score a candy apple or a box of taffy or a big bar of chocolate, wrapped in gold and silver foil, filled with raspberries or studded with hazelnuts, with a name that Jess had never heard of: Lindt or Callebaut or Recchiuti. "Very nice," Aunt Cat said later, inspecting Jess's haul, which Jess had laid out, organized first by size and then by category, on Aunt Cat's richly patterned fringed Oriental rug. Jess fell asleep that night with the taste of that marvelous bittersweet chocolate ringing in her mouth, and her hair stiff with mousse. The next morning, Aunt Cat ran a bath in her deep tiled tub and stared thoughtfully at Jess through the scented steam.

"I wonder," she began, "whether you'd like to stay the rest of the weekend?"

Jess had eagerly agreed. They'd gone for a walk in Central Park, had a dim sum brunch at the Nice Restaurant in Chinatown, and cooked a chicken potpie from scratch, rolling out the pastry on a heavy marble cutting board, blanching the peas and carrots and whisking in the cream as a woman, who Jess later learned was Nina Simone, sang softly from the record player.

On Sunday morning, Jess had gone back to New Jersey with a plastic-wrapped slice of potpie, her pumpkin full of candy, a standing invitation to visit whenever she wanted, and a secret ambition: to grow up and live in New York City, preferably in the Emerson, in an apartment with a green velvet couch and a tiled bathtub deep enough to swim in, to grow up and be just like glamorous, mysterious, elegant Aunt Cat.

When Jess met Charming Billy, her first thought was that he was another treat the Emerson had produced for her, as sweet and irresistible as one of those long-ago chocolate bars. She'd come home from her errands one windy Saturday afternoon in October and found him sitting by the elevator, just beside Mrs. Bastian's apartment. There was a battered briefcase on one side of him, a blue folder in his lap, and a graphic novel in his hands. As she'd stepped off the elevator, he'd closed his book, gotten to his feet, and looked at her hopefully. "You're not by any chance here to look at the apartment, are you?"

She'd shaken her head. "I've already got one," she said, shifting her dry cleaning from one arm to the other as she reached for her keys.

"Lucky you. It's an amazing building. Great location. You're, what? Three blocks from the subway stop?"

"Two," said Jess.

He put the book in his pocket and consulted his cell phone. "No signal," he murmured. Jess could have told him that. No matter who your carrier was, cell phones didn't work inside the Emerson. As he turned the phone off, then on again, Jess saw that he was in his early thirties, maybe a few years older than she was, and a few inches taller, with a round, amiable face and a deep cleft in the center of his chin. Under his bulky coat she could make out the broad-shouldered, thick-legged build of a wrestler, and a crest of dark hair protruding from his shirt collar. "Any chance I could use your phone?" He had a faint Bronx accent, and his blue-gray scarf matched the color of his eyes.

She paused. He rummaged through his pockets and handed her a business card. His name was William Gurwich, and he was a broker with the Hallahan Group—or at least he had a business card saying so.

"I swear I'm not a psycho killer," Billy had said, offering Jess the first of the charming smiles that had earned him his nickname. "Of course, if I was a psycho killer, I'd probably say that, too, right?" He sighed, and slumped against the wall.

"You're selling Mrs. Bastian's place?" Jess asked.

"That's the plan," said Billy. "I was supposed to meet someone here at three."

"Don't you have a key?" Jess asked.

"Oh, I do. The thing is . . ." He shoved his hands in his pockets, leaned close to Jess, and lowered his voice. "It kind of smells like cat in there, and I'm allergic to cats. It was easier to wait outside."

She nodded, noticing his watery eyes, the reddened tip of his nose.

"Anyhow, it looks like I've been stood up."

"Hang on," said Jess. She put his card in her pocket, carried her dry cleaning and groceries into her apartment, pulled her cordless phone off the kitchen counter, and handed it to him.

"Thanks," he'd said. He left a message, sneezed twice, and gave her the telephone back. "I'm going to give it twenty more minutes. That's fair, right?"

"I think so," she told him . . . and then, because he didn't seem dangerous, and because she couldn't think of a reason why not to, she said, "Would you like to wait here? No cats. And we can leave the door open in case your appointment shows up."

His smile lit up his face. "That's really nice of you. What's your name?"

She told him while he draped his coat over one of her dining room chairs. He helped her hang her dry cleaning and unload the groceries. "Wow," he'd said, taking in the apartment, the living room windows, the crown moldings and high ceilings, the ornate tilework in the bathroom. "You're here all by yourself?"

"All by myself," she told him, thinking that she'd never been so glad that it was true. She made coffee, and they sat at the breakfast bar in the kitchen, where Billy filled her in on his plans to find a buyer for Mrs. Bastian's four-hundred-square-foot efficiency that overlooked an airshaft and, in spite of the ministrations of a professional cleaning crew, still smelled like a litterbox.

"That's it," he'd said, setting down his coffee cup and looking at the clock on Jess's kitchen wall. "Half an hour. It's official. She's not coming." He picked up his coat and looked at Jess. "You want to go get some dinner?"

There was a Middle Eastern restaurant down the street, and over the next six weeks, that became their place. They'd meet there and share plates of hummus and falafel on Saturday nights that would sometimes begin with an appointment at Mrs. Bastian's apartment and would sometimes include a movie, and would always end back at the Emerson, first with long clinches in the foyer and then in the high, soft bed that had once been Aunt Cat's. After they'd made love, Billy would hold her, his chest against her back, his legs fitted into her own. Five minutes later he'd be asleep, flat on his back and snoring softly, sprawled in the center of the bed. Jess would prop herself up on her elbow and look at his face by the light that filtered in through the curtains, thinking that she had exactly the life she wanted: the right job, the right home, and, best of all, the right man to share it with.

The one problem that had emerged in their three-month relationship was Billy's failure to sell a single piece of real estate. Of course, being a broker wasn't his dream. He wanted to write. He had an MFA from Columbia. He carried a notebook with him everywhere in case his Muse spoke, and he had published a half-dozen short stories in literary magazines that you couldn't find on any newsstand but which were, he assured Jess, very prestigious nevertheless. Twice, when she'd met him at the restaurant, she found him frowning and muttering at *The New Yorker,* shaking his head over the names he knew, guys who were no-talent hacks and women who were probably sleeping with important editors.

So far, he'd accrued eighteen rejection letters from *The New Yorker,* twelve from *The Paris Review,* and at least six each from *Esquire, GQ,* and *Playboy.* He hadn't gotten so much as a nibble on Mrs. Bastian's apartment. He had been given a warning during his last performance review at Hallahan, and if he couldn't sell something soon, chances were, he'd be let go.

"It's not your fault," Jess soothed him. "It's the economy." (She'd made a point to start reading the *Times* real estate and business sections since she'd met him.)

He shook his big head sadly. "It's a buyer's market, and I'm not selling." That was when the plan had first occurred to her. He was her guy. They were in love. Love meant sacrifice, and what could she give him that meant more than her apartment? Or, at least, the listing for the apartment, which would probably be enough to impress his bosses so they'd keep him on until he got a real big break. She would roll the dice, she would risk it all. And, of course, she'd be careful to stop things before they went too far. Unlike Cinderella, she'd keep an eye on the time, and she'd know exactly when to leave the ball.

Jess ran down the stairs to the subway station and hopped aboard the train the instant before the doors slid shut. It was risky, and audacious, and possibly insane. Aunt Cat, she thought, would have approved.

The Emerson was a big brick battleship of a turn-of-the-century building that stood on the corner of 89th Street and Riverside Drive. It fit into its neighborhood, and the city at large, as if Manhattan had been built up around it. Jess, on the other hand, had slowly and painfully realized that she barely fit into New York at all.

She'd spent the steamy summer after college graduation dragging herself from one publishing house and magazine office to another, trying to make herself appear more desirable than the hundreds of other recent graduates who were competing for the same handful of entry-level openings. Aunt Cat's place would have been Jess's refuge, but her great-aunt had gone to Venice for the summer, subletting her apartment to an art historian who worked at Columbia, so Jess couldn't do anything more than occasionally walk past the Emerson, gazing wistfully into the cool marble foyer on her way to or from another horrible interview. At the end of the day, she'd take the bus back to Montclair, New Jersey, and the house that had once been her parents' and was now just her mother's, feeling bruised and bewildered, as if New York was a giant treadmill and she couldn't walk fast enough to keep from falling off.

No matter what she did or how careful she tried to be, she was forever getting elbowed on the subway, or yelled at on the sidewalk, or stumbling into some glaring hardbody in spandex at the midtown gym where Namita dragged her twice a week. "Speak up!" the turbaned guy who manned the coffee cart on the corner would beseech her when she tried to order her buttered hard roll. "Can't hear you!" the teenager with the three-inch lacquered fingernails who ran the cash register at her favorite salad bar would say.

After six miserable weeks, she'd landed a job at *eBiz* magazine, a prestigious position that, unfortunately, paid only enough for her to spend seven hundred dollars a month on rent. In New York City, that meant one of three things: multiple roommates in an illegally divided one-bedroom somewhere in Manhattan; one roommate in a decent place in one of the boroughs; or, cost-effective but worst of all, taking up permanent residence with her mother, Gloria, in New Jersey, along with Gloria's bad-tempered Pekingese, Saturday-night Jdates, and subsequent Sunday-through-Thursday despair.

Jess spent the month of August crashing on Namita's couch, in the apartment Namita shared with her cousin, investigating Options One and Two in a desperate attempt to avoid Option Three, when word came, via the Columbia professor, that Aunt Cat had died in Italy.

"Honey, are you sitting down?" Gloria asked when she'd called Jess a week after the funeral. "Aunt Catherine left you her apartment!"

Jess sank onto her wheeled chair and slid back against the carpeted partition of her *eBiz* cubicle. She still couldn't quite believe that Aunt Cat wouldn't come sweeping back into the city, her trunks and suitcases crammed with treasures—fine leather gloves, Murano glass beads, and contraband bottles of wine.

"The apartment?" she whispered.

"The apartment!" her mother squealed. "I mean, I know you were close, but this! Jess! Can you even imagine what it's worth?!"

On a bright, crisp day in September, Jess made her way into the lawyer's office, still numb from the mixture of grief, shock, and a great flaring, untrammeled joy, and signed the papers that would make Aunt Cat's apartment at the Emerson hers. The probate period was sixty days. On the fifty-third day, there was a message on her cell phone. "Jessie, it's your old man," her father's voice said. "Give me a call." She'd had to fortify herself with a dark-chocolate Lindt bar and a glass of red wine before dialing his new number and greeting his new wife.

"Jess," he'd said. His voice was warm on the phone. "I know it's been a little while . . ." The warmth of his voice was now tinged with humility. "A little while" had been since Aunt Cat's memorial service in August. She could imagine him bowing his handsome head under strange kitchen lights in some Long Island McMansion, with the phone cradled against his shoulder. "I'm going to be in the city on Friday, and it's about time I take you out to celebrate your new job. Can you meet me for lunch?"

"Hah," said Namita, lying prone on a teak bench in the gym's sauna, post-step-class, when Jess told her. Actually, what she'd said was "hah fucking hah."

"You think it's a coincidence that he ignores you for months and just happens to show up ten minutes before this apartment's going to fall into your lap? Aunt Catherine was *his* aunt, right?"

Jess had nodded. "Yes, but it's not that. I think he just wants to see me."

Namita sat up straight, readjusting the terry-cloth turban she'd wrapped around her hair. Jess marveled that it was possible for anyone to look so indignant while naked.

"Did Aunt Cat leave him anything?" her friend inquired.

Jess shook her head. "She never really forgave him for . . . for, you know."

Namita raised her eyebrow. "The hair plugs?"

Jess smiled.

"Or was it the whole ditching-your-mother-and-marrying-a-woman-who's-basically-our-age thing?"

Jess tugged her towel tighter around her chest. In her family, the events Namita had just described were usually referred to simply as The Unpleasantness.

"So will you see him?" Namita asked, leaning over to pour a ladle full of water onto the pot of hot rocks. Steam billowed and hissed.

"I'm curious," Jess said. "Don't worry, I'm not going to give him the apartment or anything."

"You want me to come with you?" Namita called through the clouds.

Jess shook her head and told her friend that she'd be fine.

Seated in a back booth at the Carnegie Deli on a cold, wet Friday afternoon, her father, Neil Norton, looked like a new penny in a fistful of grimy dollar bills. He was tall and still boyish, with a remarkable crop of thick brown hair, and a few lines at the corners of his eyes that somehow made him look better, not worse. He wore a vintage leather jacket, faded Levi's, and a gold watch she didn't recognize. His waist was slim, his smile gleaming, and he looked right into her eyes while they talked, focusing on her as if she were the only person in the room, the way he always did.

"You look gorgeous, Gorgeous!" he told her as she wiped steam from her glasses and slipped them into her coat pocket. "*eBiz* magazine. Isn't that something." She nodded, charmed and flattered, and ducked her head over the menu, wondering what she could order to show that she was a mature and disinterested woman of the world with no intention of being swayed by his sweet talk, if Namita had gotten it right. What would Aunt Cat order? She ran a finger down the menu's laminated edge while her father talked, and realized that Aunt Cat would have insisted on the King Cole Bar in the St. Regis. Aunt Cat would have known that there was no way to eat a six-inch stack of pastrami while looking like a mature and disinterested woman of the world, or really, like anything other than a slob.

When the waitress came Jess had to repeat her order for a tuna melt twice ("What's that, hon?"). Neil jiggled his legs as he demolished a Reuben, picked fries off his daughter's plate, pinned her with his insistent gaze, and asked about her job, her friends, whether she was dating anyone.

"I've got new pictures," he said, sliding a snapshot of a smiling baby across the table. "She just got her third tooth." With her curly hair and squinty eyes, the baby could have been a twin to Jess as an infant. Then again, maybe all babies looked like that. Or maybe all of her father's babies did.

She slid the picture back across the table. "How are you?" she asked.

Her father sighed and rubbed a hand over his face. His shoulders slumped inside his beautiful leather jacket. "Well, Jess, I'm actually not so good."

Her spine stiffened. Cancer? Heart disease? Had he tracked her down to tell her he was dying? "What's wrong?"

Neil rubbed his face again and described the string of bad luck and bad investments that had brought him to his current predicament. Eventually, it emerged that he'd been counting on his beloved Aunt Catherine—who, husbandless and childless, had managed to retain and increase the money she'd inherited from her parents—to, as he put it, "do something for me."

"You can't imagine how it feels for me to ask you this."

Jess braced herself, preparing for what she feared was coming: He was going to ask her for the apartment, and she was going to have to tell him no. Then she was going to have to pay Namita twenty bucks for being right. She held perfectly still as he outlined his plan, some complicated scheme designed to maximize the tax write-offs, then segued seamlessly back into apology mode.

"I know I made a mistake. You should never count your chickens before they hatch."

"Or die," said Jess softly.

Neil raised his head. His gaze hardened. "When did you get to be such a smart-ass?"

Jess gave her hair her best Namita-style toss and a little shrug.

"So that's it?" her father asked in a harsh voice loud enough to cause the waitresses clustered at the cash register to turn and stare. He pushed his empty plate away so hard that it smacked into hers and glared at her. "That's it for the old man?"

Jess got to her feet and looked down at him. At her high school graduation, she'd worn a white dress under her black gown, and wobbly high heels. Afterward, she'd sat on the front porch of her parents' meticulously restored Victorian, ignoring the barbecue out back, the cake with her name in pink icing, her grandparents, Aunt Cat. Her father was supposed to have been there, but hadn't showed up, hadn't even called. After the ceremony, Gloria had locked herself in her bedroom and hadn't come down for dinner.

Jess sat on the glider in the balmy spring air for hours as the sun went down and the stars came out and the sweet smell of grilled chicken drifted away. Her cousins and her mother's friends kissed her cheek and congratulated her as they made their way out to the cars they'd parked on the street.

It was after eleven by the time Aunt Cat came and sat beside her, elegant as ever in a crisp linen suit and a rope of seed pearls around her neck. She pulled her cigarette case and heavy gold lighter out of her bag, lighting up without asking permission.

Jess pushed her feet against the boards, setting the glider

into gentle motion. Aunt Cat blew smoke toward the gables. "He's a weak man," she announced, as if she was picking up a conversation they'd already been having. "He was a weak boy who became a weak adolescent, and I am sorry to say that life doesn't seem to have taught him much."

Jess hung her head, thinking that, weak or not, he was still her father, and he was supposed to have been there.

Aunt Cat sighed as the glider swung back and forth. "Sometimes there's no getting around it," she said. "Why don't you come visit me when camp's over?"

The day her tenure as a counselor in the Poconos ended, Jess had taken the bus to Port Authority, and then a cab to the Emerson, arriving in the entryway with two duffel bags full of summer clothes and a backpack full of books. "The fairy princess!" Del the doorman had called, and she'd smiled for what felt like the first time since graduation. She'd stayed with Aunt Cat until September, and had spent three weeks every summer for the next four years in the Emerson, pulling art books and old novels off the floor-to-ceiling shelves; soaking in the deep, tiled tub; sitting on the cushioned window seat, staring down at the park, dreaming her dreams of the city.

Now she stood up from the back booth of the deli and looked down at her father, his burnished hair and gleaming watch, sleek as some exotic bird in the noisy diner. He had the same nose and cheekbones as Aunt Cat, but that was all he'd inherited. Just some of her bone structure, none of her character. *Weak,* she thought. She reached into her pocket, groping for the key to the front door of the Emerson, and when she found it, she squeezed hard enough to bruise her palm. "That's all I got," she said.

"Now, you know, normally the sellers aren't around during the open houses," Billy told Jess on a Saturday afternoon, three weeks after she'd first raised the idea of giving him the listing. He'd been bustling around all morning, sticking flowers into vases, shoving laundry onto the highest closet shelves.

"Don't worry," said Jess. She pulled her still-damp curls out of their ponytail and threaded Aunt Cat's pearl earrings through her ears. "I'm just going to grab my purse and go to Mc-Glinchey's." McGlinchey's was the bar on the corner where, she hoped, Billy would join her once the open house was over.

"Okay," he said, glancing at the clock over the stove. "As long as you're . . ."

The door swung open and a short, angry-looking gray-haired woman in a loose sack of a dress, wool socks, and leather sandals hurried through the foyer, trailing a young woman in a navy-blue suit in her wake. "The neighborhood's really gone downhill," the older woman observed in a grating, nasal voice, glaring at Billy and ignoring Jess altogether.

"I'm Billy Gurwich," he said, extending his hand, which the woman ignored. "Maybe you should get going," he whispered to Jess, as the woman flung a fringed red-and-purple wrap that reeked of cigarette smoke on the couch, poked one stubby, nicotine-stained finger into the keyhole of Aunt Cat's antique desk, and finally deigned to notice Jess.

"You're the owner?" she barked.

Jess nodded. The woman studied her, looking her up and down, taking in Jess's unremarkable figure, her wet hair, and her big brown sweater.

"Huh. Did your parents buy you this place?"

"No. Well, actually . . ."

The woman pivoted on her Birkenstocks and stomped across the room. "Fireplace work?"

"Wood-burning," said Billy, winking at Jess.

The woman squatted to peer up at the flue. After she'd yanked the handle back and forth, she straightened up, grunting softly, and scrutinized the gilt-framed photograph on the mantel, staring at it, then at Jess. "You?"

"It's actually my aunt Catherine," Jess replied.

The woman's upper lip curled. "Well, at least you come by that hair honestly," she said. Jess's hands flew to her curls. Billy smiled weakly. The woman yanked open the refrigerator door and began to peruse the contents, lifting the jars of jam, the carton of eggs. Jess grabbed her purse and fled.

"Great news!" said Billy an hour and a half later, leaning over Jess's shoulder where she sat at the bar. There was a soccer game showing on the two television screens that hung above the rows of bottles, and the place was full of rowdy Ecuadorians, many of them in striped team shirts, who'd been swaying around Jess, singing in Spanish on and off for the last hour. Billy's round cheeks were flushed, his eyes were shining, and his hair stood up straight from static electricity when he pulled off his hat. "Toby Crider wants to come back!"

"That is not great news," Jess said. The words came out a little slushy. She hadn't had anything to eat all day because she'd been too busy helping Billy get the place ready for the open house. Then the horrible woman's questions, the way she'd pawed at Jess's things, peered at her photographs, and fingered the food in the refrigerator, as if she already owned the place, as if she had more right to be there than Jess did, had made her change her normal order of vodka and cranberry juice to just plain vodka.

Billy slid onto the bar stool next to hers, so close that their shoulders were touching. "Leverage," he said, cupping Jess's chin in one hand. "It's all about leverage. Her husband's a very big deal. Impeccable financials. If she makes an offer . . ."

"She can't have it," Jess said.

"Oh, it's not for her, it's for some kid."

"She has children?" Jess blurted. "That's unspeakable."

"Not her kid," Billy said. He rifled through his briefcase. "It's her stepson or nephew. Something. He's finishing up at Wharton, which Toby must have mentioned about a dozen times per room, and he's starting at"—more rifling—"some investment banking firm, and he needs a place fast."

"Listen, Billy." Jess swung her stool around a little faster than she'd meant to. Their knees collided. "Whoops a daisy," Billy said, grabbing the base of her chair, holding her steady.

Jess smiled at him, as the floor and ceiling tilted, and the soccer fans whooped and cheered. "I . . ." she stammered. "I don't think this is actually a very good idea."

"Cold feet," Billy said. He eased her glass away from her and put his warm hands around hers. "Cold hands, too." His smile felt like a warm blanket settling around her shoulders, like the first sip of the hot chocolate Aunt Cat used to make every winter the first time it snowed.

"Don't worry. I know you said we were just going to test the waters, but now we've got a fish on the line. A big fish. I'm going to get you . . ." He bent, smiling, so close she could feel the heat of his skin, the prickle of his cheek against her ear, and whispered a number so extraordinary it made her gasp out loud. She gulped down the rest of her drink while he beamed at her, eyebrows raised, face expectant. "So? What do you think about that?"

She smiled woozily, then leaned against him, resting her head on his firm shoulder, closing her eyes, breathing when he breathed. He smelled like wet wool and Irish Spring soap as he eased one arm around her shoulders, giving her a squeeze before detaching himself to pull out his wallet and pay for the drinks. "But where will I go?" Jess's voice was tiny, lost in the clink of

ice against glasses and the roar of the soccer fans. Billy, busy
with the bartender, either didn't hear or couldn't answer.

"You don't understand," she told Namita as they waited in
line for the movies the following Friday. "This woman. Horrible
Toby. She's like a stubbed toe."

"Let me hear it," Namita said.

Jess groaned. "She keeps showing up. Three times, so far!
The last time she didn't even call! She just leaned on the buzzer
until I opened the door."

"What does she want?"

"Measurements for window treatments," Jess said, wincing
as she remembered the sound of Toby's tape measure snapping
up and down the walls while Jess had huddled in the kitchen,
counting the minutes on her microwave clock until Toby departed. "And once she brought her feng shui consultant."

"But of course," Namita said. "Listen. Radical thought. You
could just tell her to forget it. Tell her the place isn't for sale anymore. Take it off the market."

Jess hung her head. Telling Horrible Toby that the deal was
off would mean telling Charming Billy the same thing, and she
just couldn't make herself pull the trigger, even though she'd
tried. She'd gone to the Hallahan offices that very afternoon to
make her plea in person. Billy had walked her to Citarella,
bought her a yogurt parfait, held her hands across the small
round table, and asked whether the problem was selling to Toby
or selling at all.

"Selling at all," she'd said eagerly, finally glimpsing a way
out of the mess. "I mean, I'd been getting antsy, but now that
I've been thinking . . ." She stared at her lap. "I'm just not sure
I'm ready."

"Don't worry," he'd said. "You're ready. You can do this.

And we'll find a place. A perfect place." He smiled at her and she felt herself floating away, born up into the ether on *we* and *perfect*.

Billy leaned across the table, gray eyes kind. "Tell me what you want."

She looked at him and blushed. His smile widened. "Okay, besides that," he said. "What do you want in an apartment?"

"A view," she said. "Of a river, or trees."

He nodded.

"And a neighborhood," said Jess. "Where I'd know people. With a pizza place and a bookstore and a coffee shop and a park. Maybe Brooklyn?" Billy lived in Red Hook.

He nodded. "I can show you some places you'll love," he said. "Someplace that's perfect for you. For Jess Norton, not Jess Norton's great-aunt."

She nodded. *Just right for her.* She pictured an apartment, cozier than Aunt Cat's, a one-bedroom that the two of them could afford on their own; a brownstone on a side street with high ceilings and big windows overlooking a tree-lined block, with a galley kitchen where she and Billy would cook dinner together, hip to hip. They'd walk along the snowy sidewalk in the wintertime to buy Billy a Christmas tree, and have brunch every Sunday at one of the neighborhood cafes, and fall asleep each night together, snug beneath the blankets under a skylight admitting a wedge of the starry night sky.

Eight years had passed since she'd inherited her aunt's apartment—eight years gone, as if she'd fallen asleep at twenty-two and woken up almost thirty. In all that time, she'd believed Aunt Cat's place to be her paradise, her promised land, her reward for surviving her father and New York City. But now, with Billy beaming at her, she could see it differently. Maybe the apartment was really just the round room at the top of the palace tower where the princess pricked her finger and slept for a hundred years. Now she had Billy, Charming Billy, and he would kiss her and lead her home. To Brooklyn, and a little place to call their own, a safe little nest with maybe, someday, a cradle in the corner of the bedroom, a rocking chair set in a slant of sun.

"Things are going to happen. I can feel it," Billy said, finishing his scone in three giant bites. "Stay by the phone tonight," he said, leaning close to brush Jess's cheek with his lips. She brushed crumbs off his collar, inhaling his fragrance— wet wool and soap again, with the addition of sweet bay rum cologne. Her father had worn that, too, a long time ago. "I'll be in touch."

True to his word, when she got home from the movies Billy was sitting on the hallway floor, where she'd first seen him, but looking considerably less glum. He leapt to his feet when he saw her, and scooped her into his arms. "Rich girl, rich girl," he chanted.

"Put me down!" Jess squealed as he hoisted her in the air. Her skin tingled; her heart pounded so loud she was sure he'd be able to hear. He set her gently on her feet and, after she unlocked the door, he ushered her to the couch, dropped to his knees, took her hands, and whispered Toby's price in her ear. She gasped and saw her beloved apartment blur around the edges.

"There's a hitch, though."

"What hitch?" she squeaked. His hands were still on hers, and she felt her body leaning toward his.

"She wants to close next month. I know it's last-minute, which is probably why she was willing to go so far above asking, but her stepson, or godson, or whatever, moved in with them, and she wants him out. I'll help you find movers, and storage, and temporary housing. Whatever you need, Jess. But you should know, you're not going to get a better deal than this."

Somehow, she managed to pull herself away from him and sit up straight. She looked around the room: the photographs of Moscow and Trieste and Milan, the cloisonné lamps with fringed peach-colored shades, the stacks of art books and novels, the heavy glass bowls full of nuts and candy that Aunt Cat always refilled for Jess's visits. She'd lived here for eight years and she hadn't ever gotten so much as a new set of sheets, let alone her own photographs, her own artwork or furniture. *Time to move on,* she thought. *Time to move out.* "So you think we should take it?"

His eyes were intent and his voice was as serious as that of a man taking wedding vows when he answered, "I think we should."

Jess wrangled three personal days from her unhappy boss at *eBiz,* and spent them packing up and supervising the movers, a trio of fire-hydrant-shaped fellows who spoke a language composed largely of grunts and seemed to take as their personal mission the task of folding, breaking, soiling, and mutilating every single thing she had inherited. Finally, early Friday morning, the last of Aunt Cat's mahogany sideboards and marble end tables had been wrapped in padded blankets and wrestled onto the mirrored elevator, and the final cardboard box of books was loaded onto a grimy white truck (someone had written "Wash me, please!" in the dirt across the driver's side door) and driven off to a storage facility in Newark. Jess took a quick shower, pulled on her best blue suit, wadded her wet towel and dirty clothes into a duffel bag, and stood in the middle of the empty living room, where the walls bore ghostly imprints of Aunt Cat's paintings, and the floors had grooves where the couch and chairs used to be.

She wandered over to the window. The summer before college she'd spent so many nights sitting there. She'd look down at the rustling trees of Riverside Park, at the Hudson River running beyond them, at the late-night joggers and the strolling couples, and think about the kind of life she'd make for herself. She hoped it would be something like Aunt Cat's life, with stacks of books in every room, and dinner parties each month, with red wine and down comforters, surrounded by the things, and the people, she loved. But the truth was, red wine gave her headaches and she'd never been much for parties . . . and none of it mattered because now she and Billy would make a life together.

The doorbell rang and Toby stormed into the kitchen, late, and, somehow, acting as if that was Jess's fault. Billy followed her, squeezing Jess's hand, as Toby attacked the apartment as if it were a man who'd wronged her, vigorously flushing toilets, wrenching taps open and shut, staring for long, ominous minutes at the light patch on the bedroom wall where Aunt Catherine's carved wooden dresser had formerly resided.

"You should have repainted," she said, and narrowed her eyes.

"I . . ." Jess stammered.

"We'll settle that at the table," Billy said smoothly. Underneath his down coat he wore an elegant striped suit and a patterned silk tie of heavy burnt-orange silk. The blue wool cap that Jess had grown accustomed to was gone, replaced with a camel-colored muffler that looked suspiciously like cashmere.

She reached for his hand as Toby yanked open the oven door, then kicked it shut with one Birkenstock-shod foot. Billy's cell phone rang, and as he turned his back he held up one finger and said, "William Gurwich," into the receiver. "At the table, okay?" he said into the telephone. He eased Jess into her coat, then out the door. Outside, there was a town car idling at the curb.

"Wait," she said. Billy sighed, and stopped with one hand on her back and one hand on the roof of the car. Jess stared at him, panicked, thinking, *This is all wrong.* Billy kissed her, then looked over her shoulder, up toward the Emerson, its facade glowing under the thin winter sun. "Don't worry about a thing," he said.

Forty-five minutes later, Jess found herself in a boardroom with floor-to-ceiling windows overlooking Central Park, sitting at a sleek teak conference table, signing her name again and again and again, handing over her driver's license and a copy of Aunt Cat's will, swearing and affirming that she, Jessica Hope Norton, a single woman, was the sole owner without any legal encumbrance of the property. Toby was there with her broker. Her stepson/godson/whatever was nowhere in sight. In addition to Billy, there were two lawyers, a notary, and a receptionist who'd asked if she could bring anything. "Coffee for everyone?" Billy asked, raising his eyebrows as he looked around the table. When she'd returned with the drinks, and a tray of pastries, he hadn't even thanked her before selecting the biggest muffin from the pile.

This can't be happening, Jess thought as she stared down and saw her hand moving, seemingly of its own volition, signing her name. She tried to catch Billy's eye, but he was talking to one of the lawyers. She wrote her name and pictured Toby's lip curling as she stood in Jess's bedroom, eyeballing the pictures by the side of her bed during one of her unannounced visits. "My mom was Miss Penn State," Jess explained as the other woman scrutinized a shot of Gloria waving from the backseat of a convertible.

Toby tilted the picture from side to side as if it were a glass of wine she was inspecting for sediment. "She's not that good-looking," Toby finally said. "Actually," she'd continued, making her way into the second bathroom, "I thought it was a picture of you."

Billy slid another stack of documents across the table, gave Jess a quick wink, and snickered at something on his Black-Berry. Jess wrote the date, her social security number. She accepted the check that he handed her in a heavy cream-colored envelope. All those zeroes, she thought, and tried to feel elated, and couldn't.

"Good luck," Jess said faintly. Toby got to her feet, pocketed the keys, gave a grimace that could have been interpreted as a smile, flung her fringed wrap around her, and stomped out of the room. Jess sank back in her chair and spun so she could look out at the dirty gray sky, the snowbanks spangled with condensed exhaust fumes and broken glass, the bare, bedraggled trees.

Billy smiled at her, a big, eat-the-world grin, not the sardonic half-smile she'd gotten used to, along with the down coat and the wool cap and the chapped fingers that could never find Mrs. Bastian's key on the first try. "Thank you," he said. *It wasn't "I love you,"* Jess thought. But it wasn't nothing. And maybe it was enough.

Billy stood behind her chair and rocked it back and forth. "Take a look," he crooned. "It's all yours." He sat down beside her, crossed his legs and adjusted the crease in his pants. "Just tell me where you want to start. Uptown? Downtown?"

"We can talk about it tonight," Jess said. She turned away from the window and looked into his face. "Our place?"

"Sure," he said, and hugged her, holding her close as she buried her face in the warm hollow of his neck. "Eight okay?"

"Perfect," she said.

———

That night she leaned against the brick wall of their restaurant, feeling the cold dampness seeping through her skirt. The wind blew sheets of newspaper and empty soda cans along the dirty sidewalk; a bus splattered sleet against the curb. At 8:15, Billy breezed down the block, wearing his new clothes and his old, familiar, heartbreaking smile. "So!" he said heartily, pulling off his gloves. "Have you been thinking about where we should start?"

"Wherever," she said eagerly. Too eagerly. Something flickered in his eyes, but it was too late for her to take it back, too late to stop. "I'll go anywhere with you."

He squeezed her hands briefly. Then he pulled away. "Jess," he began, taking a deep breath. "The thing is . . ."

Another bus rumbled by. Jess knew what the thing was, and she couldn't stand to hear him say it—not so close on the heels of the worst mistake she'd ever made in her life. She pulled away, trying for dignity, a measure of Aunt Cat's cool reserve, as Billy babbled about how much she meant to him, how she was a great girl but he simply wasn't in a place where he could consider anything long term, and besides, there was his writing to think about.

The check from the sale of Aunt Cat's apartment was still folded in her coat pocket, and she touched it, hoping for strength.

"I need to go now," she said.

"I'm sorry," he said. He sounded genuinely sorry, like the guy she remembered, the one she'd thought she'd cared for, the one who couldn't sell Mrs. Bastian's apartment even though his job depended on it, someone just as lost in the big city as she was herself.

"It's fine," she lied. "I'll be okay."

She swung her duffel bag over her shoulder. A cab screeched to a stop the second she raised her hand—a perfect New York moment, one of very few she'd ever had. Jess slammed the door shut before Billy could make it across the sidewalk.

"Port Authority," she told the driver. She leaned back against the ripped vinyl seat and buried her face in her hands.

She texted Namita to tell her that her plans had changed, and that instead of crashing with her, she'd be staying with Gloria for a while. She told her boss at *eBiz* that her father had died.

"Sure, honey, you can stay as long as you want," Gloria had said, trying to shove her treadmill against the wall of Jess's former bedroom. "It's just . . . do you have any idea how long that's going to be?"

"I'm not cut out for Manhattan," Jess finally said. "I tried it for eight years, and I'm just not supposed to be there." She sat on the portion of her bed that wasn't covered with stacks of printouts of profiles of her mother's potential Jdates. Gloria sat beside her and stroked Jess's forehead with her cool hand. Jess braced herself for the pep talk: *Of course you are, honey! You can do whatever you want to do!* Instead, her mother sighed and said, "So then you'll find the place you're supposed to be."

Jess began sleeping until after eleven o'clock every day, staying up all night, watching infomercials on her mother's gigantic new television set and subsisting on a diet of those sweetened, artificial-everything cereals she'd never been allowed to eat as a child. She e-mailed Namita and said she was fine. The one time Billy's number had shown up on her cell phone, she'd punched "Ignore" and gone to the kitchen for more milk. After two weeks of breakfast food and bad TV, an unfamiliar number with a 917 area code appeared on her telephone's screen and, out of idle curiosity, Jess answered it.

Big mistake. "Jessica?" Toby demanded, in her familiar grating voice. "Steven moved in last week and he can't find the spare key to the linen closet."

Jess blinked, then rubbed her eyes. On TV, an actress she remembered from two decades ago was trying to convince her that an at-home teeth-bleaching system would revolutionize her smile, and possibly even her life. "It's on the top of the little ledge, right next to the . . ."

"No, no, that's where you said it was, but it isn't there." Toby whined.

"Oh." Jess sat up straight, sending her empty cereal bowl clattering to the floor. "Well, maybe . . ."

"I think *maybe* you should just stop by sometime tonight, help him find the damn key."

"Well, but the thing is, I'm actually . . ."

"Eight o'clock. He works late. His name's Steven." Click. Toby was gone. Hopefully forever.

If life were a movie, Jess would have looked into Steven Ostrowsky's eyes and fallen deeply and immediately in love. There would have been a whirlwind courtship (during which Toby would have died, conveniently and very painfully) and soon Jess would have found herself reinstalled in the apartment that had formerly been hers, sharing it with a rising star in the world of investment banking and planning their life together. It would have been a shoe-in for the "Vows" column, with a headline involving some witty wordplay on *listings* and *love*.

In real life, Steven was Toby in male form, with the same bowling-pin-shaped body, twitchy gaze, and negligible social skills. He leaned against the door frame as his eyes darted from Jess's hair to her breasts to her hair to her hips to her chest again.

"I've looked everywhere," he said, before retreating to the living room, now full of leather-and-chrome furniture, glass bookcases filled with DVDs and compact discs, and not a single book. Jess stood on her tiptoes and ran her fingertips along the little ledge over the linen closet door and found the key on her first try. She pulled on her coat and flipped the key onto a stainless-steel assemblage that she supposed was meant to be a table.

"Hey, thanks!" said Steven, pulling his iPod earbuds free and staring at her again. Breast, hips, crotch, face, breasts. "This is a great place. Where'd you move?"

"Vegas," she said, and let the door slam shut behind her.

She took the bus back to Montclair, slept in her old bed for eighteen hours straight, woke up the next morning, washed her face, combed her hair, and got a job as a waitress ("Jess, you're wasting your potential!" moaned her mother, on her way out the door to another Jdate). She worked nights at a diner and mornings in a day-care center. ("Wiping two-year-olds' butts!" said Namita, and rolled her eyes. "This is not what we went to college for!") For six months, Jess ran a concession cart at the airport called Access-Your-Eyes, which sold knockoff designer sunglasses. ("Are you having some kind of a breakdown?" Gloria inquired over the sound of the dishwasher. "Is that what this is? Because help is available. There are new antidepressants, honey. I see ads for them on TV all the time. You don't have to suffer!")

When she was thirty-one Jess landed a position as an assistant to a professor of women's studies at the University of Pennsylvania, helping her organize a conference on reproductive rights. ("Philadelphia," Namita snorted. "Just because the *Times* thinks it's the sixth borough doesn't mean it's true.")

"You did wonderful work," the professor said at the end of the summer. "I can offer you a full-time job as a researcher, but it doesn't pay much." Jess told her the money was fine and didn't mention that she had a nest egg. She moved out of Montclair and into an apartment on Delancey Street, a walk-up on the third floor of a big brick rowhouse, on a block lined with trees whose leafy branches arched over the street. In the winter, kids pulled their sleds on the sidewalk past her front door. After walking past a little shop on Pine Street once a week for a year, she finally signed up for a knitting class, and surprised herself by enjoying it. She made scarves, then sweaters, baby hats for her cousin's kids, a shawl for Namita, an afghan of scarlet and gold for herself. There was a skylight in her bedroom, and she'd lie underneath it, bundled in the blanket she'd made, with a cup of peppermint tea next to her reading lamp, watching the flakes swirl down, thinking, *I did all right for myself. I did all right, after all.*

Three years later, Jess's building came up for sale and she decided to buy it. Her nest egg would more than make a down payment, and she'd been promoted twice at Penn, which would give her enough to pay the mortgage. "A good investment," proclaimed Gloria. "I guess it's all right," allowed Namita, who'd moved from the Upper East Side to the trendy West Village to cohabitate with an arbitrageur named Claude. On a brisk Monday morning in January, Jess pulled on her red wool coat. She went to the bank for a cashier's check, then walked three blocks to the real estate office on Walnut Street, where settlement would be made.

"Ms. Norton?" said the man behind the desk. "You're a little early." He introduced himself as David Stuart, took her coat, poured her coffee, got her settled in another wheeled leather chair in front of another conference room table. He had curly blond hair and red cheeks, as if he'd spent the weekend outside, in the wind and the sun. She imagined him towing a sled behind him, on his way to the park. There were pictures of two little blond boys in snowsuits on his desk. She added them to the picture.

"So," he said, offering her cream and sugar, "you're going to be a homeowner."

"It's not my first time," Jess said. "I had a place in New York a few years back. On the Upper West Side."

He whistled softly. "Bet you made a bundle."

"I did all right."

"But you like it better here, right?"

"Well, I guess I'd better," she said. "Now that I'm buying."

"I love it here," he told her, eyes shining as if he was trying to sell her something, as if she hadn't already come to buy. "I mean, New York's great—it's New York, right? But Philadelphia feels more like a real neighborhood to me. People hold doors for ladies with strollers. There's this cheese shop on my block . . ." But before he could tell her about the cheese shop, the Carluccis, the sellers, bustled in with their agent and a box of angel wings, crisp-thin pieces of fried dough dusted with powdered sugar. "We're so happy for you, Jess," said Mrs. Carlucci, passing Jess a pastry on a napkin.

"She's just happy that she'll be somewhere warm," her husband teased, and put his arms around his wife's shoulders.

Jess watched David Stuart lick sugar from his lips as he passed stacks of documents around the table. She passed him a napkin. He smiled at her. While she signed her name over and over, he slid his business card across the table. *Want to have lunch after this?* he'd written underneath his name and his title.

She looked at the note, then at him, then raised her eyes

to the picture of the snowsuited boys. David Stuart slid another business card toward her. *They're my nephews,* it said. *I put the picture there to keep Mrs. Carlucci from coming on to me.*

Jess smiled, flexed her fingers, and turned another page. A minute later, another business card slid into her stack of documents. *I'm thirty-two. I went to Villanova, then into the army for six years. Then . . .* But he hadn't been able to fit anything else on the card.

She bit her lip and kept signing.

The next card was brief and to the point. *Do you like Italian food?*

She thought about her apartment, how safe and cozy it was, how happy she'd been there, content with her books and her music, not lonely at all. At least that's what she told herself. Not lonely at all. She nibbled at the edge of an angel wing and piled his business cards into a little stack. Maybe it would turn into something, or maybe nothing more meaningful than a snowflake dissolving on the sidewalk. Either way, she would see. She wrote *yes* on the back of the card on top and slid it back across the table.

THE GUY
NOT TAKEN

Marlie Davidow was not the kind of woman who went looking for trouble. But one Friday night in September, thanks to her own curiosity and the wonders of the Internet, trouble found her.

Her brother Jason and his bride-to-be were registered on WeddingWishes.com. Marlie, housebound with a six-month-old, did all her shopping online, sitting on the beige slipcovered couch where she spent most of her time nursing her baby, or rocking her baby, or trying to get her baby to stop crying. So, on that fateful Friday night after Zeke had finally succumbed to sleep, she wiped the fermented pureed pears off her shirt, set her laptop on the sofa's arm, and pointed and clicked her way through the purchase of a two-hundred-dollar knife set. As she hit "complete order," she wondered about the propriety and potential bad mojo of sending the happy couple knives for their wedding. Too late, she thought, and rubbed her eyes. It was nine o'clock—a time, prebaby, when a night might just be getting started—but Drew was still at work, and she was as whipped as if she'd run a marathon.

Just for the hell of it, Marlie typed in her name and reviewed her own choices, feeling wistful as she remembered compiling her wedding registry. She and Drew had made outings of it, having leisurely brunches before driving out to the Macy's in the Paramus Mall to spend hours looking at china and crystal, silver martini shakers and hand-blown margarita glasses from Mexico.

Two years and three months after their wedding, the crystal and the silverware were still in their original boxes in her mother's basement, awaiting the day when she and Drew would move out of their one-bedroom apartment on the Upper East Side and into a place with a dining room, or at least a little more storage space. The fancy china had been pulled out twice, which corresponded to the number of home-cooked meals Marlie had made since she'd left her job as publicity director for a small theater company in Chelsea to stay home after Zeke was born.

The telephone rang. Marlie picked it up and looked at the caller ID. WebWorx. Which meant Drew. Who was probably calling to say he'd be even later than usual. She nudged the phone under a couch cushion and then, prodded by an impulse she didn't pause to analyze, turned back to her laptop, typed the words *Bob Morrison* into the "bride/groom" blank, and hit Enter before she could lose her nerve.

Nothing, she thought, as a little hourglass popped up on the screen. Over the last four years, on and off, she'd looked for Bob online, idly typing his name into one search engine or another during down times at work. She never found anything except the same stale handful of links: Bob's name listed as among the finishers in a 5K race he'd run in college; Bob mentioned as one of the survivors in his grandfather's obituary; Bob and a bunch of other graduates of a summer art institute in Long Island. Besides, if Bob ever got married, Marlie figured she'd feel it at some kind of organic, cellular level. After all the time they'd lived together, not to mention all the times they'd slept together, she'd just know.

ONE COUPLE MATCHES YOUR RESULTS, popped onto the screen. BOB MORRISON and KAREN KRAVITZ. MANHASSET, NEW YORK.

Marlie jerked her head back from the computer as if a hand had reached out and slapped her. Bob Morrison. Manhasset. That's my Bob, she thought, and then she shook her head sharply, because Bob wasn't hers anymore. They'd broken up four years ago. Then she'd met Drew, and now she was married; she was Mrs. Drew Davidow, mother of one, and Bob wasn't hers anymore.

CLICK TO VIEW REGISTRY, invited the text at the top of the page. Marlie clicked, and scrolled through the registry, her slack jaw and wide eyes bathed in the blue glow of the screen until her husband came home, looking wan and weary, and set his briefcase down next to the diaper bag. "Are you okay?" he asked. She'd blinked at him groggily and started to climb off the couch. The baby was crying again.

"No, don't worry, I got it." He managed a smile and headed toward the portioned-off part of their bedroom where Zeke slept. "Hey, little man," she heard him say. She managed to get herself off the couch and staggered toward the bedroom. I'll just rest for a minute, she thought as her head hit the pillow. She closed her eyes, and when she opened them again it was three in the morning. Drew was on the couch, with Zeke resting on his chest, just starting to open his eyes. Marlie unfastened her nursing bra, adjusted Zeke's weight in her arms, and eventually, the three of them fell asleep on the sofa, together.

"He's marrying a woman who registered for a Health-O-Meter food scale," Marlie reported to her best friend Gwen on Monday, over an early lunch at their favorite Midtown sushi place. Gwen, who'd been Marlie's friend in college and first roommate in New York, had gotten married at twenty-five and pregnant at twenty-seven, and had gone back to work in advertising when her daughter started nursery school. That day she wore high-heeled boots, fitted jeans, and a smart tweed jacket with ruffled cuffs, complemented by a gorgeous red patent-leather bag. Marlie carried a nylon diaper bag and wore maternity jeans. She'd never been a skinny girl to start with, and she was having trouble shedding the last fifteen (eighteen, actually) pounds of baby weight, which seemed to have settled themselves quite happily on her hips.

Gwen raised her eyebrows. "And we know this because . . ."

Marlie gave her the condensed version of the story while pushing Zeke's stroller back and forth with her sneakered foot: she'd been buying her brother a present, just decided to plug in Bob's name . . .

Gwen's saucer-shaped hazel eyes widened, but her voice was calm as she said, "Just decided to?"

Marlie's cheeks flushed. "Well, I was curious, I guess. And that's not the point. The point is that he's marrying the un-me! The anti-me!" She pushed the stroller so hard that it bumped into the table, spilling green tea onto Gwen's plate and into her lap. "Oh, God. I'm sorry!"

"No worries," Gwen said too quickly, as she tried to mop up the mess while keeping her cuffs dry. "It's just tea. So the un-me thing. You're basing it just on the food scale?"

"What kind of woman registers for a food scale?" Marlie asked.

"A woman who's concerned about portion size, I guess."

"A skinny bitch," Marlie muttered, handing her friend her napkin. "And if you're the person who gives them the food scale, what do you say on the card? 'Best wishes for a happy life together, PS, don't get fat?' "

"You could just go with 'congratulations,' " Gwen said.

"It wasn't just the food scale," said Marlie. "There was a plastic chip-and-dip set. Tack-ay. And beige china. Beige!" She shook her head, feeling her heart pounding, realizing she was angrier about this than she'd previously suspected. "Beige. Boring." Yeah, she thought bitterly. Like she was leading such an exciting life. Her idea of culture these days was watching more than twenty minutes of uninterrupted Oprah.

Gwen set her chopsticks down. "Okay. Listen to me. We are not going down the Bob Morrison road again."

"What are you talking about?"

"The obsession. The agonizing. The dialing while drunk."

"I only did that once," Marlie protested. Gwen's cuffs were dripping. Marlie pulled a Pamper out of her diaper bag and handed it to her friend.

"The drive-bys," Gwen continued relentlessly, pointing a chopstick for emphasis.

"It can't technically be a drive-by if you walk," Marlie said. "And, listen, Gwen, what if he was the one I was supposed to be with? What if . . ." She took a bite of dynamite roll, poured more tea, and popped a few edamame our of their shells. When she looked up, Gwen was still waiting, head tilted, eyes wide. She sighed, and said, reluctantly, "What if he was the one?"

Gwen looked taken aback, as if she'd never questioned her commitment to her own husband. She probably hadn't, Marlie thought. It was probably easy not to when your husband was tall, handsome, completely agreeable, besotted with you, and looked like a taller, not-crazy Tom Cruise. "Well, for starters, you married someone else and had a baby with him," Gwen said.

Marlie sighed. There was that. Gwen set her chopsticks down on her plate and looked at her friend intently. "Marlie," she said. "This is what you wanted. You wanted Drew, you wanted a baby, you wanted to stop working. Remember?"

Marlie nodded. She could remember, all too vividly, sitting across from her friend in this very restaurant, bouncing Gwen's daughter Ginger on her knee and avowing her desire for those very things. But Ginger had been an adorably pudgy baby who'd grown into an adorable little girl, with a collection of Little Mermaid purses and after-school ballet lessons, and Gwen, with her clean house and her nanny and her happy, accommodating husband, made it all look easy. Had Gwen's first six months of motherhood been this awful? If they were, Marlie wondered, would her friend have told her?

"I know things aren't great right now," Gwen said. "Marriages go through rough times."

"Did yours?" she asked.

Gwen shrugged. "Well, sure. Remember that fight we had about whether to take his mom on vacation with us?"

Marlie nodded, even though, as best as she could remember, that fight had ended after a day, when Paul had simply agreed to tack on the cost of another casita to their stay in Scottsdale. As for Marlie, she had thought, once or twice, late at night when she was so tired it was a struggle to get her limbs to obey her, that recent events in her marriage had transcended the boundaries of "rough time" and were edging toward "the whole thing was a mistake." Drew and his partners were in the process of launching WebWorx. Her husband left their apartment before eight in the morning and rarely got home before nine o'clock at night, and she couldn't fairly complain about it, because he was the only one bringing home a paycheck. She'd just never expected that caring for a newborn would leave her feeling so exhausted, so edgy and desperate for adult human contact beyond the ten minutes of conversation Drew could muster before falling asleep when he finally came home.

"It's going to get better," Gwen said. She glanced at her slim gold watch, smoothed her straightened hair, and got to her feet. "I know this part's hard, but trust me. You just have to live through it. Zeke's going to start walking and talking, and sleeping, and you'll be fine." She looked down fondly at Zeke, and bent to kiss his cheek. "And believe me, you wouldn't have wanted to miss this. It goes so fast."

Marlie nodded, feeling a jealousy toward her friend that was so strong and sudden that it was like being punched. She'd have given anything to be Gwen, with ruffled cuffs and beautiful boots, on her way off to an afternoon that would not include endless renditions of "The Itsy-Bitsy Spider" and three baskets of spit-up stiffened laundry; an evening that would not involve a baby who screamed and screamed, no matter how she tried to soothe him.

She meant to walk home, but Zeke was still sleeping peacefully in his stroller, and somehow she found herself walking downtown, past the bus stop and the trash cans, the grocery store and the fancy boutiques, toward the neighborhood where she and Bob had once lived together.

"Hey, Bob, meet Marlie!"

"Hah hah hah," Marlie said, holding her plastic cup of beer and looking up at the man who'd just occasioned a joke she'd heard approximately a thousand times in her life—once for every Bob she'd ever met. But this Bob didn't seem so bad. He was broad-shouldered, maybe an inch or two taller than she was, with curling brown hair and gold-rimmed glasses, a soft belly pushing against the buttons of his blue-and-green-plaid shirt, and a friendly, slanting smile. He looked like an illustration of a friendly bear cub from one of the books she'd loved as a little girl.

"Is it Marley like the singer, or . . ."

"No, it's Marlie with an *i* and an *e*."

"Oh." Bob nodded, leaning close so she could hear him over the sound of R.E.M. informing the assembled guests in the crowded off-campus apartment that it was the end of the world as they knew it. "Wanna dance?"

She shook her head. She didn't dance. Girls like Gwen— cute girls, graceful girls—they danced. Girls like Marlie stood in the corner, making caustic comments and guarding her friends' purses.

"No thank you," she said, but Bob either didn't hear or didn't care because he plucked her cup of beer out of her hand and pulled her toward the center of the room.

"No, really," she tried again, but Bob wasn't listening. He smiled and reached for her, putting one hand on the small of her back, tucking her neatly against him.

"Come on," he said. His skin was pleasantly warm, and he smelled of soap and beer and something sweet, like hay or fresh-cut grass. Even through the bass line, she imagined she could hear the beating of his heart.

Bob and Marlie stayed together until they graduated from NYU, and then they moved into a place that Marlie had found in Murray Hill. Marlie, who'd starred in every campus theater group production from *Medea* to *Hair*, did temp work in law offices and went on auditions and go-sees, trying out for everything from soap operas to experimental off-Broadway productions to made-for-cable shoot-'em-ups. Bob talked about graduate school and painted his big, colorful abstract canvases a few hours a day, a few days a week. Bob had a trust fund, thanks to a father who'd done quite well as a personal injury attorney (one big case involving a guy who'd lost both legs in a freak subway mishap, and he'd been set for life), so it didn't really matter if Bob never got a gallery to represent him, or a day job, or if he never finished the paintings he started, or if he spent most of his time making mix tapes and meeting his similarly semi-employed friends for lunches that turned into marathon Frisbee games in Union Square Park.

Marlie watched and waited, and went everywhere her agent sent her. It took her a few years to figure out, gradually and painfully, that she was a good actress, and New York City only had room for the great ones—and sometimes, not even them. She'd get the occasional callback for TV shows that filmed in New York, the every-so-often bit part, and once, a commercial for an antacid in which she portrayed Bloating Sufferer Number Three, and clutched at her belly convincingly for fourteen hours.

She and Bob turned twenty-three, then twenty-four, still in their little apartment with the kitchen full of newspapers and pizza boxes Bob could never remember to recycle, and the bed—well, futon, really—that never got made, where everything they owned had been scavenged from a street corner or do-nated by Bob's parents. Two weeks after Bob's twenty-fifth birthday, they had a talk that boiled down to Marlie asking, "Is this all you want from your life?" and Bob responding, "Yeah, and I don't see what's wrong with it." He'd sulked. She'd fumed, and gone to sleep on the couch. Two weeks later, she told her agent not to bother submitting her head shot anymore, took the full-time publicity job at New Directions Theater at 8th Av-enue and 18th Street, and moved out. *I have put away childish things,* she thought, as Bob leaned against the doorway, giving her the boxes she'd packed and wiping at his eyes. "Be good," he'd said, handing her a nine-by-nine square wrapped in plain brown paper, a portrait he'd painted of her, back when they were still in college. *Grow up,* she thought, kissing his stubbly, salty cheek and then walking down the rickety stairs with the scuffed rubber treads, past the hole that some new tenant's king-size bed had gouged out of the plaster wall. And, except for one rum-soaked weekend involving a few late-night phone calls and three trips past their old apartment, that had been that.

She'd met Drew the following summer, on a vacation Gwen had talked her into, a long weekend white-water rafting in West Virginia. In the gear shop, being fitted for her wetsuit and paddle, she'd mistaken her future husband for one of the guides. She'd peppered him with half a dozen questions about the equipment and whether anyone ever got hurt on these trips before he confessed that he was actually a Web designer from Manhattan, who'd been born and bred in the city and didn't know any more about rafting than she did. When it turned out they both worked in Chelsea, they'd exchanged business cards, and when they got home, they'd traded e-mails, then they'd met for drinks, then they'd started going out. She'd married Drew, and Bob, she knew, from a postcard he'd sent a year and a half ago, had found a gallery in the Village to represent him. "Bob Morrison, Unfinished," his show was called. She'd wondered if it was meant to be a joke. Then she'd wondered if he actually wanted her to come to the opening, or if he'd sent the card as a kind of screw-you, a way of thumbing his nose at her and showing her he'd made it as an artist after all.

Eventually she'd stopped wondering and tossed the card, thinking that things had worked out the way they were supposed to. Happy endings all around; everyone where, and with whom, they were supposed to be. So why now, all these years later, with a husband and a baby, couldn't she quit thinking about Bob Morrison? Why couldn't she stop remembering the night they'd met, how cool the spring air had been on her face when she'd left the party, how the night had smelled of lilacs, how Bob had eased her against the stairwell of that long-ago apartment, raining kisses down on her face as his hand had slid up her cheap cotton skirt . . .

You have to stop this, she told herself, pushing the stroller back toward Carl Schurz Park. She'd made her choice. She'd picked what was behind Door Number Two, and it wouldn't do her any good to think about what might have been behind Door Number One. At the park, she fed Zeke, then smeared sunblock on his plump white arms and cheeks. An hour passed with excruciating slowness while she pushed her baby in a swing and listened to the other mommies, trying to nod in the right places, trying to impersonate a happily married young mother who'd made the right decisions and was reasonably content with her life.

But that night, Drew was working late again, and, after she'd wiped down the countertops and sponged dried oatmeal from Zeke's breakfast off the floor, Marlie found herself back on WeddingWishes.com, rolling her eyes over Bob and Karen's towels and polyester-blend tablecloths. Before long, not even that was enough, and some dark impulse led her to stick one of Bob's old mix tapes into the stereo and click back to the log-in page. If you are the bride or groom, click here, she read, as the Cure's "Why Can't I Be You?" jangled in the background. She clicked on GROOM. PLEASE ENTER YOUR PASSWORD. She held her breath and typed. The whole time she'd known him, Bob's password had always been Felicity, which was the name of his cat. VERIFYING. Then, WELCOME, BOB. CLICK HERE TO UPDATE REGISTRY, read the screen. Her heart was pounding as she scrolled through Household Items to find just the thing she wanted, adding it to the list, hitting Update. One Hitachi Magic Wand, with its wonderfully suggestive shape, added to the Morrison/Kravitz wish-list. Heh. But why stop with sex toys?

UPDATE BRIDE'S CONTACT INFORMATION, invited a link. Marlie clicked, and there were the address and phone number for Karen Kravitz. Little Miss Help Me Celebrate My New Life with a Food Scale. Marlie cut and pasted Karen's information into a new window for future research purposes. Maybe she'd forward it to Gwen, who was a whiz on the Internet. Maybe Gwen would get lucky and find a picture . . .

Her fingers froze above the keyboard as another idea occurred to her. Quickly, before she could lose her nerve, she erased Karen Kravitz's name and typed in her own. UPDATE? the screen asked. *This is crazy,* Marlie thought. But the knowledge of her own insanity didn't stop her. Maybe once she saw her name and Bob's together at the top of a wedding registry that now included a food scale, beige china, and a vibrator, the obsession that had taken hold of her since she'd learned that Bob was getting married would loosen its grip, and she'd be herself again, and happy.

She hit Enter. There was a popping noise, as small and unimportant as a soap bubble bursting . . . and her screen went black.

"Oh, no," she murmured, giving the laptop a little shake. She hit Control-Alt-Delete. Nothing happened. She hit Restart. Still nothing. "No, no, no," she groaned, yanking out the power cord and plugging it in again. What if she'd broken the computer? And what was going to happen when Bob saw what she'd done to his registry?

She heard Zeke make his little crowing *eh eh eh* noise in the bedroom. She ran into the bedroom, pulled him out of his crib with shaking hands, changed his diaper, nursed him on the couch next to the black-screened laptop, while frantically trying to restart the computer with her free hand and figure out how to tell Drew what had happened. She'd gotten as far as "Honey, I'm really sorry" when she fell asleep.

———

"Marlie?"

The instant she opened her eyes, she knew something was wrong. The light. The light was wrong. There was too much of it. In his entire life, Zeke had never slept past six in the morning, and the room was too full of light for it to be that early. The light was wrong, the bed felt wrong, and that voice . . .

Marlie rolled over and felt her whole body break out in goose bumps when she saw who was lying next to her. Bob. Bob Morrison, with new wrinkles at the corners of his brown eyes, looking at her with his familiar slanting smile. She sat straight up in the bed—the futon—barely managing to bite back a scream.

"You okay, babe?" The sunlight glinted off the silver threads in his hair, and his hand was warm on her bare shoulder. "You're not getting cold feet or anything, right?"

"Right," she managed. Her heart was in her throat, and she could feel her pulse booming in her ears as she slipped one hand underneath her pajama bottoms, feeling for the line of raised flesh. No scar. Hence, no C-section. Ditto, no eighteen pounds of baby weight. And, presumably, no baby. *This is a dream,* she thought, running her hands over her hips and wondering why she had ever thought she was fat before she'd had the baby, or if she'd ever had a dream that felt this real. Everything was so vivid—the feel of the sheets on her bare skin, the faint smell of beeswax candles, the sound of traffic through the windows, even the sour just-woke-up taste in her mouth.

Bob's hand followed Marlie's under her waistband. He leaned close and kissed her cheek, then her ear. Marlie shuddered as his beard scraped the tender skin of her neck, feeling a flush of pleasure, which was quickly followed by a full-on wave of guilt. "Bathroom," she gasped. She tossed back the covers and hopped out of bed, skidding through a patch of sunlight, and stopped to twirl in front of the bathroom mirror, checking out her prebaby physique from all possible angles.

"Okay," she whispered in the mirror. "Focus." It was a dream, brought on by the mishap with the registry and possibly bad sushi. (Hadn't she thought the toro had tasted iffy?) And even though she could smell the toothpaste and the soap, could feel the slightly damp bath mat under her feet, could hear Bob padding across the floor to come find her, maybe hoping for a quickie in the shower before she headed off to work and he headed off to wherever, it wasn't real. So it wasn't cheating.

He eased the door open and looked at her with a familiar gleam in his eyes. "Good morning, sunshine."

She grinned at him. When she was pregnant, she'd had the most outrageous X-rated dreams, and one of them had started off sort of like this, and had eventually wound up including every guy on *Laguna Beach.*

He backed her up against the vanity and kissed her, once, and not for long. Then he reached for his toothbrush. "I need to get out of here."

"Oh?" This was a dream, she reminded herself. He probably just had to go downstairs, where Stephen, Talen, and Jason were waiting, wearing nothing more than their swimsuits and their smiles. "Where?"

Bob stared at her. "To work," he said, speaking slowly, as if Marlie had become deaf overnight. "Are you sure you're okay?"

Marlie nodded, looking at her hands. The left one sported an engagement ring. It was a perfectly nice diamond ring. Just not hers.

Bob leaned close and kissed her again. "Tonight," he said, his voice low and husky. "I'll make it up to you. Have a good day." He smiled and went to the closet, where he started getting dressed. "Have a good massage."

"What?" asked Marlie. Then: "Don't I need to go to work?"

He was looking at her strangely again. "You took the day off. My mother got you that gift certificate at Bliss. Remember?"

"Oh, right," she said. She nodded. He nodded, reassured, picked up his coat, and walked out the door. Marlie hugged herself and grinned, skipped back to the bedroom, and flopped onto the down comforter that was still warm from Bob's body, feeling joy flood through her. *Freedom,* she thought, in the manner of Mel Gibson rallying the Scots in *Braveheart.* Freeeeeedom! And a massage, too. What an excellent dream this was turning out to be.

Marlie spent the afternoon in baby-free bliss: skipping down to the newsstand at the corner, where the guy behind the counter remembered her name and handed her *Us, Star,* and *People* in a big, slippery stack; having a grilled three-cheese sandwich for lunch in the window of her favorite coffee shop; savoring every exquisite, silent moment of her massage. Afterwards Marlie took a taxi back to their old apartment, where she wandered barefoot through the small rooms, admiring her ruby-red toenails and noticing that the dream-Bob—Bob 2.0?—was still in the habit of leaving half-finished cups of coffee on the radiator. But there weren't any canvases, unfinished or not, propped against the walls. No paintbrushes or paint anywhere, either, no smell of linseed oil or turpentine. Weird, Marlie thought as she opened the closet, trying to see if there were any unstretched canvases in there. No luck . . . but when she slipped her fingers into the pockets of Bob's winter coat, she found a business card. Robert Morrison, it read. Director of Innovation and New Technology, Morrison Law, LLP. So Bob had broken down and gone to work for his father, as director of innovation and new technology, whatever that was. It gave her a strange, sad pang. Just for the heck of it, she dialed her own number at New Directions. Instead of her own voice, cheerful and confident, saying *This is Marlie Davidow at New Directions Theater,* there was three-toned chime, then a mechanical voice. *You have reached a nonworking number. If you feel you have reached this recording in error . . .*

Now she felt even sadder, and stranger. Was New Directions still mounting *Uncommon Women and Others*? Who was making follow-up calls to the city's jaded, cynical theater critics, convincing them that the play wasn't just a throwback gloss on *Sex and the City* because it involved more than one woman? And how long had she been asleep, anyhow?

She wondered whether Zeke was sleeping, too, or whether he'd woken up and Drew was with him. She tentatively pinched her right arm . . . then, wincing, pinched it harder. Nothing happened.

The logical thing to do would be to fall asleep again and hope that she'd wake up in the right bed (or at least on the couch in the right apartment). But after the first good night's sleep she'd had in months, dozing off seemed unlikely.

Marlie forced herself to think calmly. If this was a dream, she could wake up. If it was some kind of alternate reality, a glitch in the time-space continuum that had nothing to do with bad sushi and was possibly related to actual magic, she could figure that out, too.

She stood in the center of the room, closed her eyes, and clicked her freshly pumiced heels together. "There's no place like home," she said. She opened her eyes. Nope, still Bob's apartment. She shut her eyes again. "It's a wonderful life?" She opened her eyes. No dice.

Heart racing, mouth dry, Marlie scanned the room, looking for clues. Bob's dirty clothes on the floor . . . last Sunday's newspaper, ditto . . .

Her hands clenched into fists as she stared at the artwork-free wall. Taking a deep breath, she started walking toward it . . . then trotting. She'd worked herself up to a half-decent jog when her forehead made contact.

"Ow! Shit!"

Marlie reeled back, blinking. Her eyes were watering and she saw stars, but beyond the stars she could see that she was still, emphatically, not back home again. Then it hit her. She wiped her eyes and ran to Bob's laptop, drumming her fingers on the desk and muttering "Come on, come on," as the cranky dial-up connection stuttered its way online.

HELLO BOB AND MARLIE! read the log-in screen at Wedding Wishes.com.

She clicked on the BRIDE'S INFORMATION tab. The screen froze. SYSTEM ERROR, it read. WINDOWS WILL SHUT DOWN.

"No, no, no!" she hissed. But the connection was broken, and she heard Bob's feet making their way up the scarred staircase, and his key in the lock.

"Hey!" Bob called, said, coming through the door with a garment bag in one hand and a shoe box in the other. He frowned when he saw that she was barefoot, in her jeans. "We'd better get going. Can't be late to our own party, right?"

"Here comes the bride!" Bob's brother Randall called from the doorway of the bar two blocks from their apartment, where Bob and Marlie were regulars. Not because they'd ever liked the place—the bartender was surly, and the jukebox ate their change—but because it had two-dollar pitchers on Monday nights, which made it an affordable option for Bob's slacker friends.

Marlie winced as Randall enfolded her in a rough hug. Randall had grabbed her boob in the Morrison family dining room after Thanksgiving dinner one year, and then tried to explain away the gesture as the consequence of overwork and the trypto-phan in the turkey, while Marlie had stood there, face flaming, afraid to move lest she bump into one of the many Morrison an-tiques. She looked over her shoulder for her putative husband-to-be, but Bob had vanished. He always does this, she remembered, feeling the old frustration wash over her. Classic Bob. He'd take her to a family function, promise to stay by her side because he knew that she was shy and that his brother was a boob-grabber, and when she'd turn around he'd be two rooms away watching the football game.

Drew would never, she thought. Drew could be loud, he was frequently late, he was deeply opinionated, and he was not shy about sharing his beliefs with friends, and even less so with strangers. But at parties, he would take her coat and hold her hand. He'd stick to her side, making sure that her glass was full and that she was part of a conversation. Marlie shook her head, feeling the afternoon's unease ramping up toward panic. What if she was really still asleep, on the couch, and the baby was awake and she didn't hear him? Not likely, she knew, but every once in a while Zeke woke up and didn't cry. She'd walk into the bedroom and find him lying in his crib, staring up at her calmly with his blue-gray eyes like he was waiting for her to tell him a story.

The crowd swept her toward the buffet set up on tables along the back wall. Per usual at Morrison family affairs, there was a surplus of booze and very little food. Bob's parents were standing by the bar, looking prim and out of place, Mr. Morri-son in a sports jacket and Mrs. Morrison in two-hundred-dollar yoga pants and a beaded peasant blouse the likes of which no real peasant could hope to afford. Bob brushed past her, deep in conversation with someone Marlie didn't recognize. Marlie grabbed his sleeve and he gave her a nonchalant smile.

"Come meet my friends," he said. He steered her toward the jukebox, where she was introduced to Barb and Barry, from Ultimate Frisbee, and Karen from Morrison Law.

"Karen Kravitz?"

The woman looked startled. "That's right." She was of medium height and medium build, in a pale-blue jacket and a pair of unfortunate high-waisted blue jeans. Her hair was light brown, but her eyebrows and eyelashes were so pale and wispy they were practically invisible. "Have we met?"

So this is who Bob marries in real life, Marlie thought. Just an ordinary person, with a taste for beige china and a skewer of what appeared to be chicken satay in one hand. "Hey," Marlie said, unable to help herself, "would you say you've got about four ounces there?"

Karen Kravitz blinked her see-through lashes. "Excuse me?"

"Nothing," Marlie said . . . and then, thank God, she spotted someone she knew. "Gwen!" She shimmied and twisted through the crowd and flung her arms around her friend's neck. When she let go, Gwen was looking at her quizzically.

"Jeez, Marlie, I just saw you last night!"

"For sushi?" Marlie asked.

"For your fitting," Gwen said, looking at her strangely.

"Come with me." Marlie dragged her friend to the bathroom, which was small and dirty, with green-painted walls and the aggressive reek of ammonia. "I need to tell you something." She ran her hands through her hair, the glossy, good-smelling hairdo of a woman with time on her hands and no baby in her life. "I know it's going to sound crazy, but I'm not supposed to be here!"

"Are you having second thoughts?" Gwen asked, with an eagerness that would have been insulting under other circumstances. Her eyes sparkled as she reached into her purse—in this life, a luscious black crocodile hobo bag—for her keys. "My car's right outside. I can have you out of here in five minutes flat."

"I don't need a car, I need a computer. I have to change my wedding registry."

Gwen stared at her, eyes wide, mouth open. "You're having second thoughts about your china? Haven't you already gotten four place settings already?"

"It's not the china! My life! I'm having second thoughts about my life!"

Gwen stared at her, mouth open, eyes wide.

"Drew," Marlie continued frantically. "Drew Davidow. That's my husband. That's who I'm supposed to marry. We met him on that rafting trip, remember?"

Now Gwen looked troubled. "Marlie, we've never been on a rafting trip."

There was a knock on the door. "Ladies?" Bob called.

Marlie tried one last time. "I have a baby. A little baby boy. Ezekiel. Zeke. We named him after my grandfather." She reached into her own purse, fumbling for the wallet, and the picture she kept there, of Zeke when he was one day old, swaddled in the pink-and-blue-striped hospital blanket with a little knitted cap on his head. But the wallet she found wasn't the wallet she remembered, and when she flipped it open the only picture she found was one of her and Bob from a photo booth at Dave & Buster's, sticking their tongues out at the camera.

"Is this some kind of joke?" Gwen asked.

Marlie dropped the wallet and grabbed her friend's hands. "Help me. Help me, please," she said, her voice beseeching. "I'm not supposed to be here."

Bob stepped through the door, looking impatient. "There you are," he said, edging past Gwen. He took Marlie by the hand and led her past the dripping sink and the broken paper towel dispenser, back out into the party, as Gwen shot one last troubled look over her shoulder and left, Marlie hoped, to get the laptop that would be her salvation and send her home.

This is a mistake, Marlie thought, smiling mechanically as she hugged Bob's aunt Phyllis, who smelled of the Altoids she chewed compulsively to mask the scent of the cigarettes she thought nobody knew she smoked.

I've got to get out of here, she thought as Randall congratulated her again, allowing his hands to drift from her waist to the curve of her ass. Here own mother kissed her cheek and whispered, "Good luck." Marlie swallowed hard, almost crying, remembering how her mother had said, "I'm so happy for you" the night before she'd married Drew. The night unfolded in a parade of ribald toasts and congratulations, and finally Marlie decided that if she couldn't wake up and she couldn't get home, she could at least enjoy one pleasure denied to breast-feeding mothers and get really, really drunk.

She started with a beer, then moved to her old single-girl standard, rum and Diet Coke. The jukebox blared "Mustang Sally," and Bob's Frisbee friends clustered around a television set at one end of the bar. Marlie set down her third sweating glass on a tray full of empty plates and dirty napkins and made her way to the bar for a refill. While she waited, another way to fix things surfaced, slowly, in her rum-sodden brain. Sleeping Beauty, she thought. Heel-clicking and head-bashing hadn't worked. Maybe all she really needed to do was get Karen to give Bob a kiss.

It was, she decided, worth a try. She collected her drink, smoothed her hair, and sidled over to Karen Kravitz, who was standing in a corner with a wistful look on her face.

"Hey," Marlie said, and burped.

The other woman gave her a weak smile.

"So listen," Marlie said. "Do you, um, like Bob?"

"Sure," Karen said. Her tone was neutral. "He's very nice. You're very lucky."

"I mean, do you *like* him," Marlie said, and gave Karen's forearm an encouraging little squeeze. The other woman's eyes widened.

"What are you saying?" she stammered.

Marlie hiccupped, and silently cursed her decision to go with a carbonated alcohol delivery device. "Nothing. Never mind. Do you like art?" she asked. "Y'know, Bob's quite the artist."

"I know," Karen said warily. "He does a comic strip about the office."

"Does he?" Okay, this was good. This was something. "Are you in it?"

The other woman smiled. "Sometimes. It's more about Bob and his father." Her smile widened. "In the comic strip, Bob gets superpowers after a freak accident where lightning hits one of the vending machines in the snack room."

"Lightning," Marlie marveled. "Snack room. Wow. I'll bet the drawings are really good."

Karen's eyes narrowed. "He's never shown it to you?"

Marlie ignored the question. "He used to be a painter. In college, and after. That was what he really wanted, but it's hard, you know." *Okay,* she thought. *Bring it on home.* "I think," she blared. Oops. Too loud. She lowered her voice. "I think it's so important for women to be nurturing and encouraging. To be, you know, the power behind the throne. Or the easel."

Karen gave her a strange look. "Excuse me," she said, and disappeared into the crowd. Marlie sighed and slumped down at a table for two. When she looked up, the other woman was standing there with a steaming mug of coffee in her hands. "Here you go," she said, not unkindly. "It was nice to meet you. See you Sunday."

"Bob's a really good kisser!" Marlie called helplessly toward Karen's departing back. No answer. No surprise. Marlie hiccupped again, realizing miserably that her theoretical husband's actual fiancée might very well have thought she was proposing a prenuptial threesome.

She sighed, catching sight of Bob's familiar figure, the line of his shoulders and his worn plaid shirt, as he stood shoulder to shoulder with three of his cousins at the bar. She remembered something she'd forgotten in the excitement—the obsession, really—of stumbling across the news of Bob's nuptials. Four months before they'd broken up, she and Bob had a fight at her grandmother's eightieth birthday party. Marlie's grandmother always had something to say about Marlie's job prospects, or her appearance, and Marlie was delighted that for once she'd have a supportive boyfriend by her side.

Bob, however, had other ideas, and Jets tickets. He finally agreed to skip the game and go to the party, but he'd sulked for the entire ride up to Rhinebeck, and he'd ducked out of the living room after two beers and twenty minutes, leaving Marlie to parry her grandmother's increasingly pointed questions about whether she and her young man had made any plans.

She found Bob in his car, slouched behind the wheel with the radio tuned to the game, a third and fourth beer in the cupholders and a truculent look on his face.

"Hey. Little help in there," she said.

Bob reached down and turned up the volume without looking at her.

"When did you decide to hate me so much?" she asked him.

She'd started the question lightly, as if she were teasing, but by the end of it she wasn't kidding at all. Bob gave her a hostile shrug. Marlie was pierced with the knowledge of how far apart they'd drifted. He didn't want to be in her grandmother's house with her, and she didn't want to be in the stadium with him. He might have cared for her, might have even loved her, but he didn't—or couldn't—take care of her. And she, fed up with the joblessness and the aimlessness, the Frisbee games and the parental handouts and the half-finished paintings, was increasingly disinclined to take care of him.

The relationship didn't officially end for months, but she knew that that was the real moment when it had died.

She and Bob walked home from the bar in silence. "Are you okay?" he asked, tossing his keys onto the rickety table by the door, seeming not to notice as they bounced off the surface and slid to the floor. She nodded woodenly. When the nurse had handed Zeke to her for the first time in the hospital, she'd said, "Here you go, Mom," and Marlie had actually turned to look over her shoulder to see if her own mother was there. "I'm not sure I can do this," she'd told Drew, and he'd leaned down, eyes tender, and kissed her forehead, and said, "I know you can." She remembered the three of them in the taxi home, the brand-new car seat painstakingly strapped between them and one of Zeke's hands gripping her index finger. And she thought of Drew in the equipment shop as he'd zipped up her wetsuit and adjusted her grip on the paddle, telling her not to worry, because he was pretty sure the rapids looked worse than they were.

Late into that sleepless night, in the white cotton nightgown she'd lost in the move out of their old apartment and thought she'd never see again, she lay beside a man who wasn't her husband—at least not yet and, with any luck, not ever—and thought about Drew and her baby. She conjured their faces until she could practically touch them, could practically reach out and kiss them. She could see Zeke's fingers fanning open and shut as he nursed, the way Drew's hair curled over his collar when he went too long between haircuts.

This is what you wanted, Gwen had said. Marlie opened her eyes and looked down into Bob Morrison's slack, sleeping face. Then she touched his arm. Bob woke up with a start, eyes wide, face flushed.

"Huh?"

She propped herself up on her elbow and looked down at him. "I'm sorry," she said.

He squinted at her in the darkness. "Why, what'd you do?"

"It doesn't matter. You just have to forgive me." *Because you work for your father instead of painting,* she thought. *Because you're supposed to be Karen's husband, not mine.*

"Fine. I forgive you. Can I go back to sleep?"

She nodded, and she kissed his cheek. He ruffled her hair and rolled over. A minute later he was snoring again.

She counted to a hundred once, then again. And when the world was dark and still outside and the city streets were quiet, she tiptoed back to Bob's computer and logged on to Wedding-Wishes.com.

Her hands trembled as she clicked over to CHANGE GROOM'S INFORMATION, erased Bob and typed in Drew. UPDATE? the screen inquired.

Her fingers paused, curled over the keys. *Now,* she thought. *Now I'm going to type* ZEKE IS THE HAPPIEST BABY EVER BORN AND HE SLEEPS FOURTEEN HOURS EVERY NIGHT AND NEVER CRIES. Or DREW DAVIDOW IS HOME FROM WORK BY SIX O'CLOCK.

But she didn't type anything else. She hit Enter and closed

her eyes and crossed her fingers. Nothing happened for a minute. Then the words *Thank you, Marlie* floated onto the screen.

She went back to bed and lay down next to Bob, with his easy smile and warm hands and his smell of fresh-cut grass, for the last time, knowing in her heart that she'd wake up where she was supposed to be, curled on the couch with her son safe in his crib and her C-section scar and eighteen extra pounds back where they were supposed to be, and her husband would be coming through the door smiling his tired smile, lifting her to her feet and leading her back toward the bed they shared, telling her, "Go to sleep. I've got this."

THE
MOTHER'S HOUR

B lue, Alice thought. The September-to-January semester of the Mother's Hour had started fifteen minutes ago, on a brilliant fall morning where the gold leaves stood out sharply against the skies, and the wind held a hint of the winter to come. Alice had been trying not to stare at the pierced, tattooed, pale-skinned teenager splayed beside the radiator on the playroom's carpeted floor, but the few quick peeks she'd taken left her convinced that the girl, who'd come to Mother's Hour in a sleeve-less Sex Pistols T-shirt and low-slung black jeans, had dark-blue streaks in her tire-black hair, and a few magenta strands, too.

Alice's daughter, Maisy, wriggled in her arms. Maisy had been clinging to her like a spider monkey since they'd arrived at the community center in Society Hill. "Mommy, I'm a lit-tle shyness," she'd said. So Alice had stood in the corner for twenty minutes, next to the toddler-size table with a plastic tea set and the boxes of dress-up clothes, with her lower back throb-bing and Maisy's face buried in her neck. "Down, Mommy, down!" Maisy finally demanded. Alice set her down gently. "Be careful," she called, as Maisy ignored the other children and went trundling over to the wooden slide with her toes-in, el-bows-out walk that made her look like an indignant penguin.

Lynn, the group leader, a short, brisk woman with a silvery-blond bob, clapped her hands. "Moms, caregivers," she called. "Let's gather in a circle." The blue-haired teenager rose languidly from the floor and scooped up an adorable little girl dressed in overalls and pink high-topped sneakers, with black ringlets gathered into pigtails. "Belly kiss!" she called, and planted a dozen kisses on the little girl's convex tummy. The child shrieked in delight, dimples flashing in her cheeks.

Alice steeled herself and walked over to the slide, where Maisy crouched, scowling.

"Come on, Maisy, time to sit in a circle."

Maisy shook her head.

"We'll play later," she said, scooping her daughter into her arms.

"No! *No! Noey noey No! Play now, Mommy!*" Maisy shrieked, and kicked Alice sharply in the left breast. Alice gasped. Her eyes filled with tears, but she struggled to keep her voice calm as she carried Maisy over to the circle.

"Maisy, we do not kick. Feet are not for kicking."

"Want . . . to go . . . down! Now!" Maisy screamed, writhing in her mother's arms. Alice winced, imagining she could feel the other women's stares.

"You can go down the slide later, but right now we need to sit down," she said in the firm-but-patient tone she'd been practicing, to little avail, for weeks.

"Well!" said Lynn, giving the eight women and their charges a smile and trying her hardest to ignore Maisy, who'd ramped up into a full-on tantrum and was shrieking and pounding her fists on the floor. Lynn raised her voice above the little girl's wails. "Let's go around the circle and say our names and our child's name."

Mom One was Lisa and her daughter, a porcelain-skinned

redhead contentedly sucking her thumb, was Annie. Mom Two was Stacy, and her little boy, vrooming his firetruck over the carpet, was Taylor. Alice patted Maisy's back ineffectually and caught a name here and there. Pam . . . Tate . . . Manda . . . Morgan. The mothers, like Alice, appeared to be in their thirties, with expensively highlighted hair and dark circles under their eyes masked with sixty-dollar concealer. Any one of the diamonds on their left hands could have been swapped for a small used car.

With one mother left, Maisy finally stopped crying. "I don't like you," she said, glaring at Alice, who felt her heart contract helplessly, as if she'd been kicked there, too. "Not one wittle bit." Maisy hooked her thumb into her mouth. Her cheeks were blotchy, and her fine blond hair, which had been neatly combed and secured with pink bunny barrettes that morning, stood up around her head in a frizzy, tangled corona.

The blue-haired babysitter lifted an eyebrow and resettled the dimpled, pigtailed girl in her lap. "I'm Victoria, and this is Ellie. She's two and a half exactly." The other mothers nodded, murmuring hellos.

"And she's potty-trained, I see!" exclaimed Lynn the leader. The sitter gave a modest shrug. Alice grimaced. She'd been unsuccessful at getting Maisy to do anything with the potty except occasionally wear it on her head. Then it was her turn.

"I'm Alice, and this is Maisy. She'll be two and a half next month." She pulled a tissue out of her diaper bag and tried to wipe her daughter's face.

"Go away from me!" Maisy whined, slapping at Alice's hands. Pick your battles, Alice reminded herself, putting the tissue back in her pocket and starting a mental tally of Victoria's piercings. There was one silver ring through her lip, a diamond twinkling in her nostril, and a silver barbell run through her eyebrow, in addition to black rubber plugs that stretched quarter-size holes in her earlobes. Alice thought she couldn't have been older than nineteen.

"Free play time!" said Lynn, clapping her hands again. The other mothers, the ones with the expensive suede moccasins and diamond-and-platinum rings, gravitated toward the crafts table. Victoria resumed her slouch next to the radiator, idly twisting a studded leather cuff around one wrist as Ellie happily glued cotton balls to construction paper. Alice shepherded Maisy back to the slide and sat down next to blue-haired Victoria. She wondered what kind of mother would entrust her child to a sitter dressed like this. Probably a very hip mother, a downtown girl. Alice and her husband had recently relocated to suburban Haddonfield, where only the little old ladies had blue hair.

"How long have you been taking care of Ellie?" she asked.

Victoria raised her pierced eyebrow. "Excuse me?" Then she shot Alice a quicksilver grin. "Oh, no," she said. "I'm not the nanny. I'm her mom."

"How was your day, ladies?" Mark asked that night, trying not to sound harried as he hung up his overcoat and suit jacket and came to the kitchen to help Alice wrestle Maisy into her booster seat.

"Fine!" Alice shouted back. One of Maisy's sneakered feet caught her in the bicep as Mark finally pulled the straps around his daughter. Alice grabbed the plastic Disney princess plate and Maisy's preferred orange sippy cup from the counter. "We went to playgroup. It was fun!"

"It was not," said Maisy, abruptly going limp and sliding bonelessly underneath her straps, out of her booster seat, and down to the floor. She paused for a moment, as startled as both of her parents were at this new development, before opening her mouth and starting to scream. Mark scooped her back into the seat and tightened the straps, while Alice retrieved a steaming bowl from the microwave. Maisy's wails stopped abruptly. "Chicken noodle! My fav'rit!"

Mark frowned, loosening his tie. "Noodle soup again? Didn't she have that last night?"

"She had it for lunch today." And breakfast, Alice didn't add. "She won't eat anything else," she said, collapsing into her own chair.

"Noodles! Yommmy!" said Maisy, slurping wetly. There was clump of glue stuck in her hair, a remnant of her stint at the crafts table that morning.

"You like those noodles, kiddo?" asked Mark in the bluff, too-loud tone he always used with his daughter, the tone that, just lately, made Alice want to slap him.

Maisy ignored him, slurping away. Alice set their dinner on the table: rotisserie chicken fresh from the supermarket, a salad she'd recently dumped out of a plastic bag, and a reheated container of mashed sweet potatoes with a candied-pecan crust that she'd purchased for the unbelievable price of $9.99 a pound. For that much money, she'd thought, steering a screaming Maisy through the checkout line and ignoring her daughter's wails for lollipops, she could have bought five pounds of sweet potatoes, not to mention the butter and brown sugar and pecans, and whipped up enough mashed sweet potatoes for Thanksgiving dinner for twelve. But when? That was the question. With what time?

Mark filled his plate, then turned to his daughter. "Want to try some sweet potatoes?" he wheedled, holding out a bite on his fork.

Maisy scowled at him. "No sweepatoes! *Not eating that! I will not!*"

"Honey . . ." Alice began.

"Well, she can't just eat noodle soup for the rest of her life!" Mark said.

Maisy snatched the fork loaded with sweet potatoes and flung it toward the living room, where it probably landed on the Oriental rug—the one nice thing Alice had brought from her single-girl apartment into her married-lady home. The dog whimpered. Ever since Maisy had gotten mobile, Charlie, their sweet shelter dog, had lived in mortal terror of the little girl Alice privately called—just in her own thoughts, never out loud, never to Mark—the bad seed.

God, give me strength, Alice thought. "Maisy, we do not throw food in this house. Food is for eating. And we especially do not throw forks. You scared poor Charlie!"

"I didn't want that thing!" Maisy wailed, and upended her soup bowl onto the table. Mark shoved his chair back to avoid the encroaching tide of noodles and broth.

"For the love of God . . ."

"Please don't raise your voice," Alice asked him. "Firm but patient, remember?"

"No yelling!" yelled Maisy.

Mark sighed, picked up the bowl, and carried it into the kitchen. Alice sopped up as much of the mess as she could with a handful of paper napkins as Maisy picked noodles off the table. "Noodles! Yommy!" she said. She tilted her head back and opened her mouth wide. "Mommy, feed me like I am your baby bird," she said.

"Can't we do something?" Mark asked in a low voice as he passed Alice the sponge.

Alice dropped a noodle into Maisy's mouth. "Like what? Hire a full-time nanny? Leave her on the street corner?" She'd meant to sound like she was kidding, but when the words came out of her mouth they didn't sound joking at all. She took a deep breath and fed Maisy another noodle. "She's just . . . you know . . . spirited," she said, parroting the lingo she'd gleaned from the parenting books she devoured late at night as if they were pornography. "She's a spirited child."

Mark muttered something that sounded like *bullshit* and scooped the sodden napkins into his hand.

"We wanted her so much," Alice said the next week at Mother's Hour. The leaves outside the windows had deepened from pale gold to rust, and they rustled in the brisk wind. She'd spent ten minutes that morning getting Maisy into a jacket, dreading the day when she'd have to add a hat and boots and mittens to the routine. The mothers balanced on toddler-size chairs while their children mushed homemade Play-Doh at the arts-and-crafts table. (Maisy, of course, had refused to join in and was back on top of the slide.) "She was a very wanted child."

A few of the women nodded sympathetically. Victoria fiddled with her studded bracelet, listening intently. "I was thirty-six when she was born," Alice continued. "We went through two cycles of IVF before we conceived for the first time, and we lost that . . . that pregnancy." The word *baby* had been on the tip of her tongue, but she didn't want to say it. Pam, Tate's mother, who she knew from Baby Beethoven class, had a miscarriage at sixteen weeks. What was a positive pregnancy test followed by getting her period three days later compared to that? "Maisy was such a wanted child. And now . . ." Her voice trailed off. The private part of her brain, the place where she called Maisy "bad seed," also had repeatedly advanced the theory that the first baby, the one she'd lost, was the one she'd been meant to have, and that Maisy was some kind of changeling. Either that or a punishment. For what, Alice wasn't sure.

"It's tough," Lynn the leader said.

"Two's hard," Nora agreed.

"You ever tried whiskey?" asked Victoria.

Seven highlighted heads swung around to stare. There was a hint of a smile playing at the corners of Victoria's lips.

"You give Ellie whiskey?" Lynn asked faintly.

Victoria smiled more broadly, shoved the cuff up high on her forearm, and recrossed her long, skinny legs. "Nah. My mom used to tell me she'd put whiskey in my bottle so I'd sleep. But I know better." She hugged Ellie against her, dropped her voice to a whisper, and said, "I use cough syrup."

Someone sucked in a horrified breath. "You're kidding, right?" Taylor's mother, Stacy, blurted.

Victoria rolled her eyes. "Well, duh," she said. Alice laughed—a bright, uncomplicated sound that one of the children could have made. Her eyes met Victoria's over the knee-high table covered with fingerpaint and a vinyl Dora the Explorer tablecloth, and Victoria tipped her a wink.

"It's, you know, the same old story," Victoria told her after class had let out at noon. They'd crossed Washington Square Park for lattes from Caramel, and were sitting on a park bench with their paper cups underneath the brilliant, cloudless blue sky. Ellie sang to herself while she chased pigeons around the empty fountain and Maisy slept in her stroller, mouth open, a bubble of spit on her pink lips expanding and contracting with each breath. "I got pregnant when I was sixteen, my mom pitched a fit and threw me out of the house . . ."

"That must have been awful," Alice said reflexively.

"It was a blessing in disguise," said Victoria. "She and I never really got along. I moved in with Tommy's family."

"Tommy is your boyfriend?"

"My husband," said Victoria, sounding proud and shy. "We got married when I was six months pregnant. We lived with his mom and stepfather for a while, then with his sister and her husband, but that didn't go so well." She made a face and tugged at a strand of blue hair. "So we saved up and moved here, and Tommy works as a bicycle messenger. We're both taking classes at community college, and we found this great place in University City. Well, west Philly. It's not really that near the university. But it's not so bad." She looked sideways at Alice as the wind sent leaves rattling past their feet. "You guys could come for a playdate some day."

"Sure!" Alice said, recognizing her husband's too-loud, too-hearty tone coming out of her own mouth an instant too late. West Philadelphia was what the newspapers called a neighborhood in transition, the kind of place where Mark would drive only if he got lost, and where he'd take pains to lock the car doors until he escaped. "I mean, we'd like that," she said, more quietly. "Poor Maisy," she said, bending down to pull a wayward leaf out of her daughter's hair. "The way she carries on, I don't think she's going to have any friends unless I make some for her."

Victoria shrugged. Alice braced herself for one of the platitudes her friends, her own mother, the other mothers she knew, would have delivered. *Oh, no, she's just sensitive! Don't worry, she'll outgrow it!*

Instead, Victoria said, "She is a little bit of a drama queen, isn't she?"

"From the moment she was born," said Alice. "They put her on the table, and she looked up at the nurses with this expression of absolute disgust." She sighed. "Then she started screaming, and sometimes I think she hasn't stopped since." She shook her head. "Maybe I should put cough syrup in her sippy cup."

"Couldn't hurt," Victoria said. Ellie trotted over, beaming at her mother, with a pigeon feather clutched in one hand.

"Is it lunchtime?" she asked. There wasn't a trace of a whine in her voice, Alice noticed. How had the high school dropout, the teenage mother, wound up with this angelic child while she, who had a master's degree and a mortgage and a husband, who'd insisted on a drug-free birth and had breastfed even after her daughter bit her at least once per feeding, ended up with a shrieky, miserable brat?

Victoria glanced at her heavy man's watch, then at Alice. "You want to go get a burrito?"

In the stroller, Maisy opened her eyes. "Hungry!" she said.

"Sure," said Alice. "That would be great."

The second Friday in October, Alice rang the buzzer beside the purple door, then tightened her grip on Maisy's shoulders, looking down the street, past the glass-littered sidewalk at her minivan, which she devoutly hoped would still be there when the playdate was over. The street didn't fill her with optimism. Victoria's building looked fine, but the house next door had graffiti painted on the boarded-up windows, and the house next to that had about half a dozen guys in puffy down coats sitting on a sagging couch on the porch, staring at the sparse traffic with hooded eyes while they bobbed their heads to the beat of the music coming from a radio on the windowsill.

"Hello down there!" Victoria called from a third-floor window.

"Hello up there!" Maisy said, giggling. Victoria opened the window and tossed down a key.

"Did you make it okay?" Victoria asked as she opened her front door.

"No problem at all," said Alice, taking in the apartment.

The living room walls were buttercup yellow and the couch was draped in a cheerful plum-and-rust tapestry. A little radio played a tape of Kids' Corner, and there was an aquarium where a television set might have been. "Come see!" Ellie said, grabbing Maisy and Alice by the hands and tugging them over to the fishtank, where fish in shades of silver and blue and orange-gold swam around a tiny plastic treasure chest.

The girls played with wooden blocks on the living room floor. Victoria and Alice sat on the couch, drinking spicy tea and nibbling the sugar cookies Victoria and Ellie had baked that morning. After an hour, everyone went to the kitchen for lunch, where plants in painted ceramic pots lined the sunny windowsill. Alice sat at the table with the girls while Victoria stood at the stove in tight black jeans and a red tank top, flipping grilled-cheese sandwiches.

"I love your place," said Alice, thinking what a contrast the cozy, sunny little nest was to her own too-big house, where each and every room, from the basement to the attic, was filled with expensive toys that Maisy had either broken or ignored.

Ellie slept in a tiny room where most of the space was taken up by the washer and dryer. In a wicker toy box at the foot of her bed, she had a little xylophone, a set of ABC blocks, a handful of books, and a box of crayons. That was all, and she seemed content. Certainly happier than Maisy ever was. *I should downsize,* Alice thought, plucking at a thread on her sleeve as Victoria slid quartered sandwiches onto purple plates. Get rid of all of the electronics that lit up and whooped and flashed when Maisy pressed the right color or letter, ditch the portable DVD player that had been their saving grace on long car trips, invest in a set of fingerpaints and some construction paper, a few well-chosen board books . . .

"Hey, baby." The front door opened, and in came a man

who looked like Victoria's twin brother—tall and pale, with intricate tattoos covering both of his forearms, a knit cap pulled low over pierced ears, and a slim silver bicycle hitched over his shoulder.

"Hi, Tommy!" Victoria's face lit up as she leaned in for a kiss. Alice saw Tommy's hand linger at the small of Victoria's back, pulling her closer so that her hips bumped his. She swallowed hard. Had Mark ever touched her that way? Even before the saga of their infertility and the treatments, before sex had become something he'd scheduled into his Palm Pilot, before the baby? She wasn't sure. Victoria patted her husband's chest, pushing him gently away.

"We have company," she said.

"Oops," said Tommy with an amiable grin. He had traces of teenage acne on his forehead and beautiful teeth, perfectly straight and blindingly white. Alice wondered about his parents, back in Harrisburg, who'd presumably paid for the orthodontia, and whether they were shaking their heads over the baby their baby had had. The boy stuck out his hand. "I'm Tom Litcovsky."

Alice shook his hand and murmured her name. Tommy cadged half a grilled-cheese sandwich, kissed his wife, and headed out the door.

"He comes home for lunch?" she asked Victoria.

"Well, technically. He never gets to, you know, stay and eat anything." Victoria had never looked like more of a teenager to Alice than she did at that moment, when she smiled. "He says he doesn't like to go too long without seeing me."

"That's so sweet," said Alice.

"Sweet," Maisy repeated, with her mouth full of grilled cheese.

"I don't get it," Mark said late one night in early November.

Alice rolled over. "Don't get what?" she asked, even though she knew exactly what he was talking about. Mark had come home from work unexpectedly early that night, while she and Victoria had been making soup in the kitchen. They'd put the little girls to work dumping water in and out of a plastic mixing bowl at the sink while they chopped carrots and onions and gossiped about the other mothers in the group.

"Oh, hello!" Mark had said at the kitchen door, his gaze taking in Victoria's hair (she'd added green streaks that week), her lip ring, and the elaborate tattoo peeking over the waistband of her low-riding jeans. He'd politely seconded Alice's invitation to stay for dinner and, as they ate, he'd been on his best behavior, asking polite questions about Victoria's neighborhood and Ellie's toilet training. But once the table was cleared, Alice had spotted him in the kitchen running Victoria's silverware under the hot water for longer than she thought was technically necessary, and he'd gotten Ellie's name wrong twice.

"That girl," Mark said. "What's the deal?"

"The deal is, I met her in Mother's Hour and I like her. What's the problem?" Alice asked.

"Well, you have to admit, she's a bit of a shock to the system."

Alice shrugged. "I didn't know that my friends had to follow a dress code."

"It's not just her clothes. It's everything. I mean, Jesus, Alice, what is she? Nineteen?"

"So?"

"So what do you two have in common?"

"You mean besides our daughters, who were born a month apart in the same year?"

Mark sat up with a sigh, as if the conversation was exhausting him. He flicked on the light and leaned against the head-board. "Yes. Besides that. Does she have an education?"

"She has her GED," Alice said defensively. "She's taking classes. She's a wonderful mother. And I like her. I shouldn't have to defend my decisions."

"Okay, okay," said Mark, yanking the covers up to his chin. "I don't complain about your friends."

"My friends," said Mark, "are not punk-rock Goth girls with lip rings."

"No, they're overweight executives in Dockers. That's much better."

"I'm going to sleep," he said, turning the light off and rolling onto his side.

They lay in the darkness in silence. Five minutes passed, according to the glowing numbers on the digital clock, before Mark spoke again.

"Look," he said. "I'm sorry. If you like her . . ."

"I do," said Alice.

"Then that's fine," he said. He kissed her cheek and closed his eyes again. Lying there in the darkness, Alice remembered the way Tom had kissed Victoria in their postage-stamp kitchen that smelled of butter and toasted bread, the way his leather-cuffed hand had lingered on the small of her back.

Three weeks later, they were getting dressed for Mark's firm's annual holiday party. Maisy was shrieking in the family room ("Want my Mommy. *Want my Mommy*") while the sitter—one in a series of high school girls who, Alice knew from experience, would never return for a second stint—fluttered ineffectually in Maisy's orbit, offering toys that Maisy accepted only long enough to hurl at the sitter's head. Mark was fastening his cummerbund. Alice was sweating, pierced by her child's screams and pinched by her control-top pantyhose as she pawed through her jewelry box for the sixth time, searching in vain for her diamond-and-pearl earrings.

"You're positive you didn't put them back in the safe-deposit box?" Mark asked for the third time.

Alice shook her head without bothering to answer. She'd worn them on Thanksgiving, and put them back in her jewelry box on the dresser rather than making the trip to the bank, knowing she'd be wearing them through the holidays.

"Check your coat pockets," Mark suggested. Alice balled her hands into fists to keep from wrapping them around her husband's neck and explaining, again, that she would never pull off a pair of expensive earrings—the one thing she'd inherited from her grandmother Sarah—and just shove them in her pockets.

"Well, never mind. You look fine without them. Let's go." They tiptoed out of the house without saying good-bye, knowing that farewells would only make the Maisy situation worse. In the car, Mark laid his coat carefully in the backseat, adjusted the vents so that the flow of warm air was to his liking, and casually inquired, as he backed out of the driveway, "Has Victoria been over lately?"

"Yesterday," said Alice. She was distracted, fumbling through her beaded clutch on the off-chance that she'd put the earrings there. "Why?"

"Was she in the bedroom?"

Alice snapped her purse shut. "Oh, you have to be kidding me."

Mark held up his hands defensively, then put them back on the wheel in the nine and three o'clock positions. "Just asking a question."

"My friend is not a thief." Alice blew a strand of sweaty hair off her forehead and tossed her bag into the backseat. "I'll find them," she said. "They've got to be in the house somewhere." But even though she spent the weekend combing the house— emptying her underwear drawer, peering under the bed, even using a screwdriver to remove the shower drain—the earrings never turned up.

After the final Mother's Hour of the year, when Victoria asked if Alice and Maisy wanted to join her for a burrito after class, Alice made an excuse about having to return something at the King of Prussia Mall. For the next two weeks, there was no class. The Parenting Center was closed for the holidays. Victoria called once after Christmas. Alice saw her name on the caller ID and, feeling a strange, pinched feeling in her chest, let the phone ring.

On New Year's Day, Alice left Maisy with Mark and ran out to pick up coffee and milk at the organic grocery store. She'd grabbed a basket and was headed through the produce section when Tate's mother, Pam, a petite strawberry blond in fur-lined suede boots and a pearl-buttoned cashmere sweater, stopped her. "Did you hear?" she asked, raising her voice over the hissing spray of the misters that kept the eggplants and radishes glistening like jewels.

Alice shook her head. "Hear what?"

"Ellie's in the hospital. She hurt her head—they think maybe a concussion—and broke her wrist."

Alice's hand rose to her mouth. "Oh my God! Is she okay? What happened?"

"Nobody's really sure," Pam said. "What I heard was that she fell in the kitchen."

"Oh, God," Alice said. She thought of Victoria's kitchen, and the wooden step stool—another tag-sale find—propped in front of the sink so that Ellie could play in the water while Victoria cooked.

Pam pushed her shopping cart behind the bins of onions and potatoes. "Listen," she said. "I don't mean to gossip, and I don't want this to come out wrong, but I, well, a couple of us, we're worried."

Alice stared at her, her heart pounding.

"We're worried about Ellie," said Pam. "Remember that bump she had on her forehead?"

Ellie had had a goose egg back in November. She'd gone to her grandmother's house for Thanksgiving, Victoria had told the other mothers, and run smack into a glass door. "All our kids get bumps and bruises," Alice said. Maisy routinely sported a puffy lip, a scabbed knee, or a smashed fingernail due to one misadventure or another.

"Well, you've been to their house," Pam said, leaning one hip against the broccoli display. "Have you ever seen anything?"

Alice paused. *Victoria is a wonderful mother,* she wanted to say. But the words clotted in her throat and stayed there, and what she saw instead of Victoria's warm little kitchen with the red wooden stool was the empty space in her jewelry box where her earrings had been, and Tommy's hand lingering on Victoria's back, and Ellie's tiny finger pointing out each of the darting silvery fish in her tank as she told Maisy their names. "I . . ." she said.

Pam's face snapped shut like a fan, and she gave a single, satisfied nod. "Right. We'll be in touch," she said.

Alice tossed her groceries into the passenger's seat and stood in the supermarket parking lot, leaning against the door of her SUV with her knees shaking and her breath puffing out in the frosty air. She pulled her cell phone out of her purse and left Victoria a message. She said that she heard Ellie had fallen, that she was thinking of them, that she hoped they were all okay. She wanted to say *be careful,* or to find some way of telling Victoria about running into Pam at the supermarket, about Pam's ominous *We'll be in touch,* but couldn't think of how. All the way home, Alice replayed the conversation with Pam in her head, berating herself. She should have spoken up. She should have defended her friend. Sure, Victoria and Tommy might be young, and their neighborhood wasn't the greatest, but they were the most gentle . . . the most loving . . .

Her thoughts chased one another around her head all night. She tossed and turned, hot-eyed and sweating, kicking at the sheets, until Mark told her that if she didn't stop waking him up one of them would be going to the couch, and he had a big meeting at eight the next morning so it wasn't going to be him.

When she woke up, Alice's head throbbed, and her eyes felt like they were full of invisible grains of sand. She loaded Maisy into the car and was driving her to the aquarium when her telephone trilled and she saw a familiar number flash on the screen. Her tires squealed as she pulled to the side of the road and snatched the telephone to her ear.

Victoria's voice had none of the laughing lilt that Alice knew. "There's an investigation," she said.

Alice's heart plummeted. "Who's investigating?" she asked. "What does that mean?"

"DHS," said Victoria. "They need to examine her. To see if there's a pattern of abuse." She choked out a dry sob. "Alice, I swear to you . . . I swear to God, we never . . . nobody ever . . ."

"Of course," Alice said, hating the sweetness that had seeped into her voice like spilled honey. *Hypocrite,* she thought. *Liar.* "Of course, Victoria, you're a wonderful mother."

Victoria sounded like a little girl. "Will you tell them?" she asked. "We're at the hospital now. Will you come here and tell them that?"

Alice stared into the rearview mirror. Maisy had fallen asleep in her car seat. Her head rested on her shoulder, and the collar of her winter coat was damp with drool.

"Tell me which hospital. I'll be there as soon as I can."

The social worker was an imposing black woman with iron-gray curls and eyeglasses on a jeweled chain resting on the shelf of her bosom. She sat on a doctor's wheeled stool, taking notes. Tommy paced the length of the empty hospital room, his face pale and furious. Victoria, huddled in a vinyl chair, had twisted her body into a pretzel and was holding her knees, rocking back and forth, crying without making a sound. Ellie had been taken away for another MRI.

"It'll be fine," said Alice, patting Victoria's back. She had taken the unprecedented step of dropping Maisy off with her father at his office. "But I've got—" Mark began, looking trapped and desperate as Maisy clambered into the chair behind his desk and started pounding on his computer keyboard with both fists.

"It's an emergency," Alice told him over her shoulder as she ran back down the hall to the elevator.

"What if it's not?" Victoria asked, wiping her eyes, leaving grayish streaks along her cheeks.

"It will be," said Alice, looking at the social worker for confirmation. "Ellie had an accident. Kids have them all the time. I'm sure the judge . . . or whoever . . . they'll understand. They'll ask Ellie, and she'll tell them what happened. And really, it could have happened to anyone. Anyone who knows anything about kids would understand."

Victoria raised her splotchy, streaked face. "But what if Ellie can't tell them it was an accident?"

"I'm sure this will all be fine," Alice repeated helplessly. "Whatever you need from me . . . whatever I can do."

"Tell them we're good parents. Tell them I'm a good mother," Victoria pleaded. Tommy made a strangled sound in the back of his throat and turned and slammed his fist against the door frame.

"I will," said Alice. The social worker shot her a sympathetic look over her half-moon glasses. "Of course I will."

Victoria and Tom took Ellie home the next morning. Three days later, DHS officers knocked on their door at ten o'clock in the morning and took Ellie into protective custody pending the completion of their investigation. The next morning, Victoria showed up at the Mother's Hour alone.

"Ellie's in foster care," she said dully from her seat on the floor. She leaned against the radiator as if she couldn't muster the strength to stand. Her studs and chains and lip ring were gone, and her hair hung over her ears as if she hadn't bothered to wash or comb it. "They scheduled a hearing for the end of the month to see if we'll get her back."

The other mothers murmured sympathetically, even as they pulled their own children close.

"What can we do to help?" Alice asked.

"Could you guys write letters? Just saying that you know me. That you saw me with Ellie. That I'd never hurt her."

There were more nods and more murmurs.

"We'll do whatever we can," Alice said, and the other mothers—even Pam—nodded vigorously.

Alice wrote a letter. Morgan's mother wrote a letter. Annie's mother wrote a letter. Pam contributed a carefully worded missive in which she described her encounters with Victoria and Ellie. "Although I have not met Eleanor's father, I can attest that

Victoria seems to be a conscientious caregiver, in spite of her youth." At the end of the month, the judge ruled that Ellie could go home with her parents, but that the return would be conditional. They would be visited by a social worker each week, unannounced, for the next six months, and pediatrician's reports would be forwarded to the court until Ellie was eighteen.

The last Mother's Hour of the semester convened on the last Friday of January, beneath a stainless-steel sky. The forecast was promising six inches of snow for the weekend, and the air had a metallic bite. "We're moving," Victoria told Alice, as the children joined hands and played ring-around-the-rosy. "Back to Harrisburg. To be closer to our families, so Tommy's mom can babysit. Our social worker told us that it might improve our standing."

"But you got Ellie back!"

"For now." Victoria's eyes were hooded, and the circles beneath them were such a deep plum they were almost black. "But we'll have to be careful for the rest of her life. I think if she ever falls again . . . or skins her knee . . . or loses a tooth, and somebody thinks . . ." Her voice trailed off. Alice felt her insides buckle. What parent's care could withstand that kind of scrutiny? Certainly not her own.

"I'm so sorry," she said. The words hung limply between them. Victoria nodded and wrapped her thin arms around Alice.

"You're a good friend," she whispered. And Alice nodded, feeling tears prickle her eyelids as all of her regret, and all of her shame, coalesced in a knot in her throat.

Alice thought about Victoria on and off as the years passed, wondering where she'd gone, how she was doing, whether she was happy, what Ellie looked like now.

Maisy grew out of her tantrums by the time she started

kindergarten, and Alice and Mark had a few sunny years with their sweet little girl. They added a swimming pool to the backyard and redid the kitchen, and talked about trying for another baby, but it never happened, and neither of them was inclined to push. Alice went to Penn to get another master's—this one in social work—when Maisy started first grade, and back to work when she started third. When Mark announced, a week after their daughter's twelfth birthday, that he'd fallen in love with a woman from his office, Alice found that she wasn't surprised or even especially upset. She had, she realized, gotten out of the habit of loving him during the first few years of their daughter's life, when every minute of every day was a struggle, and while she'd learned to get along with him, she'd never learned to love him again.

He told her he was sorry. She said that she was sorry, too. They handled their divorce better than they had handled their marriage: graciously, mindful of each other's feelings, always careful, always kind.

He got the savings. She got the house. He remarried when Maisy was fourteen, and he and his new wife had twins. Alice couldn't keep herself from hoping, maliciously, that their first years would be much like Maisy's had been, so that the new wife could enjoy what she'd been through, times two, with a husband in his forties instead of his thirties. Eventually she found a man of her own, a man she felt strange calling her boyfriend and knew she would never call her husband. Jacob had been divorced twice, had three grown children, and had made it clear from their first dinner that he wasn't interested in another matrimonial go-round.

She saw Jacob on weekends, but for six years it had been pretty much just the two of them, Maisy and Alice, rattling around in the big house with the grand entry foyer that had so impressed her as a newlywed. Now Maisy was off to Cornell, and Alice was downsizing to a condo across town. There were rows of cardboard boxes lining the hardwood floors, some of them filled with the books and clothes Maisy would take to school, others packed with the bed linens and towels Alice had earmarked for Goodwill. Maisy was unzipping the sofa's slipcovers to take to the dry cleaners and Alice was rolling up her old Oriental rug when she heard her daughter gasp.

"Oh my God. Are these real?"

Alice looked over and saw, sparkling on her daughter's smooth palm, the diamond-and-pearl earrings she'd lost sixteen years before. "They are," she said faintly.

"Finders keepers!" said Maisy, snapping her fingers shut.

"They're mine," said Alice. She must have sounded sharper than she'd meant to, because Maisy looked chastened and muttered that she was just kidding as she handed the earrings over to her mother.

"They were in the couch," she said, as Alice shuffled the earrings in her palm, staring down as they twinkled under the lights.

"I lost them," Alice said. "A long time ago."

"Oh," said Maisy. She went back to the sofa. Alice slipped the earrings in her pocket. All through dinner at Maisy's favorite pizza place, she imagined she could feel their weight against her hip, the sharp edges of the faceted stones, the loops of the wires.

When Maisy kissed her good night and went to her room, Alice plugged Victoria's name into the computer. More than two thousand entries came up, and she browsed through them until she was hot-eyed and shaky, but none of the Victorias who showed up on the Internet appeared to be the girl she remembered. Of Eleanor, she could find no record at all.

At first light the next morning, Alice pulled on yesterday's jeans and her sneakers and went prowling through the high-ceilinged, half-empty rooms, past boxes labeled "Condo" and others labeled "Cornell," boxes of old family albums, her good silver, her old sweaters, leashes of dogs that had died.

She eased the front door open. The earrings were still in the pocket of her jeans. *They'll turn up,* Mark had told her. *You're a good friend,* Victoria had said. There was a sewer at the corner of their street, covered in a rusted metal grate. She remembered Maisy lying down on top of that grate on her way back from the playground two blocks away, pounding her fists against the bars, shrieking that she didn't want to walk, so many years ago. Alice bent over, looked down into the darkness, and opened her hand. The earrings vanished into the water with hardly a sound.

ORANGES

FROM FLORIDA

The telephone woke him at just past midnight, and Doug, still half asleep, flung himself across the bed to answer it. His arms tangled in the covers, and the light switch didn't seem to be where it was supposed to be. He had his hand on the receiver when the stunned, sinking feeling came over him, and he woke up enough to realize that he was alone in the bed, and the bedroom, and the house.

The telephone was still ringing. He shoved himself upright against the headboard and lifted the receiver to his ear.

"Hello?" Doug said. He kept his voice down, out of habit. In the first weeks after she'd gone, he'd had a few hour-long, whispered telephone conversations with Carrie. *Please come home,* he'd tell her. *I want to be a family again.* Her sighs were louder than his words. *I can't,* she'd say. *I just can't.*

"Hello?" he repeated.

"Did I win?" his caller asked.

It was a child's voice—whether it belonged to a boy or girl, he couldn't tell, but he knew immediately what had happened. After the second time he and Carrie had been woken up in the wee hours by someone requesting a song or asking, urgently, if they'd won, Carrie had flipped through the phone book and found that their number was just one digit away from the number for WQXT—Quickie 98. It had struck them as funny at the time—all those teary-sounding women and giddy teenagers calling in with their dedications and requests, the love songs they just had to hear in the middle of the night.

The voice spoke again, and Doug decided it belonged to a boy. "Am I the lucky caller?"

Doug looked across the empty bed. The clock on the dresser clicked from 12:02 to 12:03. "Yes," he said.

They both paused—Doug because he was astounded by his lie and the speed with which it had leaped out of his mouth, and the boy because "yes" was obviously not what he had expected.

"What did I win?"

"Oranges from Florida," Doug said. It was the first thing that came to his mind. Oranges from Florida were what Carrie's mother sent them each Christmas. He wondered, briefly, whether he'd get any citrus this December. What was the etiquette of holiday gift-giving for not-quite-former sons-in-law?

"Oranges," the boy said, sounding so disappointed that Doug was moved to add: "And a hundred dollars, of course."

"Oh, wow," said the boy. It sounded to Doug as if he were trying to work himself up to the fever pitch that disc jockeys demanded of their winners. "Wow, jeez, thank you! I never won anything before!"

"Congratulations," Doug said. "And, uh, thanks for listening."

"Thank *you*," said the boy politely, as if he were about to hang up.

"Wait," Doug said. He hadn't realized how long it had been since he'd had a non-business-related conversation with a stranger. This was certainly a weird one to start with. What was a kid doing up this late, anyhow? "Caller, are you there?"

There was a pause, a faint staticky thumping. Then: "I'm here."

"Oh, good," Doug said, improvising frantically. "We need your name."

"Joe."

"Joe what?"

"Stern," the boy said, and spelled it out.

"Very good. How old are you, if you don't mind me asking?"

"Ten," said Joe. "Is that okay? Do you need to be eighteen to win?"

"No, you're fine," Doug said, already casting about for his next question. Some dim part of his mind was warning that the boy would think he was crazy, but he couldn't stop talking. "Isn't it pretty late for you to be listening to the radio?"

"My mother lets me," Joe said. "I can listen to it to keep me company before I fall asleep."

"That's great," said Doug. "We're always glad to have listeners."

"I like Dr. Larry's Help-Line," the boy said, and sang a snatch of the show's theme song in a gruff, tuneless voice. "Someone to turn to, someone to trust . . ."

"Dr. Larry's Help-Line," Doug marveled.

"People have interesting problems," the boy said. "Last week was adult bed-wetting."

Doug couldn't stop himself—he laughed, and after a minute, Joe laughed, too.

"Okay," Doug said, "so I'll need your address now."

"Twelve Sandpiper Drive," the boy said.

Doug fumbled for a pen in the dark and scribbled the address on the bottom of the crossword puzzle he'd been working on before he'd finally fallen asleep.

Joe hesitated. "With my prize . . . can you mail it to me?"

"Sure!" Doug figured that he could download the Quickie logo and print it on stationery and an envelope, no problem. He'd buy one of those Visa or Amex gift cards, load it with a hundred bucks, and stick it in the mail, along with the oranges.

"And it'll come to me, right? Not my mom. Because I'm allowed to listen to the show, but my mom said no calling. I'm supposed to just stay in bed and listen."

"So you want it to be a secret?"

"A surprise," the boy corrected. "Is the hundred dollars regular money, or a check?"

"A check card," said Doug. "You can spend it just like regular cash." Then, without even knowing he was going to, he said, "You know what? Maybe I could drop everything off at your house." It would be easy, Doug figured. He could buy the oranges, get the check card, make a kid happy. Make somebody happy, for a change.

The boy sounded pleased already. "I can buy my mom a birthday present," he said. "A really good one."

"Sure," Doug said, feeling something in his chest ache. He'd shopped for birthday presents for Carrie, with the girls. He would take them to the mall and give them each twenty dollars to spend, and follow them around, fingering the sleeves of sweaters, nodding approval at calendars with puppies for every month or ceramic clown figurines.

"I can drop it by tomorrow afternoon," Doug said.

"That'd be good," said Joe. "So I'll see you tomorrow."

"See you then," said Doug.

For the first six months after Carrie had left him, Doug would wake up every morning reaching for her. When his hands found the stretch of sheet she had inhabited, cool and blank, the knowledge of what had happened—that she was gone, that he was now reduced to seeing his daughters on weekends and every other Wednesday—would hit him like a hammer, cracking him open again, and he'd have to sit on the edge of the bed with his head in his hands for a few minutes before he could gain his feet, turn off the alarm clock, start his day.

Time didn't so much heal his wound as cauterize it. Instead of feeling pain, he felt nothing. It was progress, he supposed, to feel as if love were a rumor from a distant planet and that life itself was like a party taking place in another room.

He got by. He was an actuary at a big firm downtown, and he went to work on weekday mornings, doing his job, paying his bills. He called his daughters every night and took them to the movies or the museum on Saturdays and he had, after a few weeks of trial and error, figured out how to cook all his meals on his George Foreman Grill. He'd spray it with Pam and fry eggs in the morning; spray it again and cook a salmon filet for lunch; spray it a third time and grill a burger or a steak for dinner. He'd demonstrated one Saturday for Sarah and Alicia, cooking them cheese omelets for brunch and Texas toast and ribeye steaks for dinner. "Good, right?" he'd asked, smiling across the table. Sarah had just shrugged, and Alicia, who he suspected was wearing eye shadow even though he thought he'd convinced Carrie that fourteen was too young, turned away from him to stare out the window, down the driveway where he'd taught her to ride a two-wheeler, and said, "Everything tastes like everything else."

There were advantages to living alone. The house looked better than it ever had. No more purses and backpacks spilling their contents by the door, no more of Carrie's shoes strewn on the floor wherever she'd kicked them off, no more straightening iron left plugged in beside the girls' bathroom sink, no matter how many times he'd patiently told his daughters that it was a fire hazard. He recycled the newspapers and his rinsed tin cans, mowed the lawn, changed the oil in the car, and separated Carrie's mail into neat stacks that he forwarded to her at the end of every week, along with notes that he labored over late into the night. *I am not sure what you want in a husband,* the most recent one had said. *I'm not sure you know, either. But whatever it is, whatever you need me to do or be, I will do it. I will try.*

Doug knew the way the world must see him—a tall man, round-shouldered and old for his years, given to frowning and plodding, so emotionally stunted he'd confuse stubbornness with love. "Even your name," Carrie had said to him—yelled at him—before she'd left. "Even your name's boring! Doug. As in slug." He'd held her shoulders until her hysterical laughter had dissolved into sobs. Later he'd said, "I can't help what I'm named," but she was asleep by then. Two weeks later she'd taken the girls, her clothes, the girls' clothes, the dog and the guinea pigs, and, inexplicably, the popcorn maker, and moved back in with her mother. Since then, he didn't think anyone had laughed in the house. Not even the kind of laughter that turned into tears.

As promised, Joe Stern was outside the white Cape Cod house at the end of a cul-de-sac on Sandpiper Drive. There was a basketball hoop in the driveway, and a basketball at the boy's feet. Doug could see that he was tall, and that he was going to be handsome when he finished growing. He had thick brown hair and a serious, reflective face that made him look older than ten.

Doug felt the boy's gaze settle over him as he unfolded himself from the car and got the oranges out of the trunk, touching their thin skins through the netting of the bag, smelling their perfume. In his pocket was the check card in an envelope with a hijacked Quickie 98 logo on the front.

"Hello," he called, advancing up the driveway. "I'm Doug Fried from Quickie 98."

The boy looked disappointed. "I thought you'd be in the Prizemobile."

"Someone else took it today," Doug said, and set the oranges down on the driveway.

The boy glanced at the fruit, then looked up at Doug respectfully. "Wow," he said. "You ever play basketball?"

"I'm clumsy," Doug confessed. "I was always tall enough, but I'm not very fast, and I can't really dribble."

"I'll bet you can palm the ball, though."

Embarrassed that he had no idea what the boy meant, Doug just nodded. Joe scooped up the ball and tossed it to Doug, who managed to catch it the instant before it whacked into his belly.

Thankfully, the boy seemed not to notice. "Here," he said, moving his fingers over Doug's. "Like this."

The ball felt disturbingly like a human head when Doug clutched it in one hand. He was reminded of his daughters as infants and how scared he'd been to hold them, fearing he'd hurt them, crush their fragile bones.

But Joe seemed pleased. "I can almost palm it myself," he said. "My dad was tall, and my mom thinks I will be, too, because I have big feet. I had to have new sneakers twice last year," he added proudly, "and my mom said if they got much bigger, I'd have to order from a special catalog."

Doug inspected the boy's feet, which seemed big but not abnormally so.

"I think," he said, "that your mom was teasing you."

"Yeah," the boy said, and sighed. "She always does."

"Did your father play basketball?"

"Yes," Joe said. "But he's in Arizona now."

"Well, I guess there are basketball hoops there, too."

"I guess." The boy sighed again, then bent to pick up the fruit. Holding the bag against his chest, he looked at Doug. "Do you need to see something that proves who I am? I've got a library card with my name on it. . . ."

"No," Doug said. "I believe you." He reached into his pocket. "This is for you, too," he said, and handed him the envelope. Joe peeked inside, folded the envelope, and slipped it into his front pocket.

"Be careful with that," Doug said. "That's a lot of money." He could hear the phantom complaints of his daughters in his ears. *Da-ad! Stop worrying! We'll be careful!*

Joe's eyes were shining. "I'm going to get my mom this perfume she wants," he said. "She tries it on every time we go to the mall, but it's eighty dollars for just a little tiny bottle, so she never buys it. She'll be surprised."

"That's really nice," Doug said.

"She's nice to me, too," Joe said. He looked at Doug more closely. "So are you a disc jockey?"

Doug shook his head. "I have more of an administrative job."

"Do you know Dr. Larry?"

"Um, I think he works a different shift."

The boy was undaunted. "Do you know Daffy Dave?"

"I've seen him," Doug said, amazed at the ease with which the lie slid off his tongue.

Joe frowned. "Is he married? Because he's always making jokes about his wife, and what a bad cook she is and stuff, but I don't think he even has one."

"I don't know," Doug said helplessly. "I never asked."

"Huh," the boy said. He set the ball down on the driveway and began rolling it back and forth with the tip of his foot. The sack of oranges slumped between them.

Doug cleared his throat. "Well," he began.

A dog's bark startled him.

"Harry!" Joe called. "Harry!"

As Doug watched, something that looked like a collection of elderly, dusty gray mopheads strolled out of the garage and came to sniff at his shoes.

"This is Harry," Joe said, patting him. "He's a Bouvier poodle mix. A Boodle."

Doug knelt and scratched the dog's frizzy head. The dog wagged his tail vigorously, then collapsed onto his back, presenting his belly.

"He likes you," Joe said.

"I like him," said Doug.

"He was my dad's, but I take care of him now."

The dog gave a lusty whine and waved his paws in the air. Joe laughed. "He's a good pet but a bad guard dog. Do you have a dog?"

"No," Doug said, leaving off the "not anymore."

"Do you have any kids?"

"Two girls. One's twelve and one's fourteen."

Joe looked impressed. "Big kids," he said. "Did they go to Michaelman Elementary?"

Doug nodded.

"Did you ever go to fathers' day at their school?"

Doug nodded again. "They have a breakfast, right?"

Joe nodded unhappily. "Pancakes and strawberry syrup. First the dads tell about their jobs, and then you get the pancakes." He knelt beside the dog and picked up the basketball again.

Doug bit his lip. Harry rolled over and started nosing at the oranges.

"I think he wants one," Doug said.

"He likes people food," Joe said, and smiled faintly. "He thinks he's human."

Doug reached for the bag. "We could try one, to see if he likes it."

Joe shifted uneasily. "He only eats out of his food dish, and I'm not supposed to invite anyone inside."

"Oh, I understand," Doug said, feeling both disappointment and relief. This solemn child pulled at his heart, and if he went inside, who knew what he'd find himself saying, or offering to do? "That's okay. I really should be going."

"Do you have other prizes to deliver?"

Doug shook his head. "No. You're my only winner today."

But it seemed Joe wasn't ready for him to leave yet.

"Maybe if we peel one and give it to him here . . ."

They had worked an orange out of the bag and were in the process of peeling it when a car pulled into the driveway.

"Oh, no," Joe breathed. "Mom."

The woman who climbed out of the battered silver car had Joe's brown hair, but none of his height and none of his solemnity. Her face was round and full and seemed made for laughing, even though her eyes looked tired. Her hair fell in tangled curls that had been gathered into a ponytail with a bright silk scarf.

"Joey? Who's this?"

"What's your name again?" Joe whispered. Doug stepped forward, feeling guilty already, as the woman's frown deepened. "I'm Doug Fried."

"And what are you doing here?" Her tone was neutral, but Doug saw that she had pulled her purse in front of her body like a shield.

"I work at Quickie 98," he said. "Your son was our lucky caller last night, and I was just dropping off his prize."

She glanced briefly at the oranges, then looked at him carefully, apparently searching his face for signs of madness or criminal tendencies. "Joe," she said finally. "What have I told you about strangers?"

"He's not in the house," the boy protested. "He's out here in the driveway, and Harry's here, too."

"Oh, of course. The dog will keep you safe," she said, and turned back to Doug, who was surreptitiously taking in the shape of her face, her sturdy-looking hands.

"What radio station did you say?" she demanded.

"Quickie 98," Doug repeated. "All hits, all the time."

She wasn't amused. "Do you have some identification?"

"I can't believe this," Joe said, spreading his arms wide in a parody of indignation. "Of course he's from the radio. Why else would he come all the way out here to bring me oranges?"

Doug fumbled through his wallet. "I left my ID back at the station, but this will at least tell you who I am," he said, and handed her his driver's license.

She squinted first at the license, then at him. "You don't have a business card?"

He made a show of searching his wallet before shaking his head. "Left them back at the station, too, I guess."

She looked down at the license. "Are you really six-foot-five?"

"Last time I checked."

"He can palm the ball," Joe said.

"Your hero," she said, and tilted her head to include Doug in a look that wasn't quite friendly, but was, at least, less hostile than the one she'd given him when she first pulled up. "I'm Shelly Stern."

"I'm sorry if I frightened you," he said.

She shook her head. "No, I'm sorry," she said, and settled

herself against the side of the car. "It's just that this is the first year Joe's not coming home to a babysitter, and I—"

"—worry about him," Joe finished, and rolled his eyes.

"Smarty," said Shelly.

"She thinks I'll burn the house down," Joe said. Without missing a beat, he turned to his mother. "Can we have pizza?"

"No," she said, and shook her head, loosing more curls from the ponytail.

Joe smiled winningly. "My treat." He raced toward the house, with Harry trotting behind him.

"Pizza," Shelly said. "One day he'll turn into a pepperoni."

"He seems like a good kid."

"He is," she agreed. "Even though he knows he's not supposed to be calling radio stations. Listen, I really am sorry for being so suspicious. Too many TV movies, I guess."

"I would have been scared, too," Doug said. "I've got kids. Daughters. Don't worry about it. Please."

Her mouth curled into something between a smirk and a smile as she looked at him, eyebrows lifted. "So, this is your job? Driving through the streets of the suburbs, dispensing fruit and goodwill?"

Doug nodded. "Something like that," he said. It had been a long time since anyone had teased him, and he wanted very much to keep talking to her. He wanted to find out what she and Joe did on the weekends, what they cooked for dinner, and where she drove her silver car every morning. He wanted to see if he could make her smile again. But he knew he had pressed his luck far enough for one afternoon, and he had no idea how to surmount the lie that lay between them.

"I really should be going," he said.

"Oh, sure," she said, and made a face. "My first grown-up in days, and I scare him away."

"Your first . . ." Doug wasn't sure he'd heard her right.

"I'm a children's librarian. I don't get to talk to grown-ups much." She gazed at the sky, shaking her head in rueful disbelief. "Grown-ups. I still can't believe I'm one. When Joe was a little guy, like maybe three, he used to come to the top of the stairs at night and yell, 'I need a grown-up!' My husband and I would just look at each other . . ." She smiled and shrugged. "Like, if we find one, we'll get back to you." She shook her head again. "That was a long time ago. How about you? Tell me about your kids?"

"I have two daughters. They're fourteen and twelve."

"Girls," Shelly said, sounding envious. "What are their names?"

"Sarah and Alicia," Doug said. "They live with their mother." He tossed out another fact, something else to show what they had in common. "My girls go to Joe's elementary school."

"So you did that fathers' breakfast thing." She looked at him with eyes the same shade of hazel as her son's. "I think it's crummy that the school keeps having them, with so many kids without fathers. It's really hard for Joe."

"It must be hard for you, too," Doug ventured.

Shelly nodded. "Not my favorite day of the year."

Doug kept looking at her, drinking her in, her little gold earrings, the silk bow against the nape of her neck, the way her hair caught the waning light. He felt light-headed and dizzy and excited and ashamed.

"So," she said, and smiled at him, then quickly looked down at the driveway, and the oranges between them. "It's getting cold out here. Would you like to come in for a cup of coffee?"

"Look," Doug blurted miserably, "Ms. Stern."

"Shelly."

"Shelly," he repeated, but could go no further.

"Come on," she said. He wanted so badly to follow her, to wrap his hands around a mug of something warm and bask in her attention.

"I'm not from the radio station," he said. She took two quick steps back, as if he'd slapped her.

"What?" she whispered. "What?"

The look on her face made him feel as if he were biting ice. "I'm an actuary," he said.

"Is this a joke?"

Doug shook his head. "Let me explain," he said, hearing the pleading in his voice. "My telephone number's just one number away from the radio station's. I was sleeping when Joe called, and when he asked if he'd won the contest, I just said yes without thinking."

Finished, he dared to look at her. Her eyes were too bright, and she was holding her purse in front of her body again.

"I'm sorry," he said. "I know how you must feel."

"Oh, no, you don't," she said. "You absolutely do *not*. You have no idea how it feels when you pull into your driveway and see some stranger standing there with your son. No idea at all." Her lips were trembling. He'd scared her, he saw, and the best thing he could do would be to leave. But he couldn't.

"I'm sorry," he said again.

"I try so hard," she said, "so hard to keep Joe safe. I worry about him; I worry all the time, and you just come waltzing up here, and he doesn't even know enough to make sure you're who you say you are! You could be anyone! You could have done anything to him!"

She glared at him a moment longer, then shook her head and turned toward the house.

Doug scooped up the oranges and followed her, thinking

that he couldn't be anyone, that he could be only himself. He was stuck that way, but it would have to be enough. He reached for her shoulder. "You know my name," he said.

She turned toward him again and looked him full in the face, her little hands balled into fists.

"You know I'm sorry."

"Sorry," she repeated, as if she'd never heard the word.

"It was a dumb thing to do. I should have just told the truth."

"Why?" she asked. "That's what I want to know. Why?"

Doug thought. "I don't know, really. I guess I wanted to do something good."

"Well," she said, glaring at him. "Next time you could maybe make a donation to the Cancer Society. Or the library. We really need a new roof."

"Maybe I will," he said, matching the heat in her voice. "But this is what I did this time, and I can't undo it now."

She looked as if she were about to say something more. Then she closed her mouth abruptly, not meeting his eyes but not running away, either. Doug was thinking of how to reassure her when the door to the house opened.

"Mom!"

Joe was standing in the doorway, with Harry poking his head between the boy's legs. A wedge of light spilled out into the early-evening darkness. "We have to get the pizza!" the boy called.

"I am sorry," Doug said one more time. He handed her the bag of fruit and started walking toward his car.

He was halfway there when he heard her behind him. "Wait," she said.

He turned to face her with his heart in his throat.

"Hold still," she said and looked him over from head to toe, examining him the way she might have measured a new piece of furniture, inspecting it for stains and scratches, wondering if it would fit through the door.

"Oranges," she said. Her voice was soft.

"Oranges from Florida," he said.

Shelly bit her lip. "I want to believe you." Her voice trailed off. "You seem sincere, and I want to believe you are. Can you understand?"

Too anxious even to breathe, Doug just nodded.

She studied his face for an endless moment. "Come on, then," she said. He held the oranges and followed her inside.

Tour of Duty

Jason and Marion Meyers were at their third college in two days, having lunch at the student union. The air was thick and hot, filled with the tortured screeches of metal-legged chairs being dragged across the tile floor. Students in the smoking section, tucked on one side of the big round room, produced a bluish cloud that edged its way out of the enclosure to hang, like fog, over everything.

Marion and Jason, mother and son, had the same thing for lunch: bagels, cream cheese squeezed out of tinfoil tubes, and overpriced, overly sweet, all-natural black-cherry soda. They nibbled their food and watched each other with identical gray-green eyes.

Marion sipped her soda and grimaced, setting the can aside. "Well, this seems like a nice one," she said encouragingly. "Beautiful campus. Do you like it?"

Jason shrugged and gave a noncommittal grunt. Ever since they'd left their home in Rhode Island the day before, Jason had communicated primarily by grunts and shrugs and long silences. None of the colleges they'd seen so far—Cornell, Bowdoin, and Amherst, each resplendent in fall foliage and ivied marble—had earned an entire sentence. With a flick of his tweed-clad shoulders and an unintelligible mumble, Jason had dismissed the swim teams and prelaw societies, the glee clubs and the frats. The quick flashes of humor that usually popped up in his conversation were absent. As he sat paging through the student paper, his broad shoulders were hunched and his face was solemn, even glum.

No surprise, Marion thought. Hal was supposed to have taken Jason on this trip. They'd planned it together over the summer, looking at maps, studying brochures, looking up admissions statistics in the Barron's guide. But Hal had gotten busy in August. A case in Ohio had taken him out of town for two weeks, and he'd been working late all through September and October, coming home after Jason was asleep, leaving before he awoke. At least, she devoutly hoped that that was what Jason thought was going on. Let him get through the interviews, she told herself. Then she'd tell him the truth.

She took a deep breath and arranged her face cheerfully. "Have I ever told you my theory about bagels?"

Jason rolled his eyes. "I can't wait to hear that," he muttered, but he was smiling just a bit.

"The excellence of a college is in direct proportion to the quality of its bagels. Good bagels, good school," Marion said. Closing her eyes, she picked up her bagel and sniffed it with the studied concentration of a wine connoisseur. "Nineteen ninety," she intoned. "A very good year." She took a nibble and chewed intently. "Not bad," she pronounced, and looked at Jason. His eyes were fixed earnestly on her face. Despite his red cheeks, still sunburned from a summer as a lifeguard, he looked very grown up. Marion pushed her plate toward her son and looked away.

"What do you think Dad had to do that was so important?" It was the most Jason had spoken since they left home at five o'clock in the morning two days ago, driving past the clapboard Colonials and curtained windows in her husband's Mercedes.

Marion shrugged. "Oh, you know how he is with those depositions, he probably just got behind . . ." Her voice trailed off. The lie sat on the table between them. Marion could almost see it crouching there, leering at her. "I know he didn't mean to hurt your feelings," she said lamely, taking little comfort in the fact that this, at least, was true. She fished in her purse, past the maps that Hal had meticulously marked with lime-green Hi-Liter, and pulled out five dollars. "Go get your old mom some of that frozen yogurt." Jason studied her for a silent moment. Then in one fluid movement he was up and out of his chair, moving toward the line, attracting plenty of attention along the way. Tall and slender, with curly reddish hair a few shades brighter than her own, he moved with a lanky grace. Two girls with big hoop earrings nudged each other when he passed them, and the girl behind the cash register stared, smoothing her uniform, fidgeting with her hair. These visits mean he's leaving, she thought. Soon he'll be gone. Her heart gave a sudden, painful twist. She closed her eyes and rested her head in her hands.

"Mom?"

Jason was standing in front of her, looking worried, with two cups of yogurt in his hands.

She made herself smile. "Just thinking."

He smiles. "Well, you must be out of practice if it takes so much effort. I got old-world chocolate or strawberry. What do you want?"

"Huh? Oh, strawberry, please," Marion said. Watching her son walk away, she thought, with a ferocity that startled her, *I will never let anything hurt him. Never.*

Their hotel in Middletown had a swimming pool. Marion made sure of that. She and Jason both loved to swim. In the water and out of it, they understood each other with a special, un-spoken ease.

Marion had always been a swimmer. "You're water-based," Hal had joked during their honeymoon, when she'd shunned golf and tennis and tanning in favor of spending hours immersed in the turquoise waters of Bermuda. He'd waded up to his knees a couple of times and floated on his back for a few moments before paddling back to shore. The truth was that the water made him nervous. He didn't like the feeling of being small in the vastness of the ocean, of being pushed and prodded by currents and waves, forces he couldn't control.

Still, Hal did his best to accommodate her. When his practice got off the ground, after he'd purchased the obligatory mini-mansion in the suburbs and the bright red sports car, he'd presented Marion with a combination in-ground pool and hot tub for her birthday. In the summer, she would often take a late-night swim to cool off before going to sleep. Sometimes Hal would come out back, sit on the edge of a chaise lounge, and watch her stroking through the warm, lit water, the muscles in her back working in clean, pleasing harmony. And later he would join her in the hot tub, where the water was shallow enough for him to feel at ease. His cotton pajamas and her damp swimsuit would lie crumpled together on a lounge chair, and the crickets would be chirping, and the air, humid and oppressive during the day, would lie on their skin like a caress.

Her three oldest children hated the water. Marion had taught all of them to swim, but it was hard work. Amy, Josh, and Lisa had to be coaxed into the shallow end with the promises of ice cream or toys, and they were visibly uncomfortable once they got there, pinching their noses shut and squinting anxiously toward the deep end as if the water was going to rise up and carry them away. Marion made sure that each could manage at least a respectable breaststroke before relinquishing them to drier sports, games that involved sticks or balls, molded rubber mouth guards and arcane offsides rules.

And then there was Jason, her baby, her surprise. Jason had taken to the water just like his mother. As a newborn, he was happiest at bath time, cooing and gurgling as Marion poured water over his plump body. He learned to swim at two and a half when, without water wings and without fear, he flung himself into the deep end of the pool and bobbed up and down like a cork, giggling cheerfully as his grandmother screamed and Hal, still clad in his wing tips and suit, jumped in after him.

That summer, on nights when Hal worked late, Marion would sometimes take Jason to the pool with her. She'd hook him over her hip and bounce him up and down in the shallow water, both of them laughing. She would fling him high in the air, and he'd land with a splash, paddling back to her, eyes wide open and arms outstretched, begging for more.

Marion knew that good mothers weren't supposed to have favorites. So she tried doggedly to ignore that, almost without exception, watching Jason swim gave her more pleasure than watching her older children do almost anything else. She was scrupulous about allotting equal time to Josh's lacrosse, Amy's singing, and Lisa's soccer. But she supposed they knew she'd always feel some slight disappointment that they weren't swimmers.

It is hard to keep secrets from your children. This was what Marion thought as she did laps next to her son in the Marriott's postage-stamp-size indoor pool. Side by side for thirty minutes they planed through the lanes, wrapped in the cocoon of the water and in their own silence.

They had dinner at a Thai restaurant near their hotel. Jason built a pyramid out of Sweet 'n Low and sugar packets, then bulldozed it with his fork.

"Are you nervous about tomorrow?" Marion asked. Jason shrugged and started arranging the sugar into a star. He worked carefully, pushing the packets along with just the tips of his long fingers. "You'll do fine. You're very articulate," she said drily, struggling to contain her frustration.

The waitress took their order. Jason asked for shredded beef, extra spicy, and kept his eyes down. He swept the star aside and started constructing a complicated-looking form involving piles of stacked sugar in a circle.

"You know, when Amy interviewed at Penn, they asked her, 'If you could be any vegetable, what would you be?' " Marion tried.

Jason's lip curled. "Stupid."

"I think she said she wanted to be an eggplant."

"Why?"

"That I don't remember."

"Weren't you there?"

"No," Marion said softly. "Your father took her." Jason started gnawing at his lower lip, vague hurt on his face. She backpedaled quickly. "But really, hon, you've got nothing to worry about. They'll probably just ask about your swimming, what you might want to study, why you want to go there . . ."

"My mom, the guidance counselor," Jason said. It took Marion a minute to realize she was being teased.

The waitress set their steaming plates down. "My, what is that?" she asked Jason, pointing to the complicated circle he'd created with the pink and brown packets. Jason smiled swiftly at Marion, then looked up at the waitress with absolute seriousness.

"Stonehenge."

The waitress laughed politely and left fast. Marion looked at her son. "Stonehenge?"

Jason nodded modestly. "It's not quite to scale, but I didn't have much to work with."

Marion smiled, feeling relief flood through her like something sweet she'd swallowed. This was the Jason she knew.

But by morning his good humor had evaporated. He sulked on the drive to New Jersey, jamming the radio buttons too hard, flicking the lock on the door up and down until Marion, preoccupied with thoughts of the telephone calls she would need to make—first Lisa, then Amy, then Josh—finally snapped at him to stop. They rode in tense silence for twenty minutes until Marion pulled off the highway.

"Drive," she said, and smiled a little when Jason looked surprised. "Go on. I'm feeling reckless."

"Fine," he said curtly, refusing to be humored. He slid behind the wheel, jerked the seat backward to accommodate his long legs, and pulled into traffic. Marion closed her eyes.

Usually, Jason was a good driver, fast and confident. But that day he was too aggressive: swinging the car in and out of lanes, growling under his breath at drivers who weren't getting out of his way quickly enough. Marion forced herself not to criticize. She dozed fitfully, waking every few minutes to find herself hurtling toward the back end of an eighteen-wheeler or swerving into the passing lane.

Abandoning the hope of falling asleep, she sat up and unfolded the map. Princeton was a tiny black speck. It looked far too small, too physically incidental to be the setting for a broken heart. She traced her finger down the turnpike, along the fragile blue lines that ran through the state like veins, trying to calm the frantic beating of her heart. Here, she thought. You are here.

The information session was held in a wood-paneled classroom with soaring ceilings and many-paned windows that still managed to be stuffy. The smell of chalk dust and nervous sweat reminded Marion of her own college days at Mount Holyoke, before she'd met Hal, when she thought she might have grown up to become a doctor or a diplomat, anything but a married housewife in the suburbs with four children and a backyard swimming pool. The difference was that now it was the parents who scurried around with forced smiles and sweaty palms, comparing test scores and GPAs, while the kids relaxed, chatting around the punch bowl. The admissions officer, a dapper, bearded man, was easily recognizable as he stood in the corner in a black-and-orange tie. With fifteen parents crowding around him, jabbering and gesticulating, he had the look of a gracious lord of the manor entertaining the petitions of serfs.

Marion supposed she should join the crowd, it being Princeton, Jason's first choice, not to mention Hal's alma mater. But instead, she toyed with her swizzle stick and found herself wishing passionately for a cigarette, even though she hadn't smoked in more than twenty years. Her headache was back, a dull throbbing at her forehead, like fists pounding on a distant door. A jovial young man in a Princeton sweatshirt walked up and handed her a large black-and-orange sticker reading "PMS."

"What does PMS stand for?" she asked.

The beaming young man barely paused. "Prospective Mother—Son," he replied.

"But I'm not a prospective mother!" said Marion. "I already am his mother. I've got papers to prove it!"

He gave her a weak smile and moved on to the next parent (PFD, which, Marion guessed, stood for Prospective Father—Daughter).

Marion turned to the woman on her right, expecting sympathy. "Can you believe this?" she said. "PMS!"

The woman spoke to Marion out of the corner of her mouth. "I'd keep it quiet if I were you," she muttered. "No sense in making trouble if you want your son to have a chance."

"Oh, come on," Marion said. "You can't believe they'd hold

it against him that I refuse to wear this!" She yanked off the sticker, wadded it up, and threw it in the trash.

The woman sidled a few steps back, as though Marion had suddenly become contagious, with her squinty eyes gleaming. "All I'm saying is I'm not taking any chances." She nodded toward a group of boys standing in a corner. "My son," she proclaimed, in a tone customarily reserved for announcing heads of state.

Marion wasn't sure which boy she meant. She nodded anyhow.

"First in his class," the woman offered. "Governor's school every summer." Her voice rose in a triumphant spiral. "Fourteen-thirty!"

Marion gave what she hoped was a knowledgeable nod. "Sounds good."

The woman was silent. Marion realized that the woman was waiting for her to reciprocate with information about her own child. "Oh, that's Jason over there," she said, pointing. Jason was talking to the sticker guy.

The woman nodded. "How are his numbers?"

"Fine!" she answered, too enthusiastically. The woman waited, eyebrows raised, but Marion couldn't remember Jason's scores. All she could remember was that her husband had gotten up early to prepare Jason a healthy, high-protein breakfast on the morning of the SATs, to shake his hand and wish him luck.

"Did he take any prep courses?"

Marion shook her head. "We did buy him a book." Her headache flared. Had the book been a guide to SATs or to colleges? She couldn't remember. Hal had been the one in charge of book-buying. "But Jason's a great kid, a very good student. Captain of the swim team."

The woman gave a barely perceptible snort and walked away. Marion sighed and tugged at her nylons discreetly. Evidently, being a great kid wasn't enough anymore. Then Jason was at her shoulder, handing her a plastic cup of punch. "They're going to start soon. Want to sit down?" he asked.

"I want to go home," she whispered, too low for him to hear her. Then the admissions officer was stepping up to the podium, and his sweatshirted assistant began flicking the lights on and off, a trick Marion hadn't seen since her own days in school. Parents scrambled toward the seats, and with a rolling surge of panic, Marion realized that this was it. They'd have another three hours, tops, on campus. Another seven, maybe, in the car, not including a stop for dinner. Then they'd be back in Providence, and if she hadn't figured out how to tell him by then . . .

Jason listened carefully as the admissions officer talked about the Princeton experience. Marion eased one of the highlighted maps out of her purse and quietly unfolded it in her lap. She ran her finger down the unassuming green that was New Jersey. Down the turnpike, over the Hudson, across the Tappan Zee Bridge into Connecticut, her finger slowed, then stopped.

She looked at her son. In his sport coat and tie, he could be any bland, bright-eyed prep-schooler. All of his little mischiefs, all of his humor, his sweetness, the detention he'd gotten in fifth grade and cried over for a week, even the scar on his chin from when he'd jumped off the lifeguard's chair and landed on a seashell—all of his history was undetectable, erased. Jason was gone, and her panic was back, and she was suddenly flushed and so dizzy that the big, fusty room in its mellow creams and browns seemed to tilt and spin. What did she have left? She'd told Jason that she wanted to go home, but there would be nothing for her there. *Ladybug, ladybug, fly away home.* Her house wasn't on fire, but her children were gone, the oldest three already, and Jason soon enough. The pool was closed up for the season, covered tight with a heavy black tarp. Her eyes filled with tears, and she bit down hard on her lip.

"Ma?" Jason whispered. Marion winced and shook her head.

"Shhh," she said. "The athletic director's up next."

The SAT woman rose to her feet, reciting her son's scores and grades, asking if they would be good enough. Her son sat beside her, clearly in an agony of shame. He wore an enormous class ring with a huge blue-red stone set in the center. Even from a distance, Marion could tell the stone was fake.

"And," the woman trilled in a high buzzing voice, "he was a Westinghouse Science finalist."

The admissions officer was trying not to smile. Marion made a strangled noise, and when she looked down she saw that she'd crumpled the map in her lap. Jason was staring.

"Let's go," he whispered, and she nodded, easing past the knees of disgruntled Westinghouse Science finalists, out of the building, down a slate path, through a gate to where they'd parked at a meter on Nassau Street. There was something special about the gate, Marion thought, something important, but she couldn't remember what. Was it that the students weren't supposed to walk through it until they've graduated? Or that the parents were never supposed to walk through it at all? Too late. She stood by the car door and extracted her keys from her purse. "I'll drive," Jason offered, but his mother shook her head.

"Go to the gym and find the swim coach. I'll meet you here in an hour."

Jason shoved his hands into his pockets. "Tell me what's going on," he said. "Please."

Marion took a deep breath. "Your father," she began, and her voice caught in her throat. This is all wrong, she thought, and started coughing. "Ma?" asked Jason, and patted her ineffectually on her back, as if she'd swallowed a mouthful of water. I should sit down with him, somewhere private, explain this reasonably.

Jason was talking, and Marion forced herself to listen. "What about Dad?" he asked. "Is he sick?"

Marion's chest loosened, and she managed to suck in a breath. "Oh, no," she said. "Oh, Jason, nobody's sick." She drew another shaking breath, let it out slowly, and said what she hadn't let herself say for days since Hal had told her. "It's just that your father is moving out."

For a moment the two of them stood silently, looking at each other, posed like swimmers at the end of the pool, holding on to the concrete ledge, readying themselves for the turn. In the distance, Marion could hear the staccato rhythms of a campus tour, the gunshot of the guide's high heels along the slate path, the rhythm of questions and answers.

"He's planning on moving out. He'll be gone when we get home," she said. Jason's face flushed. He balled his big hands into fists.

"Ohio," he said dully. "All that time in Ohio. Does he have a girlfriend there or something?"

Marion shook her head, feeling incredibly weary, more tired than she'd been after labor, or the sleepless nights with each of her new babies. "It's nothing like that, Jason," she told him. "It's just us. Your father and me. That's all."

She reached for his hands. She said his name softly, to comfort him. She thought to tell him that none of them knew, she least of all, and how scared she is about being alone, and how letting her son go will be the hardest thing she's ever done; harder, even, than losing a husband.

Jason pulled his hands away from hers. "I don't know anything!" he cried. Each word was wrenched out of him as if by force. His voice cracked. "Not anything!" At the top of a tall stone tower, a bell tolled, and suddenly mother and son were engulfed in a flow of bodies, as students burst out of their classrooms and streamed outside, calling and laughing.

DORA ON THE BEACH

"Hey." Dora Ginsburg slowed her pace, pulled off her earphones, and looked up at the two teenage girls in bikini tops, shorts, and flip-flops standing in front of a shuttered custard stand. The girl who'd spoken sauntered across the boardwalk to Dora. She was tall and rail-thin, with rib bones pushing against the waxy white skin of her torso, a white handbag made of cheap imitation leather tucked under her arm, and a necklace reading "Amber" in curlicued gold script around her neck. The girl following behind her was shorter and stockier, with broad shoulders and solid thighs and the same unhealthy pallor.

Sisters, Dora thought. There was nothing except the ink-black hair and the fishbelly-white skin to link them, but still somehow she knew that the two of them were sisters.

"Yes?" she asked, marching in place to keep her heart rate up. "Can I help you?"

"Can she help us," the tall girl, Amber, said to the shorter one. "Why, yes, I think she can." The shorter girl murmured something Dora couldn't hear, and shuffled her feet. Dora could see the curving edge of a tattoo—a heart, or a butterfly wing—peeking past the scrap of cloth that covered her right breast.

Their clothes, she thought, would be completely inadequate if the temperature dropped. It might be seventy-five in the sunshine, but it was, after all, just ten days until October, and the nice weather wouldn't last. Her own outfit—loose white shirt, pale blue cotton-blend clamdiggers, and white rubber-soled orthopedic walking shoes, with two inches of Supp Hose in between—was much more appropriate.

Amber, the tall one, shoved her hands into the pockets of her minuscule shorts. "We've got a problem," she said in a thick New York accent, and tilted her face at Dora, chin first.

"What's that?" They were probably lost, Dora thought. They weren't going to rob her, not in broad daylight. And if they were, they wouldn't get anything but the little music player she'd bought herself, her keys, the cell phone she'd never quite figured out how to use, and the *Philadelphia Examiner* she still bought, even though the paper seemed to be falling apart, bit by bit, shedding its book reviews and Sunday magazine and all the columnists she liked. Reading it was a bit like having lunch with a friend who'd developed leprosy and would arrive minus a few fingers or the tip or her nose, and you'd have to be polite and pretend not to notice.

Amber snatched at Dora's hand with her pale, bony fingers. Dora tried to pull it back, but the girl's acrylic nails dug into her skin and held her tight as she turned Dora's hand over and studied her Medic Alert bracelet. "Well, Dora Ginsburg, it's like this. My sister and I are experiencing technical difficulties." She dropped Dora's wrist and stretched her bony arms over her head. "With our accommodations."

Dora nodded, then looked sideways, scanning the boardwalk for sunbathers and strollers, for anyone who'd notice what was going on. But everything was quiet except for the gulls squawking and the roll of the waves. It was 10:15 in the morning. In July or August the boardwalk would have been jammed from Ventnor, where Dora lived, all the way down to the last casino in Atlantic City, but now summer was over. The lifeguard stands were boarded up, the hotels were half-empty, and while the casinos were still full of little old ladies who'd spent twenty-five dollars for a bus ticket and ten dollars in quarters, most of the snowbirds who lived in her condominium had already packed up and headed to Arizona or Florida for the winter.

"So do you need . . ." Dora's voice trailed off. "Directions?" she asked hopefully.

The girl with the tattoo—Dawn, Dora remembered—fiddled with the strings on the side of her bathing suit bottom underneath her shorts. Amber shook her head curtly. "Nah. We need a place to stay." Her voice was as harsh as the seagulls' cawing, her eyes as hard as two pebbles.

"Oh!" Dora felt relief flood through her. "Well, there's the Radisson, just up the boardwalk. And . . ."

Amber grabbed Dora's wrist again and pulled her over to a bench on the edge of the boardwalk. She pushed Dora's shoulders until she sat down, then she sat beside her, with her naked thigh flush against Dora's blue pants leg. Dawn trailed them reluctanctly, dragging her feet. Dora's music player slipped out of her hands and bounced underneath the bench. "How about your place?" Amber said. "How about"—she grabbed Dora's wrist again and flipped her bracelet over— "3601 Brighton Court?"

Dora tried to wriggle sideways, but Amber kept one arm around her shoulders and one hand clutching her wrist. She opened her mouth to scream, then closed it. The wind was blowing. Nobody would hear her. And who knew what this crazy girl would do if she tried to call for help? Instead, she gave a foolish smile and said, "I'm not really set up for visitors."

Amber bent down and reached into her big scuff-marked purse. Dora felt something hard jabbing into her ribs. "You feel that?" the girl whispered, her breath hot in Dora's ear. "You know what that is?"

Dora moaned. Dawn slipped off her flip-flops and curled her painted toenails against the gray planks of the boardwalk. Then she bent down, picked up Dora's music player, and offered it to Dora. Amber snatched it away.

"Amber . . ." the girl said.

Amber ignored her. "My sister and I have been watching you. Your building's back there, right?" She pointed her chin at the Windrift, a glass-and-stone high-rise tower half a mile away, where Dora had an apartment. "Nice," she said. Her thin lip curled away from her crooked front teeth. "With a swimming pool and everything. Very nice. You've probably got a pullout couch for when the grandkids come to town."

Gooseflesh dotted Dora's arms. There'd been a rash of robberies over the summer—*push-ins,* the police called them on the news. The victim would be coming home, unlocking the doors of her apartment when someone would come up behind her, push her through the opened door, take what they wanted, and break the rest. One woman had suffered a heart attack in the middle of a robbery, Dora remembered. *Critical condition,* the news had said. "We'll have advice on how to keep yourself from being a victim coming up after the break," the perky newsanchor had promised, and what had Dora done? She'd turned off her set. Of all the nights to go to bed early!

She locked her knees so the girls wouldn't see them shaking. "I'll take you to my apartment," she said in what she hoped was a reasonable, conciliatory tone. "You can take whatever you want. I've got a TV set and some jewelry and some cash. You can have it all as long as you won't hurt me."

"Come on, Amber," Dawn said softly, as she tapped her flip-flops against her thigh. "Let's just go home."

"Nobody asked you, Dawn," Amber said. She shoved the muzzle of the gun harder against Dora's side. Dora gasped, knowing she'd have a bruise there the next morning. Ever since she'd started taking blood thinners, everything gave her bruises.

"You can't do this," she blurted.

"Sure we can," Amber said with an icy grin. "We just did."

Dora didn't have sisters. Her husband, Sidney, had been dead for two years. And Sam, her only son, had called her the week before to say that he was dropping out of graduate school to work as a party motivator at bar and bat mitzvahs.

"So all the dancers are Jewish?" Dora had blurted, after Sam had finished explaining that he'd be earning a living by dancing for crowds of thirteen-year-olds in what Dora just bet was an embarrassing outfit. Her son, who hadn't even danced at his own bar mitzvah!

"No, Ma," Sam told her wearily. "Two of the other dancers are black. Nobody cares whether we're atheists or Hindus or what, as long as we keep the party energy up."

Dora sat on her couch, the phone in her hand and the TV remote control in her lap, with no idea at all of what to say. "I don't understand . . ." she began.

"There's something else I need to tell you," Sam said. "Kerri and I are splitting up." Dora slumped against the throw pillows, suddenly dizzy. She wondered how her son had chosen the order in which to break the news: I've dropped out of my Ph.D. program in order to gyrate to Kool and the Gang and, oh, by the way, my wife and I are getting a divorce.

"Sam, no," she said.

Her son sighed. "It's a done deal." There was a pause. "I'm sorry, Ma."

"I like Kerri," Dora managed.

Sam had sighed again. "Yeah, I like her, too."

She hung up the phone and started to cry, weak, helpless tears streaming down her wrinkled face. She'd gone wrong with Sam, somehow, but she wasn't sure when, or what it was she'd done wrong, or failed to do in the first place. One minute she'd been twenty-one years old, dizzy in love and saying "I do." A minute later and she was thirty-three, the mother of a perpetually sullen, closed-mouthed seven-year-old and the wife of a man who had secrets of his own.

She'd been making dinner one Wednesday night when the telephone rang, and on the other end of it was a woman whose voice she'd never heard before. The woman was laughing: a gaspy, desperate, distinctly unamused sound. She was laughing and saying, *You keep him, I don't care. Stay with him. Better you than me.* Dora had listened to her laugh, holding the pot into which she'd just dumped a cup of rice, thinking that she hadn't known there was a competition. When Sidney came home he kissed her, same as he always did, and that night, it being a Wednesday, he made love to her, same as he always did. Dora never mentioned the telephone call. Not then, not over the years and decades that followed, not even in the midst of their worst fights, not even after her miscarriage, when the doctor had come to her hospital room, asking whether they wanted to know the gender of the baby they'd lost, and Sidney had said no without even looking at her, as if it was his decision to make.

Sidney had died when he was sixty. Diabetes had taken its time with him, first shutting down his kidneys, then leisurely robbing him of his vision, then his toes, and then his left leg, until he'd ended up on a hospital bed looking like a pile of sticks beneath a blanket. He had a morphine drip in his arm and, near the end, he called some other woman's name. Who's Naomi? one of the nurses had asked, and Dora had lied. My middle name, she said. He calls me that sometimes. The nurse had nodded sympathetically. They'd patted her shoulders and called her *poor thing*.

And then Sidney was gone, and Sam was in New York City, and Dora was alone in the house in Silver Springs.

Where? she wondered, after the men from the Salvation Army had finished hauling thirty years of her life out the door—the sofas and dining room tables she and Sidney had picked out together; the paintings and *objets* that had come later, when Sidney had insisted on a decorator.

Where? She remembered her honeymoon in Atlantic City, all those years ago. They'd stayed in a little hotel right on the ocean. She remembered the bed with chipped blue paint on its metal headboard, and how the people in the next room had pounded on the wall when they were making love late one night, and Sidney put his hand over her mouth to stifle her giggles. She could recall the feel of the sunburn she'd gotten on her cheeks, the taste of fried fish and cold beer, taffy from one of the stands on the boardwalk, saltwater washing over her knees, and seaweed tangling in her toes as Sidney scooped her up and carried her into the ocean, out past where the waves were breaking.

After the house sold she'd decided on two condominiums: one in Clearwater, for the snowy winter months, and one in Ventnor, a few miles from where she'd honeymooned, much nicer for retirees than Atlantic City, the agent had said. It was a one-bedroom unit in a building with a doorman and underground parking, a swimming pool with water aerobics for seniors five mornings a week, floor-to-ceiling windows giving her a beautiful view of the ocean. September was her favorite time of year. The air was clear, the water was warm enough for wading, but the children had gone back to school, leaving the beach and the boardwalk quiet enough for her to walk for hours if she wanted, alone with her thoughts and her memories.

"Lunch first," Amber said. She kept her arm around Dora's shoulders and the gun jammed in her side. She instructed Dora to lead them to her apartment building, where her car was parked. The two of them marched along the boardwalk with Dawn trailing a few yards behind, pausing every few minutes to lean against the railing with the wind blowing her hair back, staring dreamily out at the sea.

Dora found that she could barely walk, her knees were shaking so badly. Help me! she wanted to scream at the occasional passersby. Save me! The trouble was, anyone who saw them wouldn't notice anything out of the ordinary—just a little old lady out for a stroll, enjoying the last of the season's sunshine with her two tattooed, bikini-clad granddaughters who, let's face it, didn't look any trashier than most of the girls she saw on the beach in the summertime.

Amber turned her head over her shoulder. "Dawn, what do you want for lunch?"

"I don't know," Dawn mumbled. Dora led them to her Camry in the Windrift's underground garage, an empty concrete space that seemed full of ominous shadows and strange noises. She groped in her pocket, and dropped the car keys twice. Amber finally grunted in disgust and bent down to scoop up the keys.

"After you," she said. Dora got behind the wheel. Amber sat in the passenger's seat, seat belt unfastened, one hand in her purse. Dawn clambered into the back.

"Where do you want to eat?" Amber asked her sister.

Dora saw the other girl shrug in the rearview mirror. "I don't care," she said.

"Seafood it is," said Amber. "And margaritas." She cocked an eyebrow at Dora. "You know a good place?"

"Leo's on the Pier?" Dora suggested. She'd never been there, but she'd driven by the place a million times. It had kind of a honky-tonk look, with strings of red chili-pepper shaped lights around the doorway and music pounding so loud that Dora's car windows shook as she drove by. Better yet, it was always crowded, even in the off-season. Each diner would be a potential witness to her kidnapping. Maybe the girls weren't even old enough to drink. Maybe the waitress would ask for IDs, and when Amber opened up her bag, she'd see the gun glinting inside, hurry to the kitchen, and call the police.

"Just a sec." Amber rummaged in her purse. Dora's heart froze, until Amber pulled out two long, fringed T-shirts—one pink, which she tossed to Dawn in the backseat, one purple, which she balled up in her own lap—and, unbelievably, a Zagat's guide. "Leo's on the Pier. Yep, here we go. This 'bustling, waterfront emporium' boasts 'oversize drinks' and an 'anything-goes vibe,'" she read. "Locals swear by the 'fresh-grilled fish and steamed lobster,' naysayers 'roll their eyes' at the 'ditzy servers' and 'tacky nautical décor.'"

"What's a naysayer?" Dawn asked.

"A stick in the mud," Amber said curtly. She turned to Dora. "Let's ride."

"Would you ladies care for anything from the bar?"

Dawn shook her head. "I'm not supposed to drink," she said.

The waitress raised her eyebrows at Dora. "Oh, nothing for me," Dora said hastily, and wrapped her arms around herself. Amber had requested a table on the deck, and she and her sister seemed perfectly comfortable, but Dora was wishing desperately for a sweater.

"Three margaritas, and if none of you drink 'em, I will," Amber said, and gave a shark-like grin. "I'm on vacation." Dora held her breath, waiting for the request for ID, but the waitress just saluted the three of them with a tip of her order pad and vanished through the swinging doors into the restaurant. Dora cleared her throat twice before she could get the words to come out.

"I need to use the restroom," she whispered.

"Oh, right, right," Amber said, nodding. She'd pulled on her own shredded T-shirt dress, and seemed to be in a jolly mood, perhaps because she'd successfully hijacked Dora, perhaps because there was liquor on the way. "Old people pee all the time. Urinary incontinence," she said, her voice a touch too loud for Dora's comfort. "You go ahead." Dora shot to her feet. She'd walk toward the bathroom, then slip into the kitchen and find a cook or a waitress . . .

"Dawn, you go with her," Amber ordered.

Dora's heart sank as Dawn pushed back her chair and slowly stood up.

"Don't forget your purse," Amber said, cutting her cold eyes at the item in question.

Dawn sighed, picked up the purse, and trailed Dora to a pair of doors that read "Buoys" and "Gulls."

In the bathroom, Dora fumbled the lock into place and sank down onto the toilet. She could see Dawn's pale calves and flip-flops, standing motionless in front of one of the sinks. The girl's voice floated through the thin wooden door.

"I'm sorry about this," Dawn said.

"Not as sorry as I am," Dora muttered.

When she opened the door, Dawn was staring at herself in

the mirror. The curved edge of the tattoo was still visible beneath the neckline of her T-shirt dress, and her hair gleamed under the bright bathroom lights as if it had been oiled. Her gaze met Dora's in the mirror, then slid away.

"Can't you get her to stop?" Dora asked. Her lips trembled, and she saw herself in the mirror, reflected under the unforgiving light, pale and frail and timid as a mouse. The very look you'd expect from a woman who'd lived forty years with a man in love with someone named Naomi, whose son was checking out of his marriage to dance for teenagers.

Dawn looked down and snapped the ponytail holder that was wrapped around her wrist. "It'll just be for a few days," she said. "I think."

You think. Dora washed her hands and the two of them returned to the table, where Amber was waiting and three lime-green drinks in salt-rimmed glasses were melting in the sun.

"No sofa bed?" Amber asked, scowling at Dora's living room, taking in the couch that faced the windows, the small television set, the framed wedding picture of Sam and Kerri, as if she expected a pullout couch to materialize under her furious gaze. After lunch Amber had told Dora to drive them to Target, where the sisters loaded up a shopping cart with what Amber deemed "vacation necessities." There were bottles of suntan oil, nail polish and nail polish remover, spray cheese and Pringles, three-packs of nylon bikini underwear, nightshirts, sanitary napkins, beach towels, a bicycle lock, a silver-and-blue boom box and half a dozen CDs, wide-brimmed straw hats, an inflatable reflective raft with cup holders built into the armrests, and a pair of hot pink hooded sweatshirts that read "Ventnor." All of it had been paid for with the credit card Amber plucked from Dora's wallet with a magician's dexterity.

"Damn. We should've bought that air mattress, Dawn."

"It's okay," Dawn said, setting a few of the shopping bags down on the coffee table. "We can sleep on the floor." She looked at Dora hopefully. "Do you have sleeping bags? Or extra blankets or something?"

"Well, I'll take a look, but . . ."

There was a knock at the door. Dora's heart leapt. Salvation, she thought. Even if it was Jehovah's Witnesses, or the condo association president inquiring about her dues . . . Two feet from the door, Amber's voice hissed through the room. "You say anything and you'll be sorry."

Dora pulled the door open. Her next-door neighbor Florence Something, one of the Windrift's few year-rounders, stood in front of her with a smile on her tanned face and a Saran-wrapped paper plate in her leathery hands.

"You've got company!" she burbled, peering over Dora's shoulder to the living room, where the girls, still in their fringed T-shirt dresses, were lounging on the couch. Dawn had a copy of the AARP magazine open in her lap. Amber held the remote control, pointed at the television set sideways (like a gun, Dora's mind babbled), and was flicking through the channels so rapidly they were a meaningless blur, but Dora could tell that she was listening to every word. "I was baking this weekend, so when I saw you all come out of the elevator, I thought to myself, I thought, Florence, I bet those girls would love some of my magic bars!"

"Thank you," said Dora. Florence passed the plate into her hands. Dora looked at her, trying to send a message with her eyes. *Help me. I'm in trouble.*

Florence just squinted over Dora's shoulder. "Hello, girls!" she chirped at Amber and Dawn. "Your granddaughters?" she asked Dora.

"Long-lost stepchildren," Amber drawled.

"What's a magic bar?" Dawn called from the couch.

"Oh, they're delicious! My grandkids' favorite! You start with crushed graham crackers and melted butter . . ."

The telephone rang. Dora jerked toward the kitchen, but Amber was too fast. Uncoiling her skinny body from the couch, she crossed to the kitchen in three long strides, snatched the telephone, and raised it to her ear. "Hello? No, I'm sorry, she's unavailable at the moment. May I ask who's calling?"

Dora knew that it had to be Sam. He always called her toward the end of the month, to use up the minutes on his cell phone.

"I'm a friend of your mother's." Amber's voice lifted flirtatiously, while Florence continued to discourse upon the making of magic bars. Dora leaned against the wall with her heart beating like a trapped and desperate animal. Amber tucked the telephone under her chin and flung herself back onto the couch, swinging her legs over the armrest, winking at Dora while she chatted. "No . . . no, a new friend. What?" She giggled. "No, not everyone who lives here's an old lady."

Florence made a noise like a cushion suddenly deflating— hmmph!—and shook her frosted-blond hair. She had on one of her matchy-matchy outfits: pale-pink clamdiggers with pink espadrilles and pink lipstick. Around one wrist, she wore a silver charm bracelet with tiny black-and-white photographs of each of her grandchildren. Dora found herself wondering whether Dawn and Amber would have picked her over Dora if they'd seen Florence first and, strangely, found herself feeling both relieved and resentful at the prospect.

"Where in New York? Do you go out a lot?" Amber was asking Sam. Dora gave Amber an impatient look and stretched out her hand for the phone, knowing the girl wouldn't give it to her. "Okay, well, nice chatting with ya. Yeah, I'll tell her you called." She hung up the phone and grinned indulgently. "Sit down, Dora. Take a load off. Have a magic bar. Rest up. Later, we're gonna go to the beach."

"Oh, it's a perfect evening for that. You'll get a lovely sunset. Such nice weather we're having. Unseasonably warm!" Florence burbled.

"You and Dawn?" Dora asked faintly.

"And you, too." She wrapped her arms around Dora's shoulders and squeezed the flesh of her upper arm. Hard. "We wouldn't go anywhere without you."

It was two o'clock in the morning by the time they made it back to the apartment. Amber and Dawn had confiscated Dora's cell phone, unplugged the telephone in her bedroom, and, after much debate, decided to line up four dining room chairs against her bedroom door, reasoning that she probably wouldn't be able to open it, and that even if she did, the noise of the chairs falling would wake them. "Sweet dreams!" Amber called, and Dawn murmured something that sounded like *Sorry*. Dora leaned against the door and listened to the two of them bickering over how to inflate the air mattress that silly Florence had been only too happy to lend them, along with a set of sheets, a travel alarm clock, and another plateful of Magic Bars.

She staggered over to her bed on legs that felt like overstretched rubber bands and collapsed onto her back. The day had been filled with more activity than she normally had in a week: the lunch out, the shopping trip, the sunset on the beach. Then they'd gone back up to the apartment so the girls could take showers and apply frightening amounts of makeup and wriggle into miniskirts and tank tops, then out again, first to a restaurant Amber had found listed in her Zagat's as having the best crab cakes on the shore, then to a club, then a club inside of a casino, then an after-hours club, where Dora had sat on a shaky-legged barstool in her clamdiggers and graceless walking shoes, feeling the music pounding through her, burrowing into her bones.

Now that she was finally alone, she forced herself to breathe slowly and think. It seemed unlikely that the girls would kill her—not after Florence had seen both of them, and Amber had talked to Sam on the phone. Still, better safe than sorry. She flicked on the bedroom light and found pen and paper in her bedside table, wondering exactly how to begin. "To whom it may concern," she finally decided. "I am being held hostage in my own home by teenage girls. Their names are Dawn and Amber. I don't know their last names." She listed every detail she could think of—Amber's necklace, Dawn's tattoos, their ages (she'd learned that Dawn was eighteen and her sister was nineteen, and that they both had fake IDs). She added her best guesses for height and weight and wrote that they lived in Queens, where Dawn was enrolled in cosmetology school and Amber did "this and that." She added her name and telephone number beneath the notation "If you find this please call the police." She made two copies of the note and left one beneath her bedside lamp, where whoever found her body would be sure to see it. There was an envelope that had once contained a power bill in the top drawer of her desk. She slipped the second copy of the letter inside, weighted it down with one of Sidney's old watches, cracked open her bedroom window, and tossed it out into the night.

"Hey."

Dora opened her eyes and looked down. She was in her own bed with the covers pulled up to her chin. The sun was shining through the curtains, and she could hear the wind and the waves outside. It was another lovely September morning on the Jersey shore. Maybe the whole thing had been a bad dream.

"Hey."

Dora propped herself up on her elbow and saw Amber standing in the doorway with her dingy white purse tucked under her arm. She had declined her sister's offer of sunscreen the day before, and her cheeks and legs and forearms were a painful-looking orangey-pink.

"Yes?" Dora whispered.

"I can't figure out your coffee machine," Amber whispered back.

Dora felt that she was still enveloped in a dream fog as she pushed herself out of bed, walked to the kitchen, measured beans into the grinder, and flicked the machine on.

"Fancy," Amber observed. Standing barefoot in a neon-green nightshirt, her stiff black hair flattened against one cheek, she smelled of cigarette smoke and liquor. Dawn was still sleeping. The indistinct lump of her body was curled on its side on the air mattress, underneath Florence's comforter. "You got any creamer?" Amber asked through a yawn.

"Are you going to shoot me if I don't?" Dora asked on her way to the refrigerator. Amber grinned.

"Nah, I'll just rough you up a little." She leaned back against the counter and drew in a hissing breath as she hoisted herself on top of it. "Sunburn."

"Sorry." Dora lifted the coffeepot and thought about what would happen if she threw it in Amber's face and ran for the door. Too risky, she decided, looking into the girl's eyes, which didn't seem sleepy at all. She poured two cups of coffee instead.

Amber eased herself off the countertop and sat down on one of Dora's dining room chairs, wincing as the backs of her legs came into contact with the upholstery. She wrapped both hands around the blue ceramic mug. "Look," she said. "If you want to know why we're here, it's for Dawn." Amber's accent turned "for Dawn" into something that sounded a lot like "fall down."

She cut her eyes toward Dora's living room, where her sister was still sleeping, then swallowed a mouthful of coffee, grimaced, and reached for the Wedgewood sugar bowl.

"We'd been planning this vacation for a long time, but then we had to use the money for something else."

"For what?" Dora asked.

"Not drugs, if that's what you're thinking," Amber said. Dora felt her face flush, because *drugs* had been exactly what she was thinking. "Dawn was pregnant. With Lester Spano," Amber said, making a face to let Dora know exactly what she thought of Lester Spano. "She thought they were gonna get married or something. I said to her, 'Dawn, Lester Spano is not who you want to have kids by and spend the rest of your life with.' Shit, I wouldn't even go to a movie with Lester Spano. But Dawn, she's, you know." Amber lifted her bony shoulders in a you-see-how-it-is shrug. "Romantic or something."

Her New York accent thickened as she told the story. "So she's buyin' little baby booties, she's knitting mittens, for God's sake, and suddenly Lester Spano is nowhere to be found, and his cell's disconnected and his mom says she doesn't know where he went—she said this to Dawn, and then I went over there and she said it to me, so I knew she wasn't lying." Another shrug. "Five hundred dollars. And that was with the sliding scale, and with a bunch of freaks screaming at us. 'Baby-killer, baby-killer.' " She smiled thinly. "You can just bet nobody was screaming at Lester Spano." Another smile. "I gave 'em his address." She twirled the sugar bowl in her hands, rattling the spoon against its rim. "So, no more Jersey Shore, except we'd already bought our bus tickets, so I thought, why not? I thought, maybe it would cheer

Dawn up to get out of town. And I knew I'd find us somewhere to stay." She took another sip of coffee and nodded, satisfied. "I'm good at figuring things out."

"You . . ." Dora swallowed. She had begun to imagine this as some kind of prank, a stunt; she thought that Amber had done it on a dare and conned her sweet, dim sister into coming along for the ride. But now . . .

"I take care of Dawn," Amber said, and raised her chin pugnaciously. "She's a little bit . . ." Her voice trailed off as she looked toward the dim living room.

"Slow?" Dora ventured.

"Not slow," Amber said sharply. "She got better grades than I did. She's not slow, she's . . ." She combed her fingers through her hair, trying to rearrange it, and crossed her bony, burned legs. "I don't know. I don't know what she is." She gave up on her hair and spooned more sugar into her mug, with her shoulders hunched and her mouth mere inches from the steaming liquid.

"Maybe she's depressed," Dora said.

"Maybe that's it," Amber agreed. "Over Lester Spano, who isn't worth the gas it takes to go see him." She slurped her coffee and slumped in her seat. "But it's not workin'. She loves the beach. I thought she'd be cheered up by now. But she keeps talking about him. Lester. About how she always thought she'd go on a nice vacation with him."

Dora poured herself coffee, then stared at the girl across the table. With her makeup smeared off and her hairdo deflated, Amber looked softer than she had on the boardwalk. She was a teenager, just like Sam had once been, just like Dora herself had been, once, a long time ago, and she was pretty, underneath the hairspray, the junky jewelry, the gangster-girl façade. She had fine features, a broad mouth, eyebrows as delicately arched as birds' wings above her black eyes. With her hair down around her shoulders and her eyeliner scrubbed off, she could have been the niece or granddaughter of anyone at the Windrift, one of those girls who went to a good school, and who did not claim her vacations at gunpoint.

"How about your parents?" she ventured. "Can't they help?" Amber snorted dismissively. She flicked one slender hand in a shooing gesture in front of her eyes, then reached into her purse. Dora's heart lurched. But instead of a gun, Amber pulled out her Zagat's guide again and yawned, taking care to cover her mouth, as she flipped through it one-handed.

"This place," she said, thrusting the book at Dora. "Snacks on the Beach. It says they've got pineapple pancakes. Dawn likes pineapple."

The next three days passed in a blur of restaurants, afternoons on the beach, late nights in a series of hot, noisy, smoky, crowded nightclubs where the thudding bass lines would echo in Dora's brain until morning. She'd sit at the bar with Amber beside her, holding her big white purse in her lap. "Go dance," Amber would tell her sister, and Dawn would walk slowly toward the dance floor, close her eyes beneath the flickering lights, and stand in one place, hips swaying back and forth at the same languid pace whether the song issuing from the speakers was slow or fast, whether there was anyone in front of her or not, like she was dancing in a dream.

On the third night, the girls forgot to put the chairs in front of her bedroom door.

Dora lay on her bed with her heart hammering in her ears as the television finally clicked into silence. She crept to the door and crouched there with her ear pressed against a spot just above the doorknob, listening to the girls' sleepy conversation, which finally trailed off. Amber snored lightly as she slept. Her sister's breaths were deep and regular. Dora turned the doorknob by millimeters and tiptoed into the living room, where she peered down at the girls, sleeping side by side on Florence's air mattress. Amber's purse was on the table next to the couch. Dora picked it up, slung it over her shoulder, and crept into the kitchen, where she pulled her telephone out of its cradle.

Who to call first? The police? Should she call her son?

Dora stood in the darkness and realized that no matter who she called, she'd sound foolish. *Yes, officer, two girls from New York. They are holding me hostage. Where are they right now? Actually, they're on my living room floor, sleeping. Tomorrow I'm supposed to take them to the new George Clooney movie, because Dawn likes George Clooney.* ("He looks like Lester," she'd told her sister, and Amber had said, "Oh, for God's sake, he does not!") *Then we're going on a helicopter ride over Atlantic City. To be perfectly honest, I'm sort of looking forward to it.*

She set the telephone back in its cradle and froze when Amber rolled over, muttering in her sleep. Dora forced herself to take slow breaths and count to a hundred before unzipping the white purse.

There was a gun in there, just as Amber had told her. A squirt gun, a cheap thing made of pinkish plastic with a chipped white trigger, filled with water, Dora supposed, to give it that genuine handgun heft.

She laughed at herself softly before slipping the gun back into Amber's purse. She listened to the ocean wind whipping at her window, not the soft breezy kiss she'd imagined when Atlantic City first occurred to her, or the still, humid night air in Clearwater, where she spent her winters. The wind blew hard in the darkness, dangerous and fierce. She could hear night noises through her window: traffic, the far-off wail of an ambulance, the water rolling onto the sand, the girls breathing. Dora hung the purse back over the dining room chair and crept back into bed.

———

"Come on," Amber said, tugging at her sister's hands.

"I don't want to."

"Come on!" she repeated. Dawn shook her head and crossed her arms above her life vest. Dora could see the edge of the tattoo on Dawn's chest. She knew what it was now—a heart that had once held the word *Lester*. Dawn had told her the night before, on the beach, that Amber was going to pay for her to have it lasered off.

"Seriously, Dawn!"

Dawn closed her eyes and shook her head at the same dreamy pace she shook her hips at the dance clubs. The pilot yelled something Dora couldn't make out as the rotors chopped at the air above their heads. Amber spoke urgently to her sister, then shrugged, and raised her voice.

"Dora, you tell her!"

Dora looked at Dawn. "It'll be fine," she said, looking at the girl intently so that she'd know that Dora meant more than the helicopter ride. "You're going to be all right."

Dawn shook her head again, with her black hair rippling against her lightly tanned cheeks. Her lips moved, and Dora made out the words *I'm scared.*

"You'll be sitting right next to us. Right between us," Dora said.

Dawn seemed to consider this before giving in. "'Kay," she said. Dora helped her fasten her belt, and she leaned over, forehead pressed against the window, as they left the ground. Amber had to yell to make herself heard above the helicopter's blades, but Dora could read her lips. *Thank you,* the girl was saying. *You're welcome,* Dora mouthed. And when Amber reached across Dawn's lap and took her hands, she squeezed right back as they rose over the buildings and the boardwalk, the sand and the water, up into the endless blue sky.

NOTES ON STORIES

I began this collection half a lifetime ago, when I was eighteen. I've always loved short stories, such as those from Stephen King and Andrew Vachss to Ann Hood and Amy Bloom to Kelly Link to Ray Bradbury and Harlan Ellison, and I've been writing them, and publishing them here and there, for years.

In this collection, the stories are arranged chronologically, starting with the youngest character (Josie Krystal, her first summer back from college) and ending with the oldest (Dora, widowed and retired and living on the beach.) I think each one illustrates a particular moment in a character's life and illuminates the choices men and women make about how they love, and who, and why. Here's a little more about each one.

Just Desserts and *Travels with Nicki* (1990)

There's a Sharon Olds poem that I love in which the narrator describes seeing her parents at their college graduation.

> *I want to go up to them and say Stop,*
> *don't do it—she's the wrong woman,*

he's the wrong man, you are going to do things
you cannot imagine you would ever do,
you are going to do bad things to children,
you are going to suffer in ways you never heard of,
you are going to want to die. I want to go
up to them there in the late May sunlight and say it

But she doesn't.

I want to live. I
take them up like the male and female
paper dolls and bang them together
at the hips like chips of flint as if to
strike sparks from them, I say
Do what you are going to do, and I will tell about it.

Or, as my mother still likes to say, "It's all material."

My parents split up when I was sixteen. When I was seventeen, I headed off to Princeton, which had (and has) about the best creative writing program for undergraduates in the country, to tell about it. I wrote about my parents' divorce, and wrote about it, and wrote about it, and wrote about it. My joke about college is that everything I wrote had a single theme: *My parents got divorced, and it hurt.* Freshman year: My parents got divorced, and it hurt. Sophomore year: My parents got divorced, and it really hurt. Junior year: Did I mention that my parents got divorced? Senior year: No, I'm not over it yet! (I think we should all bow our heads in gratitude that I didn't go to graduate school.)

I must have written hundreds of pages about families and divorce, daughters and divorce, fathers and divorce . . . you get the idea. *Just Desserts* and *Travels with Nicki* were written for a course with John McPhee, who was the most patient and generous teacher I had. These stories were about the only things worth saving from that period of my life, creatively speaking. I still have John McPhee's original notes on *Travels with Nicki. Polish it up,* he wrote. *Publish it. Your sister will sue. But you have a great defense. You know how to tell a story.*

The Wedding Bed (2006)

I wrote this piece recently, to revisit the fictionalized version of my family and complete Josie's arc. These days, the books about single girls in the city that are dismissively called chick lit get a lot of flak for the Cinderella fantasy they allegedly embrace—the way their heroines muddle through the pain and poundage of single-girl existence, wisecracking all the way, until Prince Charming appears and Takes Them Away from All of That. I've written two novels that end with wedding bells. But does a marriage, and a man willing to proffer a ring and promise forever, necessarily equal happily-ever-after? I think Josie would beg to differ. I know for sure that Nicki would.

Swim (1989/2006)

When I was in college, I spent a summer working in New York City. One of the free weekly newspapers there had a fiction contest, which I entered and won, with a short story called *Swim,* about a young woman who graduates from college with a degree in English and few marketable skills. She sets up shop ghostwriting personal ads, and one of her clients falls for her. (It was an enormously comforting fantasy, one that I could embroider endlessly back when I was a soon-to-be college graduate with a degree in English and few marketable skills.)

"Find me that story!" my agent demanded.

I tried . . . but I couldn't.

My version of record-keeping involves bundling piles of documents—rough drafts, tax returns, photographs, diplomas—into big plastic shopping bags, which get stacked on my third floor, just down the hall from the guest bedroom. I went through all of my bags and couldn't find *Swim*. Nor could I remember which free weekly in New York had printed it. All I remembered were the bare bones of the story: The girl in New York. The classified ads. The title.

I started from scratch this past year, over a long weekend in Los Angeles in my favorite hotel in the world, the Regent Beverly Wilshire (or, as I—and Laura San Giacomo in *Pretty Woman*—call it, the Reg Bev Wil). I set it in L.A., because that's where I was, and gave it a few modern updates (online dating as opposed to ads in the *Village Voice*). *Swim*—or, as I've been calling it, *Swim 2.0*—is the result.

Meanwhile, if anyone reading this was living in Manhattan in 1990 and remembers the original story, or even who printed it, I'd love to know.

Buyer's Market (2005)

Part of promoting a book is sitting for interviews—and, maybe because writing is such a distressingly boring thing to watch, a lot of times the interviewers want to visit the writer's house. "We want to see you in your element," they say, in a way that always makes me feel like some kind of expensive but useless, exotic, flightless bird.

You try to be a good sport and take everything that gets written with a sense of humor, but it's hard not to feel a little invaded. (Because, really, what woman wants to be judged on the contents of her refrigerator or whether her bedroom's sufficiently clean?)

I once had a reporter sneak into my closet, find clothing with price tags still attached, and report on the prices in her story. Sadly, she was so pleased with her investigatory coup that she failed to note that the outfits were borrowed for a photo shoot. To this day, I don't think I've managed to convince my mother that I do not, and never would, actually purchase a $2,100 sweater. And the scene where Toby picks up Jess's mother's photograph and sneers, "She's not that good-looking . . . I thought it was a picture of *you?*" True story—and too good not to use.

This is a love story, but it's a love story about both a person and a place, about dreams and memories, and about what you get when you let them go.

Good Men (1997)

I spent a lot of time in my twenties thinking about love and marriage and what gives two people the impetus and the courage to decide to link hands and jump off the cliff (I had a pretty jaundiced view of the institution. See Story Note One).

Good Men has the same characters as my first novel, *Good in Bed*—Bruce, who is sweet but a bit of a slacker, and Cannie, who's funny but kind of a control freak, and Nifkin, the small, quivery, spotted rat terrier, who is, of course, perfect in every way. This story was actually written before the novel, in my spare bedroom of my Philadelphia apartment, on the Mac Classic I'd had since college, at night, when I was still working full-time as a reporter for *The Philadelphia Inquirer.* It occasioned a lovely rejection letter from *The Atlantic.* ("Dear Ms. Weiner, While you are obviously a writer, this isn't quite right for us.")

The Guy Not Taken (2005)

A few years back, I was on www.weddingchannel.com buying a wedding present when I happened to accidentally type in the names of every guy I've ever dated. (And don't look at me like I'm a freak . . . you know you've done it, too.)

I typed in the names, and lo and behold, one of them popped up, with a wedding date and a registry and all.

So, of course, I emailed his registry to my best friend, and we spent a giddy evening making fun of his and his betrothed's crappy taste in china, and that was pretty much the end of it.

Except it wasn't.

A long time ago, I read a Stephen King short story called *Word Processor of the Gods,* in which a man inherits a computer from his dead nephew and ends up using the Delete key in ways the good folks at Wang had never imagined. I started thinking about the magical possibilities of online registries. What if you could make your own additions and deletions? What if you could, say, erase the bride's name and type in your own? What if you hit Enter and woke up the next morning in bed with your ex?

And so a story was born.

This piece took a few funny detours along the way to publication. When I first described Marlie registering her ex for a Hitachi Magic Wand, my agent, who's my first reader, sent the story back with a note reading: "What is this?"

Okay, I thought. She went to Catholic school from junior high through graduate school. Of course she's not going to recognize a name-brand vibrator. I kept it in, and sent the story to my editor in New York, who sent it back with the exact same note in the margin . . . at which point I realized that I am a pervert.

This story was originally published by *Glamour* in the fall of

2005 and was optioned by DreamWorks shortly thereafter. A screenplay's in the works, and even though it's early, I understand that in the movie Marlie will not be a mother, as the concept of a mother semi-willingly wishing away her child has been deemed too disturbing for the filmgoing public. As my real-life child would say, "In-ter-est-ing."

The Mother's Hour (2006)

A lot of what I've written has an element of answering the question "What's the worst thing that can happen?" This isn't necessarily because, as one critic memorably suggested, I am a masochist (at least I hope I'm not). It's just that I think the most interesting dramatic possibilities come in moments of crisis. So I put my protagonists through the wringer by asking: What if your ex-boyfriend writes a column about your sex life? What if your sister steals your boyfriend? What if your baby dies?

One of my current preoccupations as a mother is the standards parents hold themselves up to, the way mothers judge themselves and one another, the debate between working versus stay-at-home mothers, those who stay in the city versus those who go to the suburbs, those who hire nannies versus those who opt for day care . . . and on and on and round and round it goes. This story touches on some of the tension implicit in the choices, and the sacrifices, that modern mothers make, and takes up my old favorite question, slightly tweaked—"What's the worst thing you didn't do?" I think this is as close to a horror story as I'll ever come.

(Interesting side note: This was almost published by a women's magazine that was fine with everything except the ending. Would I consider changing it, the editor wanted to know. I decided not to. I think, given the circumstances, and the choices the characters made, it ends about the way it should).

Tour of Duty (1992)

My mother actually told me that my father was leaving on our way back from my interview at Princeton, at the Vince Lombardi service area on the New Jersey Turnpike. ("Well, where was I supposed to tell you?" she demanded, when I pointed out that this was perhaps not the most appropriate venue for such a revelation.)

This was the first story I ever got paid for. *Seventeen* published it in the fall of 1992. They paid me $1,000, which was an unbelievable amount of money, especially given that I was earning $16,000 a year at the time. I used the check to buy a couch from Ikea.

Oranges from Florida (1994)

My brother Joe used to fall asleep listening to talk radio, and that's where the idea for this one came from. It was also an interesting challenge to write from the perspective of a man and view the end of a marriage through his eyes.

Redbook published the story in 1994 (they retitled it *Someone to Trust,* for reasons I never understood).

Dora on the Beach (1998)

I wrote an early draft of this story years before my second novel, *In Her Shoes,* but I think it contains the germ of the idea that formed part of that story: a girl with a surplus of chutzpah and a lack of funds heading to a resort community and, essentially, kidnapping a grandmother so she'll have a place to stay.

It almost got published twice, but was turned down by two different magazines. (I think the main character wound up being too old, and the teenage girls too unlikable. Plus, the whole abortion thing might have been a little too much.) Like *In Her Shoes,* it's also a sister story, a story about secrets and the redemptive possibilities of love.

ACKNOWLEDGMENTS

Thanks first and foremost to my wonderful agent Joanna Pulcini, without whose persistence, sharp editorial eye, and big heart, large chunks of this book would still be stuck in a Kohl's bag in my guest bedroom. Joanna once again went above, beyond, and all the way to Cape Cod in service of these stories, earning my solemn pledge: No more house arrest! (And I promise I will quit archiving my short stories in shopping bags.)

I'm grateful to my teachers in high school and my professors in college: John McPhee, Joyce Carol Oates, Toni Morrison, J. D. McClatchy, Ann Lauterbach. I'm also grateful to the editors who initially polished, and published, some of these stories: Adrienne Nicole LeBlanc at *Seventeen,* Dawn Raffel at *Redbook,* Sarah Mlynowski at Red Dress Ink, and Daryl Chen and Cindi Leive at *Glamour.*

Thanks to everyone at Atria Books, the best publisher a writer could hope for: Judith Curr, Carolyn Reidy, Kathleen Schmidt, Gary Urda, Lisa Keim, Kim Curtin, Jeanne Lee, Christine Duplessis, Craig Dean, Nancy Inglis, Nancy Clements, Linda Dingler, and Davina Mock. Thanks to Suzanne Baboneau at Simon & Schuster UK for phenomenal support across the pond, and to Regina Starace for a beautiful jacket.

My editor, Greer Hendricks, is worth a price above rubies for her smarts and skills and endless patience, and her assistant, Hannah Morrill, is a gem. My publicist, Marcy Engelman, is a superstar. I'm grateful to her and her team: Dana Gidney, Jordana Tal, and Samantha Cohen. Thanks also to Jessica Fee for the great job she does setting up my speaking engagements.

Thanks to everyone at DreamWorks and at Parkes/MacDonald Productions for falling in love with "The Guy Not Taken" (but not, thankfully, for messing with his online wedding registry). Thanks to Andrea Cipriani Mecchi for her friendship and for making me look so good, to the eternally calm Algene Wong, and to Tracy Miller for her hard work on tight deadlines.

Finally, thanks to the people who make my writing life possible and my real life so much fun: Jamie Seibert, Mary Hoeffel, and Terri Gottlieb, who hang with Lucy, and my indefatigable and very good-humored assistant Meghan Burnett, who will someday be a publishing powerhouse and way too important to take my calls.

Jake Weiner is not just my brother, he's also my film agent (and a darn good one, too). My sister Molly, brother Joe, mother Fran, Nanna Faye Frumin, Uncle Freddy and Aunt Ruth, and sister-in-law April Blair are all excellent red carpet dates. Love to my b.f.f., Susan Abrams Krevsky, and to Sharon Fenick and Alan Promer, Phil DeGennaro and Clare Epstein, Alexa and Craig Hymowitz, Craig and Elizabeth LaBan, Debbie Bilder and Lee Serota, Olivia Grace Weiner, Renay Weiner, the Gurvitz family, Todd Bonin and Sara Leeder, Warren Bonin, Ebbie Bonin, and all my friends and relations for the love, support, and material. Most of all, a thousand kisses to Lucy, for being her sunny, funny, sassy self, and to Adam—the guy I took.